SEVEN SISTERS

MYSTERIOUS CHARM: BOOK 7

CELIA LAKE

 Created with Vellum

ALSO BY CELIA LAKE

The Mysterious Charm Series
Outcrossing
Goblin Fruit
Magician's Hoard
Wards of the Roses
In The Cards
On The Bias
Seven Sisters

Find a complete list of all my books at celialake.com/books.

Sign up for my newsletter to be the first to hear about future books and learn about fascinating bits of research. Happy reading!

ABOUT SEVEN SISTERS

What if you had ancient magic on your side?

Vivian has become a trifle bored with the routine of her inquiry agency and her commitments to the fae-blooded community. When a young man asks for help stopping mysterious events at a boarding house his uncle runs, she takes the case.

Cadmus knows a great deal about classics and ancient Greek, but this is beyond his ability to translate. He'll do anything to keep his home safe and give his nephew a proper start in life. If he must, Cadmus will even wrestle with his quite sensible fears of unfathomable magical beings.

Dangerous flowers, ghostly figures, and spooky lights were bad enough, but then Cadmus stumbles across one of Vivian's most closely held secrets. If they don't learn to set aside their old habits and trust each other, things could end horribly for everyone else in the house.

∾

Join Vivian and Cadmus near Oxford in 1922 as they take part in a seance, dive into the past, and just possibly dance into a new future together.

ONE

"Vivian? Do you have time to see someone this afternoon?"

Vivian glanced up at her assistant. "What sort of someone?" All she had waiting on her desk was finishing a report for the Minister of Flora and Fauna about some investigations into perfume ingredients of dubious origin. That had not quite been her usual line of work, but it had involved a satisfying amount of subtle conversation.

"It's a young man, Farran Michaels. He was at school with Anthony, and he's been worrying over something." Eleanor shifted from one foot to the other, her mist-blue skirt swaying with it. She was nervous, then, as that was one of her most obvious tells. It made Vivian frown, because she couldn't think what would make Eleanor that uncertain about asking her.

"That is not like you, Eleanor. I suppose he is in your sitting room at the moment?" That would be the house two doors down, to be precise, which Eleanor ran with the same precision she ran the office, keeping her younger siblings firmly in line. It served them all well, generally, since

Eleanor had been widowed young, and she'd lost both parents around the same time.

Eleanor met her eyes, unexpectedly fierce. "He's a good sort, Vivian, and he doesn't know what else to do." A personal interest, then, and possibly a personal problem. Eleanor was usually straightforward, innately practical, and utterly resistant to bribery, among her other virtues. For her to suggest that much, the boy was not only a good sort, but had her willing to extend herself on his behalf. Curious. Very curious.

"What does Anthony think of him?" Anthony was Eleanor's brother, the youngest by a few years, and a bit of a pet in the family.

"Oh, looks up to him no end. Farran's thoughtful, willing to help out. I'm sure Anthony would have failed his Materia classes without Farran."

That at least gave Vivian a place to start. "What have you told him about me?"

The younger woman shrugged, slightly, both feet steady again. "That I work for you, and that you know quite a few people who might be able to be of some help, and perhaps you could suggest someone."

"Someone?"

"From what he's said where I could hear - and I'm sure that's not the whole story - there is something quite queer going on. The type of thing you would find intriguing, cousin. And you don't have any cases that need your direct attention at the moment."

Eleanor calling on their relationship, that meant quite a bit. They were quite distant cousins, as their people counted it, and Eleanor's line of the family were much more likely to go to one of the Five Schools, and to find positions in the web of connections and businesses that kept Trellech and the rest of the magical community humming.

It was true she had no pressing cases at the moment. They came and went, and early autumn was often quieter, she'd found, for some reason. More people out on hearty outdoor walks, less cooped up by rain and inclined to plot and make trouble. Vivian took a deep breath. "More tea, please. For two."

Eleanor beamed. "Thank you, Vivian. Five minutes."

Precisely five minutes later, Vivian had put the papers on her desk away. She moved to settle in one of the easy chairs looking out the window, down toward the river. She heard the knock, and called out "Come." The single precise word.

A young man held the door for Eleanor, who had the tea tray, and who set it down, pausing to see if she should stay. Vivian nodded minutely, and then held out her hand. "Vivian Porter."

The young man took her hand, bowed over it with a kiss in the air above it. Old-fashioned manners, then, even by her standards. That was intriguing by itself. "I am Farran Michaels, Madam Porter. I appreciate your time." It was a rather impressive presentation for a young man, even allowing for how his voice quavered for a moment when he said her name. He couldn't be twenty yet, if he'd been at school with Anthony.

She smiled at him. It would not put him at ease, of course, but that was not the point. "Eleanor tells me you have a curious situation?"

Michaels nodded. "It's my uncle." He tried to figure out how to begin. "I am just out of school, Madam Porter. I began my apprenticeship in June. I have been living with my uncle the past six years, we're the last of the immediate family. The family estate is called Thebes, just outside Oxford, quite a large manor, two wings and the main house, twenty two bedrooms."

He took a breath before continuing. "For the past decade or so, Uncle Cadmus has run it as a boarding house. Mostly for scholars and researchers who want to be convenient to the university, but still live in the countryside. Also artisans. There are outbuildings and such. One person made items out of stained glass, another was a painter, and so on. There's a coppersmith right now. The estate has plenty of space, Uncle Cadmus started it as much to use the space as anything else."

That was an intriguing setup. Vivian hadn't had much to do with boarding houses since her own apprentice days, too many years ago. But the mesh of personalities - or the lack of such integration - could present unique concerns. "And what does your uncle do, besides run the house?"

"Oh, Mrs Cooper does all of that. She's excellent." He took a breath and then added something obviously important, but delicate. "She's deaf - it's relevant to the story. But she does the cooking, and the ordering. There are women from the village who come in every day for the cleaning and the laundry is sent out, and all. Very civilised. Not fancy, Madam Porter." And she could tell he was looking at her, with her elegant suit jacket and skirt, her hair precisely so. "It's home. And comfortable."

Vivian inclined her head, considering that. "That is a fine thing for an old house, to be comfortable," she said, looking to put him more at ease. "But something happened?"

Michaels nodded. "Two weeks ago, I went back for a few days, my master was working on something that meant I couldn't be in the house or workshop. And - the feeling of it had changed. All weekend, I kept hearing people telling stories about..." He searched for the right word. "It sounds quite odd."

"Do tell me. I've an interest in folklore." It covered a variety of sins and pleasures, folklore.

He was a pleasant and obliging young man, and he was looking for her help, so of course he would tell her. "First, there were some odd events. Some sounds, but Mrs Cooper swore she'd seen things - the kind of thing you'd think were ghosts, except that Thebes - our Thebes, I mean - has never been haunted."

"Not requisitioned during the War as a hospital or anything like that?"

"Oh, no. I mean, the East Wing were people doing War work. Something to do with publishing, I wasn't told what. I suppose they wouldn't have, though, especially to a school boy. And the West Wing had several nurses, from one of the hospitals nearby, and one of the hospital administrators, quite a scary woman."

There was something charming about him, the way he knew and owned his age. From her perspective of three score and three, it was almost refreshing.

"It wasn't just that, though. There was something curious with the greenhouses. Plants blooming out of season, or - differently. Mrs Gollard got quite a nasty rash from what should have been a perfectly normal orchid. And there were some stories about queer lights in the gardens at night."

"Nothing obvious, but - you know the property well, and it's not as it should be." The way the young man was talking, he also had a certain sensitivity to magical energies that was not common. Even by her standards. More to the point, the way he talked about the way the feel of the place had changed suggested it was not something anyone had nurtured in him, and not something he was used to discussing with other people.

That made her decidedly more curious. Not just at what was going on, but why this young man talked about what he felt in a way much more like she'd expect from a cousin. She offered him an encouraging smile, to continue.

Michaels let out a long sigh. "Yes, that's it exactly, Madam Porter. Uncle Cadmus says I'm fussing over nothing, and I should put my head down and focus on my apprenticeship, I have a lot to learn." He grimaced. "I'm not at all good at it."

She raised her eyebrow, but didn't press. "What were you hoping for, when you came to talk to me?"

Michaels looked up, visibly uncertain now, the easy manners shifting into nervous fiddling with one of his cufflinks. "I'm not sure, ma'am." He glanced at Eleanor. "Mrs Norton, her brother and I are friends, and he suggested I tell him about it, talk it through. Mrs Norton heard, and said you might be willing to help. But I'm not sure what kind of help you can offer, ma'am."

Vivian nodded. "Is there space in the boarding house at the moment?"

"Oh, yes, ma'am. Several nice rooms. Two en-suite. Why?"

"Do you think you can forget you met me? Except perhaps very briefly as Mrs Norton's employer?"

Michaels went wide-eyed at that. "I think so, ma'am." Gathering himself, he added, "It's only this conversation, right?"

Vivian laughed. "Just the one conversation to ignore having, yes. Quite simple. I think I will see about taking up a room for a little while. Your story intrigues me, and the things I need to work on right now can be done there. If your uncle asks, you can say you know I've an interest in folklore. I may need to mention I heard about the place from you via Eleanor here."

He bobbed his head.

"Write down the address for me, please. Does your uncle have one of the journals? I know they're rather dear yet."

That got her wide and earnest eyes again. "No, ma'am. He doesn't hold with some of the new magical devices. Not until they're tested. He - well, Classics people, ma'am, the ones I've met aren't in a hurry for new things as a rule."

"I suppose that has a certain consistency, docsn't it? A letter will do just as well."

"Can I - anything else, ma'am? And um, payment." He went beet red.

"You're a young man. If you have money it's probably in some sort of trust until your majority, yes?" And he was nowhere near inheriting yet, if he wasn't yet twenty.

He bobbed his head again.

"Traditionally, I'd say you owe me a favour, to be collected later. But as you're still under age, that seems a tad unfair. For the moment, you have presented me with an interesting question, and that will do. I may ask you to help if there is a future question where your skills or knowledge would be of assistance, but you are not bound to do so." She kept her voice even, precise.

It would be very easy to use the phrases that would make it a binding agreement. They hovered at the tip of her tongue, like a hummingbird. But she was neither her mother, nor her grandmother. And Eleanor would disapprove if she made it binding, and Vivian could not bear that.

"Thank you, ma'am. Of course. If I can be of help, usefully of help..."

She smiled, inclining her head. "Let Eleanor know how to reach you, if I need to get a note."

Eleanor picked up the cue immediately. "Off you go, Farran. If you stop by the house, there's biscuits in the tin."

Michaels stood, made a slight polite bow, and let Eleanor show him out. Three minutes later, she came back in. "So. Usual things for a case away?"

"Help me pack, forward the mail, and water the plants, yes."

"What's the story?"

"Oh, the same cover story will do. Folklore research."

"I'll search out a collection of suitable journals and books to supplement your shelves."

"There was that recent article by - Wenna Newton, wasn't it? On the various surviving legends about Fair Rosalind?"

"Quite, and that might be helpful regarding the manor. No reason not to help them along a bit if it won't cause trouble."

Eleanor laughed. "Or divert attention."

"That too, that too." With that, they settled in to figure out the details of the necessary arrangements.

"Good morning, Mistress Gladstone." Vivian nodded politely at the woman behind the counter of the bookshop. It was one of five shops along this street owned by the cousins. Most of their kind had preferences of whether they used the bookshop, the apothecary, the tea shop, the milliner, or the shoe shop to get to the back stairs. Whichever they picked, the back hallway would bring them to their real goal, the upstairs spaces. Vivian vastly preferred the bookshop, not least because it was the easiest to explain if someone saw her disappear in there for hours.

Not that she usually stayed that long. She had limited patience for some of her cousins. Many, if truth be told. Eleanor had been a delightful breath of fresh air when she'd come to work for Vivian five years ago.

The older woman nodded, and said "Good reading, Mistress Porter."

"I'm quite sure it will be." That was the code that meant she could go straight up, without having to sidle her way back and avoid other customers. Given permission, she made directly for the stairs, following the twist of the corner. She felt the magic settle around her, as the warding recognised her permission to be here. The stairs came out in a small foyer, dappled with sun. She paused, setting her hat and her small basket on a hook on the wall. She turned to smile at the large elder bush spreading out along the short wall opposite the stairs from its large round wooden half-barrel of a pot.

"Afternoon, Alfred. You're looking well." Which he was, by his standards, though decidedly less humanoid than the last time she'd seen him, only a few weeks ago.

The branches rustled slightly. She suspected he'd be taken off to Shropshire by spring, to mind the doorway to the Realm he'd chosen. They'd get some much younger bush in, one who was still able to walk about the upstairs rooms and speak English. Some of the younger cousins were balking at the delicacy and patience needed to speak with less verbal guardians. Vivian knew it had been giving Alfred rather polite fits, as well as leaf spots.

"Which way is Luned?" Easier than searching for her.

It took a moment, a sort of coiling effort, but then the right hand branch quivered.

"Thank you." She made the small gesture of gratitude. Since she could see he'd been properly watered that morning, she nodded and went down the right hand hallway. As she walked, she listened for the conversations in the side rooms as she went. Two of the rooms were occupied, but from the little she could hear through the doors, they were the ordinary sorts of social gatherings the cousins preferred to have with no outside ears. The third door down, she glimpsed a flash of a white flower with a purple ribbon on the half-open door, and knocked on the door frame.

"If your name isn't Vivian, go away." The voice inside was sharp.

"It is. Morning, Luned. Bad night?"

Vivian pushed the door open, stepping into the small room. Two chairs were pulled up by the window over the street, allowing them to see out, though charms blocked others from seeing people inside. Luned was not sitting, but instead was stalking back and forth, the heels of her shoes tapping on the wood floor and her hair bobbing with the movement.

"Something the matter?"

"The Belin are upset but entirely uncommunicative beyond a small fall of rocks and a bit of flooding from a river being dammed. The foxgloves are suffering some kind of blight in the Midlands. Alfred's successor is not quite ready to take over, and we really should get him moved before the end of the summer, he's gone thoroughly sessile the last fortnight. And now you want to talk to me, and I'm quite sure it's not to take half a dozen matters off my plate."

Very sharp, then. Vivian spread her hands. Pacifying Luned wouldn't work, it never did, but she could at least not add fuel to the fire. At least there wasn't anything worse, though the Belin might be a worry.

"I've got a job, I'll be out of touch except by journal for the next... oh, few weeks, at least."

"And what about the new and full moon offerings?"

"Eleanor will handle those, she's had plenty of practice." Vivian kept her voice steady. "And she's quite skilled at handling the mail, you know that."

"And where will you be, then? Somewhere luxurious, no doubt?" Luned still resented that transatlantic trip Vivian had had to make for a case last year.

"A boarding house for wayward academics near Oxford." It came out sounding rather prim.

"That manor?"

"No, though the chance of hearing some of the gossip from the area does appeal." Vivian wasn't sure what she'd hear, as she wouldn't be terribly near the mysterious manor that had reappeared after several centuries of magical absence, which was a bit north of Oxford proper. Certainly, she wouldn't be close enough to overhear chatter in the local pub or wherever the researchers were sleeping and dining.

"What sort of case?"

"Ghosts, odd flowers showing up in the greenhouse, lights in the gardens, that sort of thing. Just enough to be intriguing, and my primary work at the moment is some background research and reports, nothing I can't take with me."

Luned wheeled around, and looked Vivian up and down, then blew out a breath. "I can't forbid you to go."

"No." Vivian was patient. She was the elder here. More to the point, she'd set up her life so that a quite limited list of people could tell her what to do. The Grandmothers, not that they ever had, precisely. A few of the senior aunts, but generally only the ones with good sense. She worked well with Luned, but that didn't mean Luned could order her around.

"You'll have your journal? In case there's a problem?" There was a decided note of frustration in Luned's voice, along with resignation.

"I will. There's no portal there, but there's one a mile or two away. Easy enough to get to, if there is an emergency."

"What are you telling them you are?"

"Well, they will assume I'm fully human. No need to glamour my eyes." Hers were a pale green, unlike Luned's rather more obvious yellow. "A spinster folklorist. Wenna Newton's done some work in the county, so I've read up on what she did so I can do something else."

"Folk music, isn't that her thing?"

"Yes. Ghost stories might be too on the nose, if they've been seeing something, but perhaps stone circles, or I'll stumble on something suitable." She waved a hand. Half of folklore research was listening to whatever people wanted to tell you about, and she felt it was better to let them talk. People could be quite helpful that way, without ever realising it.

"You'll think of something. You always do." It was grudging, but at least Luned had stopped pacing.

"Can I take anything on while I'm there? Routine paperwork, that sort of thing?"

"Oh, would you make a clear copy of the counts for the year? Up to whenever you do them? Your handwriting is so much more readable."

Not Vivian's favourite thing, but manageable. "Of course. Bring them round tonight, or have Eleanor send them on, whichever suits." It would at least give her an excuse to get out of difficult conversations if she needed one, or an excuse to go in search of conversation, as needed.

Luned huffed, and then leaned back against the wall. "Do you expect difficulty in Oxfordshire?"

"Not particularly, but - something about it, it made me curious. And you know I like to follow that up."

"Anyone else, I'd wonder if there was a handsome man involved."

"You know what I think about that. I've never minded a charming gentleman, but..." Vivian shrugged. "The ones who are actually my age aren't able to keep up with me, the ones who can are - well, they're the ones hit hardest in the

War. And the younger ones are entirely too young. Farran is the young man who asked for my help. He was charming and well-mannered, but barely out of school. Though he might make one of the younger cousins a suitable partner, in a few years."

"You don't usually think much of young men."

Vivian shrugged. "I've seen rather a lot of them get themselves in no end of trouble. I prefer them once they've figured out trouble has consequences and costs. But this one's got a keener sense for the," she angled her hand slightly, just so, "the feel of a place than most. I wouldn't be surprised by a lost kinsman somewhere back, honestly. I find I want to figure out if it's general or just his home territory. That makes a difference."

Luned snorted. "I suppose there's sense in that." She rubbed her face, most unlike her.

"It really is bad, then?"

"Nothing settled after the War, and the number of lords we lost, too many places aren't properly tended to."

"They're getting sorted, aren't they? Just more slowly than we'd like?"

"Some of them. We're having to go quite far afield to find appropriate heirs for some of them. Or the lord of Ytene, the heir there was halfway around the world, and he's only just settled in now. Thankfully, he has enough of the landsense to know what's needed now he's home."

"And some of them don't." It wasn't a question, but more an expression of despair at the state of the world.

"Some of them never had the landsense." Which was the best word they had for it in English, even if it was unsatisfactory. "Some of them had it shattered, in the trenches. Some of them don't feel it's important, and it's not a thing you can explain. Even if we could tell them, the Silence forbids what we'd want to say." Luned made a sharp gesture with her hand, the flash of fingers thrown out, spread wide, averting unwanted magics.

"Look, I don't know how long this will take me, but once I'm back, let me take some of it on."

Luned looked up, eyes brighter under dark hair. "You mean it?"

Vivian knew she'd regret that, but it was the right thing to do. "Enough to give you a break, at least. A proper break. Maybe a trip on one of the transatlantic liners. Nothing to do but be charmed and eat and drink well for a fortnight."

"Ah, now that's a bribe. And perhaps a glimpse of our ocean cousins?"

"Well, if that's what you want, you could go up to Scotland. But that's increasingly chilly this time of year. You know they'd let you join them."

Luned shivered. "Not in the cold, thank you very much. I don't know how they manage."

"And they have no idea how we manage roads and big houses and automobiles. So there we are."

It made Luned laugh. "I suppose. And we are very good at what we do, aren't we?"

"Excellent." Vivian grinned. "So. I'll write. You'll write. You can pop up to Oxford if you need to, or I can come down."

Luned let out a long breath. "Stay a bit? Tell me about your research?"

Vivian nodded, finally moving to the chairs by the window. "Animal, vegetable, or mineral?" Any of the three would occupy them nicely for a few hours.

THREE

Cadmus glanced out the window for the fourth time in three minutes. He hated this part of running the house, but there was nothing for it. He wanted to be upstairs with his books and his papers and his notes, rolling around in the elegance of Greek words that perfectly illuminated some nuance of meaning or context. He felt like he was himself, there, using his skills to craft something of use, bringing greater understanding. Everywhere else, he felt awkward, as if he'd been broken in the distant past and mended poorly. Or perhaps work-hardened would be a better way of thinking of it, where the next blow of the hammer, when it came, might shatter him into fragments. He didn't know how to fix it, he had tried everything he did know, and none of it had worked.

But if there was one thing classical authors had taught him, it was that hospitality mattered, that doing it properly was what made society work. Even if this was not at all the sort of hospitality most of them meant. He wasn't a ruler in some citadel. He wasn't even some outpost on a long trade road, far away from any other home. He was in a modestly large country home, convenient to Oxford and her spires. Nothing special, except to him. And Farran, he supposed.

He glanced around, frowning again, at all the things he only noticed when he was waiting for someone. He couldn't do a thing about the spot of staining on the ceiling, from the bad storm two years ago. Or the way the bookshelves had a bit of a sag to them. But the dust, above them, that spider web, he could ask Mrs Cooper to make sure the day help saw to that.

In another time, in another world, it would have been Farran's mother overseeing the place. Or his own sister. They'd been brought up to manage a house and staff. Delia, his sister-in-law, had a wonderful way with hosting. She was the creator of a cosmos in miniature, making him think of the way the Greeks saw the universe, as a great and intricate ornament. And Thera, his sister, she'd had a gift for making a space feel comfortable. She had been queen of all the little touches that encouraged one to linger and enjoy the beauty of a room. Or better yet, at least as far as he was concerned, the ones that encouraged one to curl up with a book in a comfortable chair.

Cadmus was fine with ancient etiquette. He understood about offering cool water to wash the feet, not behaving like Penelope's awful suitors, and being pleasant to people just in case they were a god in disguise. About how when people came together for the Mysteries, everyone was welcome, poor and rich, woman and man, slave and free.

The modern expectations baffled him, and had since he was a schoolboy. He'd done all right when they were in school, when things were either explained properly, or were mysteries to everyone. He'd done better when he'd learned to wield hammer and anvil and been trained in how to share the forge with others.

But the sort of ordinary social expectations that kept happening, those he had never mastered. There were codes to the flowers, with nuances that he always got wrong, even when he used the reference books. The colours he liked weren't fashionable, and he couldn't figure out why. And he had no idea how to plan a menu for other people, or make sure the laundry got done promptly. Never mind how to tell it was done well beyond the most obvious lack of stains.

That was why they had Mrs Cooper. He said a prayer to Hestia, every day, thankful that Mrs Cooper was here and knew what she was doing. Even if there were cobwebs in the corners sometimes, there was always plenty of tasty food on the table. Linens were washed and hung to dry and put back on the beds, on a regular cycle.

But they still needed someone to handle the accounts, and to be the face of the place. He couldn't say the accounts were easy at the moment, nervously counting what repairs they had money for and what they didn't. But he understood how the rows and columns of numbers worked, and how to set money aside for future needs. Cadmus was presentable enough, he supposed. He knew he didn't look like much. He was no one's idea of a heroic visage, being shorter than average, and with hair that was going salt and pepper in a very undistinguished sort of way. He supposed it matched the water stains and cobwebs.

Most importantly, though, he was the only person who could meet a new resident. One of the men at the club had called him out on that, saying he should call them boarders or guests, and neither of those felt right. It was the wrong nuance. A resident had a stake in the house, even if it was different than his. Being a boarder implied a very merce-nary transaction, one that made him uncomfortable. They were not guests, not in the Greek sense of xenia, because they would be here for quite a long time, some of them.

He let out a breath, glancing out the window again, and finally seeing the cart pull up. He'd asked John, the gardener, to pick her up at the station, with her things. There was no portal nearby, unfortunately. Ann Porter was rather a mystery to him. She'd mentioned in her letter that she knew a friend of Farran's, and Farran had suggested the place.

Cadmus had asked Farran, who had shrugged in the way only a young man could shrug, and said she'd asked for a place to stay while doing some research. Cadmus couldn't help thinking there was more to it. He'd been around Farran, day in and day out, barring when he was away for schooling, since Farran was six. His nephew's little deceptions were entirely visible to him. Even if he had no clear way of teasing out what they were, they were there, like a crack in an urn that had been carefully turned towards the wall so it wouldn't show to guests.

The bell startled him out of his thoughts. He hurried to answer the front door, pulling the second, silent bell pull to let Mrs Cooper know someone else was responding. Working the latch, which was sticking again in the autumn damp, he finally got it open to manage a respectable, "Madam Porter? I'm Cadmus Michaels. Do come in, welcome to Thebes."

Before him stood a woman. Not a young woman, nor an old woman, but someone in the range of ages he was awful at guessing. Forty, perhaps? Less grey in her hair than he had. He knew some people used dye, or illusion charms. Other people laughed about it, at his club, or in the shops.

If it was dye, it was better than most people's, the brown had a richness of tone that reminded him of some of the shading on the better redware he'd seen. It had a depth of colour that was rather striking in contrast to her pale green eyes. She wore small wire-framed glasses, perched on her nose, and she was tall enough to be looking just a little down at him, like she was examining him. Her clothing gave the impression of a certain asceticism, all sensible navy blue fabric with little in the way of decoration.

He offered his hand, and she shook it, without hesitation. "Thank you. I gather my trunk is being brought around."

"John will leave it in the kitchen hall until you see the rooms." He'd already got off his expected lines, and it made him feel suddenly awkward, like he was speaking out of turn. He took a deep breath. "The usual way of things is, actually, usually people confirm they'd like a room here. I hope Farran explained how things work?"

"That you have a number of long-term residents, that meals could be provided or not as I choose. And about my primary concerns which have to do with location."

"Ah. Yes." Cadmus swallowed. "Let me show you the rooms I thought you'd prefer, first. If you like them, we can discuss from there while John brings your trunk up."

She nodded sharply, then just waited, with an unsettling patience.

Cadmus gathered himself. "This way. May I take your bag?" She had a small carpet bag with her. She shook her head. "Thank you, no, I can manage."

He wondered, not for the first time, about her background. There was something of an exceedingly competent nanny about her. She seemed the kind of person who might soften occasionally at night or when dealing with some new scrape, but the rest of the time would have a strict schedule and high expectations. She wasn't quite old enough to be a terrifying aunt, but he rather thought she was preparing to take on that role in a few years.

He led the way up the main stairs, hoping she saw the faded and somewhat scarred wood of the bannisters as welcoming rather than dingy. They had been much battered by the last two generations of children in the house, and the scratches wouldn't buff out anymore.

"The guest rooms are in the east wing, on the first and second floors. The west wing are the family rooms, and the staff." Cadmus was never sure what to tell people when.

"I gather there aren't many family?"

"Just myself and Farran, who you've met. He's only here sometimes, he's apprenticing with a talisman-maker in Oxford. We have a live-in housekeeper." This was the delicate part, and more than one person had stormed off once they met her or sniffed and disappeared, never to come back. "That is Mrs Cooper, I'll introduce you once you've seen what you think of the room. And there are three women who come from town for the daily cleaning work. Laundry is sent out on Monday mornings, and is back on Wednesday evening."

He brought her down the hallway to the end. The best room open had a good view of the gardens, and perhaps this mysterious woman would like that sort of thing. It had its own bathing room and water closet attached, rather than sharing across the hall. He supposed the colours wouldn't bother her, they were muted blues and greens, nothing startling.

He opened the door. "I thought you would prefer this suite. En-suite facilities through that door like you requested, and a view of the garden from the desk. Do take your time and look around." This was the point at which he usually withdrew, to wait in the hall. She swept into the room, and he felt pulled along in her wake, to stand awkwardly in the doorway as she inspected the space.

She began by walking slowly once around the room, clockwise. She opened the door to the en suite, and then continued, before repeating the circle again, looking much more closely.

This second time, Madam Porter pulled drawers out of the bedside table. She sat on the bed, very primly, her feet hanging just above the floor for a moment before she stood again, as if floating down to earth. Then she opened a window, making it clear she was one of those women who approved of a brisk breeze while sleeping or airing the room out. There were worse things, so long as she understood that it did not suit with having the fireplace burning.

When she sat at the desk, she frowned, tapping something he could not see. "This desk, one of the legs is unsound. Is there an alternate that could be moved in here? Perhaps slightly larger?"

That was not the best of omens, Cadmus had a whole system of them by now, but it was not the worst, either. After a moment's consideration, he offered, "We have a few others not currently in use. If you'd like to use one of them instead, we can move it."

She nodded sharply, and stood, her skirts swirling. Cadmus was caught for a moment by the fabric. It wasn't behaving quite like the ones he knew, cotton and linen and wool. Not cheap cloth, for all it wasn't colourful or decorative, he suspected, it had a heft to it that wasn't like the clothing of the other women residents. The detail nagged at him, as details sometimes did, until he firmly set it aside as a thing far too indelicate to enquire about. She kept moving, checking for dust on the mantle and the state of the fireplace. That done, she disappeared into the bathing room, and he could hear her turn on the tap. She was in there long enough he was sure she was testing the hot water.

At least they had no shortage there. His brother had put in the best of the magical boilers before his death. The water itself came from one of the local rivers, and got run through a series of pebbles and sand to filter it down to the highest purity.

She reappeared, making one more pass of the room, peering into the corners. Cadmus was glad the cleaning women from the village had enough pride in their work. The other women he'd shown had checked some of these things - the men rarely noticed - but none had been as thorough as Madam Porter.

"It will do nicely." She offered a particular kind of host-gift. "That is a lovely view, thank you. I will most certainly enjoy it." He couldn't make sense of her tone, which was warmer now, but not exactly friendly. It was like there was still a great distance between them, made up of barbaric formalities that Herodotus would have done far better with. "Your nephew mentioned you preferred coin to a cheque."

"If it's not a bother." He cleared his throat. "You should meet Mrs Cooper first."

She took a step, as if to follow him, but stopped as soon as she realised he hadn't moved. "Is there a problem?" Her tone was clipped again. Then, she seemed to realise. "Your nephew mentioned Mrs Cooper is deaf. I do know sign, though I am rather rusty, and I learned in an isolated community up north, so I suspect my accent is rather queer. As it were." Her tone had turned almost confiding for a moment, before she shifted back to brisk practicality. "Would you be able to help with a few questions about the meals? I'm not sure my vocabulary is up to all of it."

It felt like he'd swum out to sea and got caught in an

undertow. He gawped, then managed a cautious, "Mrs Cooper will appreciate someone else to talk to, I'm sure." It sounded entirely feeble, even as he heard it come out of his mouth.

"Quite so." Cadmus made sense of the words, but couldn't make sense of the situation at all. He realised with a start he hadn't even mentioned the mealtimes. "Hot meals are eight, one, and half-six, for residents who wish to eat together. Otherwise, Mrs Cooper can arrange a tray or packed lunch."

Madam Porter nodded again. "Quite sensible. Do introduce me, then?" It was as if they were working off entirely different expectations of how this went. Hers were not illogical, but they kept flat-footing him.

He hoped she wasn't one of those people who had a list the length of her arm of foods she wouldn't eat. That never ended well. Even worse were the people who would only eat food one specific way, usually boiled to mush.

He wondered where she'd learned sign. Most people had no idea about it, or worse, considered it to be degraded or infantile or whatever other insult they wanted to apply. For her to come out with it that promptly, well, he wasn't sure what that meant.

"Has she been with you long?" The question jolted him out of his thoughts.

"She came when I was ten."

FOUR

MONDAY AFTERNOON

T he kitchen was, in many ways, the best preserved part of the house. Cilix, his brother, had had it redone around the turn of the century, fully modernised and laid out sensibly. There was a large wooden work table in the middle, and all the space to cook a formal supper for two dozen if needed. Not a thing they did now, thankfully.

Mrs Cooper was seated at one end of the table, where she could see the door. More importantly, she could see the charm lights that flashed above it when someone went through the frame, or answered the front door, or other such things.

He wondered what Madam Porter would make of her. Mrs Cooper held everything together, but he admitted that she looked more than a bit shabby. So did he, if it came to that. They couldn't afford to replace clothing just because it had gone a bit faded. Most of what they wore had migrated to a sort of dull beige and muted grey. Mrs Cooper's apron was fresh and clean, except for a splash of something shockingly yellow near the pocket. Turmeric, by the colour, so she must have been making up a curry for Mistress Cole, who had a fondness for them.

Cadmus waited for Mrs Cooper to meet his eyes, and then signed. "This is Madam Porter. She approves of the room." He was careful to spell the name precisely. Then he added, "She signs and she has questions."

That brought a raised eyebrow, and then Mrs Cooper aligned herself subtly, facing Madam Porter, and her fingers moved again. "Good afternoon. Is your room good?"

"Thank you, yes. Mr Michaels is changing a," Here her fingers paused before she gestured with her fingers, outlining the shape of the desk.

Cadmus shifted, making the sign once, for Mrs Cooper, and then again, facing Madam Porter, so she could catch it. Odd word not to remember, but if she was as rusty as that that could explain it. He knew he could forget a perfectly simple word in Greek when his mind was caught by something else, and he'd been reading Greek since he was eight.

"Yes, thank you." That was clearly to him. "I had a question about the food." Madam Porter turned her head for a moment, to see if he was following. He nodded, though he moved into the kitchen to make it easier to see her hands move.

If she had expected to sign, that might explain the dark clothing. He had no idea if she were the kind of person who thought about the benefits of contrast, and but her pale hands stood out clearly against the navy suit.

She went on, a bit more smoothly. "How do you arrange the food?"

It was not a question Cadmus had expected her to ask. Few people thought about that sort of thing, especially anyone who'd been in the kinds of houses Madam Porter's clothing suggested. She might not be wealthy herself, but she certainly knew how a large house worked, even if it was a boarding house now.

Mrs Cooper began explaining, her hands moving slowly, repeating a phrase here or there when Madam Porter queried. They went through several exchanges, then Madam Porter said, "I'm quite pleased so far, can you help me with some vocabulary? I can fingerspell, of course, but it's the class of thing I want to convey."

Cadmus blinked but nodded. "Of course. Can you explain to me?"

"I do not eat red meat, or blood pudding or blood sausage or liver or kidneys. Beef stock is acceptable if it's part of a different dish. I do eat chicken and fish, and most anything else."

Cadmus nodded, and let her begin, gesturing slightly with a hand. She made something of a fumble of it, getting as far as 'red meat', clarifying it as 'beef' and then getting stuck on the blood pudding and blood sausage. Cadmus shifted easily, explaining.

It made Mrs Cooper raise both her eyebrows, and then ask bluntly. "Not Jewish? Or foreign?"

Madam Porter shook her head. "My family has been here since before the Romans, some of us. Those foods do not agree with me."

"Nothing else?"

"Those are the only things." Cadmus watched her fingers. Her gestures were otherwise precise and sharp, but when she signed, there was a curious shift. It was as if she were working against some invisible pressure, just a hint here and there, where she didn't fully extend a finger, or made a motion smaller than he would have. He was sufficiently distracted by this that he glanced up to realise they were both looking at him with remarkably similar patient looks.

It was terrifying. He knew for a moment what it must have been like at Eleusis, when the sheaf of wheat was thrust up high, when the glance of the Gods turned towards the initiates. Possibly benevolent, but never safe.

Cadmus took a deep breath. "Is there a problem?"

"I believe you were..." Madam Porter glanced at Mrs Cooper, whose fingers moved. "Day-dreaming, yes. I've promised a list of foods I eat and don't eat. If we could see to the formalities, I could settle in."

"Do let me show you to the household office." Here he was back on somewhat more solid ground.

She made her farewells politely to Mrs Cooper. Cadmus had to approve, even if he wasn't sure what to make of this strange self-possessed woman. She understood how to be a guest, and the liminal space of being a resident in someone else's house.

He showed her back up to the library, where it looked out toward the garden. He opened the door in the panelling, letting her into the small household office. He settled in the cracked leather chair on his side of the desk. "You are welcome to use the library, the music room. There is a piano there, though please keep all music to between three in the afternoon and eight in the evening. The other parlours and rooms on this side are available to residents as well, or the terrace in good weather."

Madam Porter perched on the other chair, placing her carpet bag tidily at her feet and drawing out a leather portfolio. "Is there anywhere I should avoid?"

"The west wing, beyond the hallway. Those are the family rooms."

"Should I expect to see much of the other residents?"

"Most of us gather for supper reliably on Wednesday and Sunday, other than that it will depend." He considered, trying to remember that what he'd forgotten to cover, since they were doing this all out of proper order. Cadmus concealed his confusion by taking out the paperwork he'd prepared last night, and handed it over. She shifted her glasses to read the agreements closely, giving him a moment to find his equilibrium once more.

"Oh, yes." He remembered. "If you drink, it is by your own arrangement. I provide a locking cabinet for wine with meals, and other items may be stored in your room. Drinking in excess is treated like any other issue that affects other residents."

It got a little dry snort from her. "I have some familiarity with living in community, and I expected something of the kind. That will not be a problem." Whether it was because she did not drink, or whether she avoided excess, he could not tell. It might be either. Asceticism was a possibility, but he hoped not. Ascetics were rather tiresome to live with.

"Food in the rooms is implied by the trays..." She was clearly working from her own mental list.

"There is a storage cupboard, enchanted against pests. There are sound dampening enchantments on all rooms, but louder sounds do carry somewhat, or anything that rattles the walls or floor. You are welcome to have guests but please be considerate of the others." Then, taking something of a risk, he ventured, "You are rather younger than most of our residents. We may be too quiet a household for you."

Something in that comment made her eyes twinkle, though she didn't say anything about it. "When is convenient to meet them?"

"Perhaps a summary now, and introductions as you meet? I will be at supper tonight."

Madam Porter nodded. "First, is the formal mode of address the usual thing here?"

"It is as you prefer. Madam Etna, Mistress Cole, Madam Gregson, and Herr Professor Balsano prefer the formality. Emma Jacobs, Danae White, and Healer Richard Danegeld are all inclined to be less formal after the proper introductions. Mistress Price, it depends on how she feels about you."

"Herr Professor?"

He supposed the name stood out. "Austrian, not German." It made a difference to some people. "He keeps largely to himself, he is a lecturer in 19th century history of magical theory at the university. He takes many of his meals there, and is often in his rooms working when he is here."

"A pity. I do like a spot of spirited academic discussion with my meals."

"Do you indulge? Mistress Price is an academic, and Emma Jacobs is a librarian."

Madam Porter smiled, and looked charmed for a moment. "Folklore. Specifically, the plants mentioned in various surviving folk songs and tales, and their associations. Something a tad deeper than simple practical knowledge, though I certainly have no objection to more time in a garden or stillroom when I've the opportunity. I would be delighted to talk to Herr Professor Balsano if he has time and inclination, I suspect there is some overlap."

Cadmus nodded. "I am a classicist by preference."

"Something else before that?"

"I was in the Colonial Service in Afghanistan for three years, but I found it did not agree with me." He'd said it so many times since then that the phrases felt almost entirely truthful, and didn't stick in his mouth the way it once had.

"Ann, then." It took him a moment to realise what she was saying.

"You would prefer that?"

She nodded. "Might as well begin as we mean to go on. And I do think it is a tad awkward to be formal with someone one is living with, even in a setting like this. Unless you prefer otherwise?"

Madam - no, Ann - was very certain of herself, carrying him along in her wake. It was very like Mrs Cooper, now he thought about it. It may have been a terrible mistake to introduce them, even if it was a necessity.

He shook his head. "It does get a tad confusing, with Farran sometimes here, to both be Mr Michaels. Please, do call me Cadmus." He couldn't refuse to match her, there. It would be rude. Inhospitable. Then he remembered. "Oh, and there's Robin Aelfdane, he's our last resident, pardon."

That got a sudden narrowing of her eyes, as if she'd had a sharp headache strike her for just a second. Then her expression smoothed out as if there had been nothing there. "An inch or two taller than I am, improbably blond hair, emerald green eyes?"

It described the man perfectly. "Will, um, will that be a problem?" He hoped not. Robin not only paid up promptly, but he was generous about sharing around a bottle of wine or port, and a pleasant conversationalist at supper.

"Very distant cousin." He couldn't make sense of her tone for a moment, then she went on, more evenly, "Anything I should know about the others?"

"Madam Etna is a spiritualist. She will likely try and talk you into a seance, but she has been told, very firmly, that she may ask once, and only once. If she gives you any trouble, please tell me and I will take care of it."

"Is she one of the dark room and apparition sorts, one of the levitating sorts, or a table rapper?"

"Board and planchette, by preference, or mediumship."

"Hmmm." It was a thoughtful sort of noise, and gave him no clue what she thought about spiritualism. Or his permitting such a person in the house. Though she seemed familiar with at least some of the variety. "The others?"

"Mistress Cole is getting on a bit, her mind wanders sometimes, but she's very pleasant. She used to do a particular kind of apothecary work, rather fiddly in the measurements, but she might like to talk about the plants with you. She does like a nice curry, so if you're inclined, let Mrs Cooper know and she can make extra. Madam Gregson is a widow, and she lost both her son and husband in the War. She didn't want to keep up the family home. I don't think she'll give you any difficulty."

"But she does to you?"

"She rather dotes on my nephew, and he finds it a bit frustrating at times, though of course he is polite about it."

"I suppose someone might. He's a very well-mannered young man, a credit to you and his upbringing. Though of course I only met him briefly, at Eleanor's."

Cadmus nodded, then felt he should finish the list. "Andromache Price is a researcher in literature, affiliated with St Hildegard's. Mediaeval tales, I believe, but I'm afraid that's not at all my period. Danae White makes rather wonderful copper hammered jewellery and art objects, very Arts and Crafts in the better senses. She has a workshop in one of the outbuildings on the grounds. Richard - our Healer - serves at the clinic in town, of course, and he has been kind enough to consult on our little infirmities."

He counted on his fingers. "And Emma Jacobs is a librarian, though I'm afraid she'll tell you she spends much of her time maintaining their records rather than enjoying the books."

"I gather that's a necessity in a well-run library. Better it be done well, if someone has to do it."

Cadmus nodded. "She's been kind enough to see to things in here, and suggest some adjustments."

"That seems a most congenial group, thank you." She then stood, almost abruptly. "Supper is at half-six?"

"Yes. I'll let Mrs Cooper know to set a place. It is fish tonight, in cream sauce, and vegetables."

With that, his new resident nodded once, smiled pleasantly, and turned. He listened to the sound of her footsteps on the stairs fade away, then shook his head and retreated to his study.

FIVE

MONDAY AT SUPPERTIME

Vivian felt the preliminaries had gone quite well, really. Once her trunk had been delivered to her room, she spent a pleasant enough hour arranging everything to fit the seeming she wanted to present. Here was the row of serious-sounding folklore texts, and just one or two of the volumes of amusing stories and songs. Her array of suitably dull-coloured suits and frocks, sedate enough for a woman of middle age and a bookwormish bent, hung in the closet.

She had a set of scarves and shawls of modestly brighter colours folded precisely in the dresser. They were precisely the sort of thing a female secretary or assistant might be gifted by those with less taste than money. In this case, with a resident spiritualist, they might be just the thing.

Her underthings matched the rest of the clothing, which was made of sensibly heavy-weight silk and linen and wool, depending on purpose. Nothing at all like her usual preferred dresses and outfits, of course, but her work required the utmost attention to detail.

There was not one thing in these rooms that would

make anyone think she was anything other than what she wanted them to see. The other items were all tucked in the secret compartment in her trunk only she could open. She had her ritual case and robes, her journal, the ancient chatelaine with the keys she needed for her various roles. She might well be here long enough to need the ritual items, at least. Now the trunk was locked and firmly charmed to stick to the floor at the end of the bed until she alone released it.

She redid her hair, in a looser bun than earlier, and checked the collar of tonight's deep green dress. Then she chose an unchallenging grey shawl from the drawer, and arranged it on her shoulders. Vivian was not looking forward to the delicate dance that might be required with cousin Robin. She did rather wonder what he was up to here. She was certain he wouldn't tell her. No more than she'd tell him her intentions. He was not the sort of cousin one trusted.

She glanced at the clock on the mantle. Twenty-five past six, and time for her to go down.

When she entered the dining room, Cadmus was standing at the head of the table, the far end. There was something about the way he stood, comfortable in the space, that she found intriguing. The man in a habitat beside the library. "Ann, good evening, come in. We thought we'd put you here, by Madam Price and Mistress Jacobs, seeing as how you have academic interests in common."

Vivian nodded, smiling. "Ann Porter. Please, do call me Ann," she said, easily giving the name she used while working on cases. Her last name was common enough not to be distinctive. "Folklore, though I promise I won't be asking you to listen to endless verses of song. I'm rather more interested in plant references and such."

It was the kind of sufficiently opaque research that occasionally produced fascinating conversations, but most of the time lead people to murmur something polite and change the subject. Either suited her nicely. The elder of the two, closer to Vivian's actual age of sixty-three, nodded, salt and pepper curls bobbing. "Andromache Price. Specialist in women's literature of the mediaeval period, particularly those reflecting the interaction of the domestic and political sphere."

"Marie de France, I assume everyone says? Or wasn't there an argument about whether the Pearl poet might have been a woman?"

The other woman was more like Vivian's apparent age, in her mid-forties. She had dark hair pinned into a flat bun at the nape of her neck, and round wire-rimmed glasses, in an unusual shade of copper. Vivian suspected charms and enchantments on the metal beyond the usual sort for eyeglasses. "Oh, goodness, don't get Andie started, we'll be here until midnight. Emma Jacobs, do call me Emma." She was pleasant, and quite comfortable engaging someone new.

She settled in her chair, smiling pleasantly, and Cadmus said, "I broke open a bottle of wine, since it's your first night. A glass?" She nodded, and then settled in to look back at her companions.

Andromache was leaning back, eyeing Vivian. "And what do you do, Ann?"

"Nothing like formal research, like yours. I didn't attend university." There were several ways the ensuing conversation might go, and all of them were potentially informative.

"You don't disapprove of academic education for women, I hope?" There was a definite note of challenge there.

"Oh, goodness, no. I've had to make my own, and it's rather a lot of hard work, isn't it? I've always rather envied the women who had a chance to spend time with others, discussing the details of their field. I'm afraid I've been rather solitary by nature, other than seeing a few cousins, and various connections related to projects."

"Have you been living in Oxford? Anyone we might know?"

"Oh, no, I live in Trellech. I'm here for the research, the folklore. And of course, the things one can hear in Trellech are very well documented, aren't they? I got rather interested in the area thanks to that manor that popped back up. I thought a change of scenery and a chance to focus on the Oxfordshire tales might do nicely."

"Mmm." That was Andromache, looking thoughtful.

Regrettably, that was also when Robin Aelfdane swept in, wearing a long frock coat that trailed out behind him, in a particularly vivid peacock blue. "Cousin! Goodness! I scarcely believed it when Cadmus mentioned your name."

Vivian smiled, and extended her hand. Robin took it, made a fussy air kiss over the top, and then beamed at her. It was all falsity. He was up to something, she was entirely sure. Too loud, too flashy, too much false gaiety not to be. He did always prefer to distract from what he was actually doing with a grand show.

"We must catch up, sometime later. It wouldn't be fair to bore everyone."

Emma was leaning in. "Cousins?"

"Quite distant." She and Robin both said it at the same moment, and he grimaced before his face smoothed out into easy bonhomie.

"I'll let you get to know the others. Ah, Richard, I had a question for you."

One by one, the others filed in, more than Vivian had been led to believe generally took supper together. She was quite certain they were all here to examine her, and see what they thought. She went through the motions with each, making pleasant comments, inquiring after their particular interests, offering small tidbits of generally accurate personal details that were not the whole truth.

That included Madame Etna, who looked her up and down as if sizing up exactly what tack to take in convincing her to agree to a seance. At that point, Cadmus moved to the bell pull. He rang it, and sat down. "It is hooked up to a light, in the kitchen, when we need something."

Mrs Cooper brought in the first course. Vivian had worried it would be the worst sort of middling British food. Rather, instead of a Brown Windsor soup or some jumble of vegetable ends, it was tomato soup, with just the right touch of seasonings and cream. Nothing expensive, she was sure the tomatoes had been put up from a garden's abundance a month or two ago, but well done.

The main course was, as Cadmus had mentioned, a fish with dill cream sauce, quite tasty, and she suspected really rather suitable to the larger number of women present. The men took extra servings of bread and butter, she noticed, or the potatoes. There was a simple bread pudding, to round out the meal, with apples, raisins, and just enough spice for flavour.

As the meal finished, the charm lights dimmed, as if some other magic was draining them, leaving the room largely lit by the three candles in the centre of the table. Then a door slammed. A flash of something white, luminous, and apparently made of flowing fabric crossed between the long dining table and the single door out.

"She comes! She comes! She comes!" That was Madame Etna, and the comment was almost entirely predictable.

Vivian strained her senses, trying to feel for any shift in the magics of the room, or the house, that might suggest this was some legitimate ghost. She had found no particular stories about hauntings in her research about the house so far, but it had only been a boarding house for a few years. She could feel nothing like that, though certainly she was not an expert in ghosts or their hauntings.

The apparition floated from one side of the room to the other, past the door, before hovering in mid-air. The longer Vivian looked at it, the odder it seemed, having no particular sense of appendages at all. It was more like a fantasy of a ghost or phantasm than the thing itself.

Though, to be fair, she had vastly more experience with selkies, merfolk, various lineages of dwarves, and the plant-allies like Alfred and his people than with ghosts. If this were a ghost.

The others in the room had, according to their personalities, shouted or backed away, or observed closely. Andromache and Emma were observing, as were Richard, and the Herr Professor. Robin, she noticed, was shifting away from it, not from fear, but as if he didn't want it to focus on him. She considered standing, and approaching it, but she thought that would be too much too soon for her new compatriots.

And besides, then it disappeared, as quickly as it had appeared. If it were a trick, done with smoke and mirrors and backlit fabric, she could not see how it was made. If it were a charm-illusion, all of them - bar Mrs Cooper, who seemed an unlikely sort to create that kind of thing - had been in the room, actively participating in conversation. Farran might have returned unannounced, but she had seen his discomfort with the unexplained events already.

It suggested some particular cause, recently introduced to the house, but that was as far as she got.

"Do, please, sit down, everyone. Wine?"

Cadmus's voice was wavering, Vivian noticed, showing that he had not cared for that at all. But he would carry on, stubborn and determined, in the best and worst traditions of the Colonial Service, whether or not it had agreed with him.

SIX

MONDAY AFTER SUPPER

"We must gather in my parlour!"

Cadmus barely managed to restrain a groan. He took a breath, and tried to think what Odysseus would do. There were worse models, at least Odysseus was known for his elaborate schemes and they often turned out well. Eventually.

"Please, Madam Etna, let us make sure everyone is all right." He looked around the table. Everyone was beginning to settle again. Ann Porter was looking intrigued rather than terrified, peering over the rims of her glasses. It would be rather awful if she fled after less than five hours in the building, so that was slightly reassuring. "Is everyone well? More wine, anyone?" He held up the wine bottle, Richard and Emma both extended their glasses, and he topped them off, then poured another glass for himself.

He took a deep breath, looking around the table. "I'd say that was unexpected, but it isn't really. I beg your pardon, Ann, I should have warned you we have had some, some, unexpected events here. Almost none have been dangerous.

The greenhouse might have been an unfortunate fluke." It sounded feeble to him, Merlin knew what she made of it.

"Unexpected?" Ann leaned forward. "No history of ghosts, then?"

Cadmus found it frankly embarrassing to try and explain. Even ignoring the fact - which he really couldn't - that residents had left whose coin they couldn't afford to lose. "No, no history of ghosts or hauntings or anything more than the usual creaks of an old building with many people living in it."

"And the greenhouse?"

"There was an orchid in the greenhouse that gave Mrs Gollard - she's no longer a resident - a nasty rash, and it shouldn't have. It turned into a different variety. There have been some odd lights in the gardens. Things moved around in the library. There might be an innocent explanation, but when I've asked, no one has said it was their doing, And now - this."

Ann narrowed her eyes, and Cadmus got a sense of something shifting in her, not that he could figure out what. "Madam Etna, do you believe it was a Presence?" He could hear the capital letter in her voice. He'd thought better of Ann Porter, but he supposed folklorists were nearly as likely to be bogged down in whimsy as a spiritualist.

Madam Etna drew herself up, as best she could - she was not a tall or naturally imposing woman - and then said, "You know of my art?"

Ann nodded. "I'm quite aware of the very real skills required, yes. You have lived here some time? Is there a new sense of a Presence? Or something changed?"

That got Madam Etna pursing her lips, before she said, "I would need to consult my spirit guide."

"May I inquire as to the identity of your spirit guide?

I'm afraid I had quite a difficult experience a few years ago with..." Ann pursed her lips. "One of Boudica's daughters, I think the claim was." Cadmus got the distinct sense that she had begun hunting, and it was rather like watching an invisible hound and its quarry. Fascinating, and decidedly unsettling, not least because it was suddenly not the nonsense he had initially assumed.

"You are not a believer?" The retort came sharply.

"In that case, no. I asked the usual sort of clarifying questions, and the woman had absolutely no answer for things that would be quite normal for a spirit from those times." Ann fluttered her eyelashes for a moment. "There were some sort of claims about an elephant. And visions of her troops being seen in the midst of one of the London railroad stations, or something of the kind. And nothing she said about food made any sense."

Whatever Cadmus had expected her to say, it had not involved elephants. He rather thought someone had got Boudica confused with Hannibal, which made even less sense. Madam Etna clearly was put off her usual routine as well, so at least it was not just him that she discomfited. She drew herself up, then with as much dignity as she could manage said, "My guide is nothing like that. We refer to her, respectfully, as the Grey Dancer. Not by some such name as Esmerelda or Roland or Montmorency."

Ann shook her head. "Of course not." There was a flicker of something in her eyes, too fleeting for Cadmus to make sense of. This whole conversation was going entirely too fast for his comfort. He was no Odysseus, he knew that, for all he wished he could summon the man's adaptability.

"Perhaps not tonight, however, Madam Etna. You will - you will," he cast around for some acceptable explanation. "You will surely want to prepare, properly? A day of silent reflection, haven't you said you prefer that for matters of significant weight?"

Madam Etna drew in a breath, sharp enough that all her jewelry shivered. "I must consult the charts, the moon phase, the planetary alignments, for something so important, our dear home." She narrowed her eyes. "And to see how our newest resident takes to the space."

Ann spread her hands. "Entirely appropriate, Madam Etna. I may make a few short day trips to begin my research, but I would be glad to attend if desired."

Seeing that some sense of detente had been reached, Cadmus cleared his throat. "You are all welcome to stay, of course. Ann, perhaps I might show you something more of the house?"

Ann rose, moving gracefully. "That would be most kind, yes. Thank you for a most interesting welcome, ladies and gentlemen." She glanced down the table. "And my dear cousin. We must catch up at some point."

It sounded, to Cadmus, at least, more like a threat than affection. He hurriedly coughed. "The moon rise is really quite lovely from the garden windows. This way?" He wished people would not be so complicated, and Madam Ann Porter seemed very complicated indeed.

Thankfully, she followed him out, quickly enough. Once they were well away from the dining room, he said, "I do apologise for Madam Etna, she takes the whole thing so very seriously."

Ann waved a hand, looking vastly more relaxed than Cadmus felt. That was wrong, too. It was his home, he had lived here from before he was born. She'd not even spent a night here, how could she be so at ease? Still, having offered a sight of the moon, he was now committed to showing her the gardens by moonlight. He walked, and she kept pace with him.

"You have previous experiences with spiritualists?"

There was a sharp nod. "You permit Madam Etna to remain. May I ask your own - views of the topic?"

"I allow anyone who keeps the house rules and keeps up with their account to remain." He didn't have much choice about that, not really. Then he swallowed, and said, "There are a lot of spiritualists around. More now, since the War. She seems much less, much less..." Then he couldn't figure out what the proper adjective was.

"Does she do seances regularly here?"

"Oh, no. Not for clients. She and several others share a little flat in Oxford for that sort of thing. Tasteful garden with many moonflowers, floral wallpaper. Very Edwardian. She only does seances here for herself and other residents."

"May I ask which usually indulge?" There was an odd note to the last word.

"Madam Gregson, Mistress Cole, Danae White and occasionally Richard Danegeld, and your - cousin?"

"Very distant cousin." Ann's voice was prim and clipped again.

"Is that, pardon, but you are staying here. Is that going to be a problem?"

"His line of the family have, one might say, different priorities than mine. In a number of areas. We will sort ourselves out without damaging your home, I promise."

"Would he keep the same promise?"

There was a long pause. "I am not sure he would think to make it, but he does not..." Her voice dropped off, as if she was considering how much to say. "He would consider your house neutral ground, and it would be impolite and also imprecise to cause damage in that case."

That was not at all reassuring, but Cadmus rather suspected he had wandered into something untranslatable. It certainly seemed a rather complex sort of family, and he hoped that Ann was more of an Agamede than a Medea. The interest in plants was optimistic, in that regard. He gathered himself, and finally managed, "Well, I suppose that's something. I sometimes sit in on the seance too." He felt he had to confess that, or - well, or she'd realise as soon as they actually sat down for the seance.

"Why?"

It was a sharp question. Everything about her was sharp. "I don't believe, but I don't disbelieve, either. I have - I do not have enough evidence either way."

"Not your first ghost, then?"

That type of question flung him back to the mountains of Afghanistan, as it always did, and he shivered. He kept it to just the one shudder, this time, barely. His jaw snapped shut, it must be loud enough for her to hear. "This way." Fussing with the outer door to the garden gave him a chance to regain his composure, even as he scolded himself silently for being made of such brittle metal.

She waited until he'd opened the door and gestured her out, then moved to stand on the broad terrace behind the house. The garden stretched out in front of them, entirely dark except for the light from the few rooms on this side of the house with lights on. "The garden. The back, there, is the orchard."

The moon was waning, but still close enough to full there was plenty of silvery light. Ann tilted her head, and he could see her frowning for a moment.

"Is there a problem?"

"Oh, no. I'm curious, though. Is there a building that

way? I thought I caught a glimpse of something in the moonlight."

"There are deer in the forest, of course. And other animals. Badgers, rabbits, foxes. There is a folly off that way, though. A modest tower. My father used it as a reading room, it's still in quite good repair."

"Indeed." Then she nodded at him, once more. "Thank you. I'll see you later."

Before he could say anything, never mind ask what she meant, she had ducked back into the house.

SEVEN

TUESDAY, OCTOBER 10TH

The next morning, Vivian rose early. She wanted a chance to get a sense of the place before the other people were up and about.

There was no sign of movement as she left her room, pressing her hand to the door to seal the lock to her magic, as well as turning the key. She listened, then went down the stairs, heading for the library. There was no noise in the breakfast room, either, and she could not yet smell food set out.

There was no one in the library when she opened the door, but the way the chairs had moved suggested people had been there some little time the night before. Perhaps discussing the apparition, or whatever else it might be. She went directly to the shelves, looking for books of local or familial history that might be of interest. She couldn't read them all now, of course, but she could note which books were there.

Five minutes later, there was a tidy list in her own personal shorthand in the pocket notebook she kept for such things. There were no gaping holes in the collection, but neither were there works which immediately struck her as relevant to the problem. She would have been uneasy if there had been no books on local folklore or ghost stories, or no works of family history. Either might suggest that someone in the home was hiding something, perhaps something significant.

The books were, however, exactly what she might suspect. She could not decide, for the life of her, if that was a good thing or not.

Letting out a puff of breath, she tucked her notebook back into the concealed pocket in her skirt, and turned to go look out the windows. She had been standing there for perhaps a minute when she heard a gentle little cough.

Turning, she saw Mistress Cole by the door. "I saw the door, I do hope you don't mind, were you in the middle of something? Oh, were you reading, there are so many nice books in here. And some rather odd ones, but I suppose that's the way of an old library, getting out of step with the fashion."

One of those women, clearly, who had to narrate the world in order to make sense of it. Or as much sense as she wanted to, which was not as much as Vivian might prefer. Vivian took a breath, and pasted on her charming and approachable smile. "You're Mistress Cole, of course. We didn't get an opportunity to speak much last night."

"No, no, you were very much enjoying your conversation with the younger women. You professional women, you do like to chat. That's a thing, isn't it now, how you make your little nests of who talks who, and what you talk about."

Decidedly fluttery. "Oh, I enjoy a wide range of conversation. Are you an early riser, then?"

"Oh, I barely sleep these days, but I don't mind. I get to

see the sunset and the dawn, and that's a thing I'd never have thought I'd say when I was a schoolgirl, always wanting to lollygag in bed. Is that the word I mean?"

"I think so, yes. Did you want something? I don't want to disrupt anyone's usual routine, that wouldn't be kind at all." Vivian was quite capable of the same sort of twittery pleasantry in return. It was, in fact, an essential method of parts of her work.

"Oh, I just came to let you know that Mrs Cooper has put breakfast out, and to offer to show you. If it was you here, but who else would it be, the others aren't down this early, or don't come down to this part of the house until they've had a nice bit of strong tea to wake them up. Do you eat much in the mornings, Madam Porter?"

It did make Vivian smile. "Oh, please do call me Ann, if you'd prefer, Mistress Cole. I do appreciate it. Perhaps I might ask you a few more things about the house? What the custom is? A new boarding house is always rather a mix of discovery and fearing one's put one's foot in it entirely. And I do like a nice breakfast, not too filling, but something to keep me going."

The older woman considered for a moment. "Ann." There was no offer for Vivian to use her first name, but that was all right. It was a small step on the right path. "And of course, dear, I'm glad to help. And Mr Michaels is a fine man - Michaels senior, I mean - but he is a man, and there are so many things he doesn't think to mention."

Vivian nodded. "My little suite is quite well decorated."

"Oh, that would have been Mrs Cooper's doing. Most of it, at any rate. Or it would all be leather and wood. Or possibly marble, and that's a horrid cold substance, isn't it. It's a terribly sturdy sort of house, actually, for all they worry about it."

"All they worry?"

"Mr Michaels and his nephew. And I suppose Mrs Cooper, too, but I can't make sense of any of that. They taught me enough to say please and thank you. I wouldn't want to be rude, that would be horrid, but I just don't understand how it makes sense to other people, all the things with the hands."

"I know a bit of sign language, and the woman who taught me pointed out it's not that different from talking to someone with a strong accent. From the highlands in Scotland, say. You learn how to make sense of it, bit by bit."

"You sign? Oh, goodness, where did you learn that? I didn't think it was a common thing at all, but if a professional woman like you knows that kind of thing, well, it must have some use, mustn't it?"

Vivian considered. The accurate answer to that wasn't an option, and this was in fact the sort of woman who would recognise dissembling more quickly than most. The twittery women so often did notice things out of place, whatever else they might or might not do. "Oh, I learned from a distant cousin - she lives in a village, quite remote, up north, where a number of people sign, and I was collecting folklore from the area. I'm not fluent, or not as much as I'd like to be, but enough to get by, with a bit of help."

"Goodness, you mentioned, but I didn't realise, how brave, travelling all those places you must go to get stories."

"I admit, I'm a bit more interested in the house. You mentioned it was quite sturdy?" If she could redirect Mistress Cole, all the better.

"Oh, yes, so many of these old houses, they have bits of stonework dropping off, or horrid leaks in the corner of the room, or some such. But for all Mr Michaels worries about it, it seems to be the general upkeep. A place that's had a few hard years, not a decade or two of neglect, or more. Or worse, gilding the lily - that's the term I want, isn't it? Making the place look good without tending to the bones."

Vivian rather felt that Mistress Cole's metaphors were getting more and more mixed. "No, I do see what you mean there." Vivian kept her voice pleasant. "And there's no tales, nothing of the unexpected?"

"Well, there haven't been, but perhaps the family's all been dreadfully practical, not noticing the subtler influences? I mean, I'm quite sure that Mr Michaels, kind as he is, isn't the sort to welcome, well, the gentler touch."

There were a dozen ways Vivian could guide that. She decided on a mild approach. "But he comes to the seances?"

"Oh, yes. He takes hospitality very seriously, I think. Which is a good thing for a man, isn't it? Not at all common these days, not the way it used to be. But we should talk to Madam Etna, certainly. She's the one who knows about the spirits."

Vivian had assumed that's where Mrs Cole would end up, certainly. "At lunch, perhaps, if there's a chance?" She made the suggestion gently.

"Oh, she might not wish to talk. She regularly spends whole days in silence, fasting, to sharpen her senses."

Vivian suspected, based on her previous experiences of such mediums, that it was instead an excuse to curl up with a pleasant novel and a plate of sandwiches and bonbons and not be bothered by anyone. She couldn't blame the woman for that, certainly. Mrs Cole certainly seemed kind, but perhaps a bit tiring, the way she tended to chatter on.

"Emma suggested I might talk to you about some of the plants you worked with?" Vivian made the suggestion to try and guide the conversation a little easier to manage. Thankfully, it worked, with a few tidbits about the mechanisms of action of particular plants she might well find useful for other projects.

EIGHT

TUESDAY AT SUPPER

C admus was prepared to let out a sigh of relief after supper that day. Ann Porter seemed to be settling in well enough. The difficult residents tended to turn up at his office promptly at nine in the morning after their first night with a list of desires. Some of those were legitimate, of course, something no one had noticed was broken or loose or not working correctly.

But with the difficult ones, there were a host of less sensible requests. The sun was too bright, could he alter that? But no, not with additional curtains, that was too much work, opening and closing them. Others were shocked they could hear the sounds of other people in the building in the hallways. The idea that their rooms could be managed with charms, but a long hallway was not worth the effort and the upkeep in the magic, seemed beyond most of them.

He had lost his temper with someone a year ago, enough to snap "It is a home with near a score of other people living here. Some people find that enjoyable," at Mr Lothington, who had complained about the noise repeatedly. He rather regretted the sharpness, but not the fact Mr Lothington had left the following week. The man had been exceedingly demanding, and rather unpleasant to Mrs Cooper.

At any rate, Ann had made no undue demands. Cadmus had been able to spend the entire day working on his current translation project, and then spend supper letting other people talk. It was really most pleasant.

There were only four of them tonight, Cadmus and three of the women. And Richard, at least briefly. But Richard had had to excuse himself when he was called away to a patient as they were finishing.

The other men had been busy with other things, in Trellech, he thought. Various matters of business. And he gathered Andromache and Emma were attending a lecture together. It was a fine thing that they got on so well, they'd both seemed a bit lonely when they moved in.

Robin Aelfdane had mentioned something about a supper out with a friend in Oxford. Cadmus wasn't sure what to make of their interactions, those two cousins. They didn't look much alike, either, but quite distant cousins might well not. He certainly knew distant cousins who looked nothing alike, though usually those were so distant they didn't necessarily recognise each other, much less treat each other dubiously.

Ann was dark haired, trim and tidy, and probably in her mid-forties, though he was a lousy judge of a woman's age even when she wasn't wearing cosmetics. Robin was noticeably younger, perhaps thirty. Not the same generation, then, or near enough not. And he was tall, rangey, and quite blonde. Also a much sharper dresser, favouring eyecatching jeweltone colours.

At any rate, it meant supper was Cadmus himself, Ann Porter, Mistress Cole, Madam Gregson, and Madam Etna, who had slipped away after the entree was removed, claiming a headache.

Ann was having a pleasant conversation with Mistress Cole, something about the local sights, he couldn't quite hear the details. They seemed to be doing well enough, and that was a kindness. Mistress Cole could be quite wearying, the way she went on, but she meant well.

He waited for a lull in the conversation, then offered a "Perhaps we might take the tea into the orangery? It's quite a pleasant night out for the autumn."

Ann nodded, and said "I'm afraid I was so busy settling in I didn't get to explore the gardens today, and it's supposed to rain tomorrow."

Trivial, but pleasant. Cadmus arranged the tea things on the tray, and carried it along. Turning into the hall to the orangery, he stopped dead after two steps. Something was terribly different about this hallway he'd walked down every day for decades, and he was transfixed.

The paintings on the wall, the various landscapes painted by esteemed ancestors and associates of the family, they had changed colours. Where the hallway had had the calming greens and blues of hills and rivers, a farming scene, a field with sheep, there was now a riot of competing colours. They almost made his eyes hurt, bright oranges and glaring reds. Even the blues had a sharpness to them, like the colour the sky in Afghanistan had been before everything went horribly wrong.

He managed to set the tray down, rather than drop it, and then held out his hands. "Beg pardon, ladies, but I believe there's another curiosity here. Please, stay where you are." He did his best to use his voice of authority, such as it was, but they did stop, peering down the hallway.

"Is something the matter, Mr Michaels?" That was

Mistress Cole. Ann, he realised, was looking from side to side.

"I presume this was not a hallway dedicated to the Fauvists?" Her voice was more amused than otherwise.

"No, it was not." He added to Mistress Cole. "The colours of the paintings have changed. Not the form, I think, at least not in principle." That would require closer examination, and he was not sure he wanted to venture it. He wondered then if this was temporary or not. Most of the paintings had sentimental value, and not much else. They showed the house, the nearby lands, the occasional ancestor. But there was one painting of particular note, an early Turner. He didn't want to sell it, but knowing he could had let him go back to sleep more than one night.

Mistress Cole harrumphed. "Paintings should stay as they're painted, silly things." She shook her head. "I will get back to my knitting then."

Cadmus waited for her to go, expecting Ann would leave too. Instead, she stayed where she was, looking from side to side, at what she could see down the hall.

"You're not frightened?" He would be. Well, he was, honestly. But she had much more right to be, it was a strange house, she knew nothing about any of them, so any sensible person would be packing her bags.

She was not packing her bags. Perhaps, then, she was not sensible. His brain tried to turn it into one of those ridiculous sentences from a grammar book, where the basic premise was repeated in a dozen different constructions.

When he managed to rein in his mind, she was looking at him. Very patiently. Then she said, and he suddenly suspected she was repeating herself, "Not at all. I find it an interesting mystery."

"You're sure?" It sounded feeble, even to him.

"Nothing so far that I've seen has been remotely dangerous. You mentioned that there was an orchid, in the greenhouse?"

"Yes. But she had an unusual allergy. Long before that incident, I gather. And she's really quite all right now, Richard made sure of that."

Ann considered. "Look, all these things, they really are quite curious. Do they scare you?"

Cadmus considered, carefully. "They're unsettling. The house hasn't changed much, all the years I've been here."

"All your life?" The question was casual enough, but Cadmus felt himself bristle.

"Most of it. Mother ran a small tutoring house here, so I didn't go away to that. Five years at Schola, of course. And then I was in the Colonial Service for a few years, but other than that, yes. Here. Or near enough to be back every fortnight or so."

Ann nodded. "And no ghost stories?"

"Oh, the usual range in the village, I gather. You'd likely know better than I."

"Ghost stories are, in fact, an entirely different genus than folklore. As a rule."

The thought diverted him. "Do you classify them with Latin names? Or - Gaelic? Or does it depend where you are?"

"The classic system is numbers, actually. Invented by a Finn. Antti Aarne, still quite a new system, only a decade or so old."

"Oh, that sounds rather intriguing, I do appreciate a thoughtful classification. Do you have a copy?"

She flushed. "I'm afraid it's in German. I gather there's someone considering a translation."

Cadmus waved a hand. "I'm a classicist. Much of our professional literature, such as it is, diverts through German. I can muddle along well enough, at least with a dictionary."

She tilted her head for a moment. "Is that why Herr Profesosr Bolsano is here?"

"A favour for an acquaintance." Cadmus admitted. "He was - having some trouble finding someone who would rent to him. As if he were to blame for the War."

"Not at all military, I gathered."

"Goodness, no. What we'd call a conscientious objector, or near enough, I think, though I've never pressed him on the details. I did confirm that he has permission for long-term residence and all that, of course."

"Has he been here long?"

"Oh, a year. The last one to join us was - " Cadmus counted back. "That would be your cousin, I think." He considered. "The odd occurrences began sometime after that. At least a month."

Ann nodded. Then she blurted out, "I'm sorry. I just remembered something. Do excuse me."

NINE

TUESDAY AFTER SUPPER

"Cousin." Robin was lurking outside her set of rooms, leaning against the wall. He was the picture of the man of leisure, a royal blue suit with a bright green pocket square and waistcoat, hair slicked back. "We really should catch up."

Vivian glanced around, considering. Inviting him in was just encouraging him in half a dozen ways Robin should never be encouraged. But they did have things to say to each other that were better done in private.

"Half an hour."

"I brought those marzipan treats you like so much."

"Bribing me will not help you."

"You say that, and then I give you nice things, and you invite me in."

Vivian snorted, then reached to unlock the door, then ushered him in. "You're lucky this isn't one of those boarding houses where men aren't ever allowed in a lady's private rooms."

"Come on, Viv. We're cousins."

She closed the door, sharply. "Don't call me that."

"Are you on a case, then?" He slunk over to the easy chair by the window, lifted it six inches in the air with a wave of his hand, and turned it around to face the desk, leaving her the less comfortable chair.

"I am living in the Oxford countryside for my health, of course."

"So no recent burning passion for folklore then."

She waved a hand. Actually, the folklore was a long-standing interest. Or rather, figuring out the ways in which the stories she knew from her foremothers had been changed and warped by the passage of time and human culture. "Why are you here? I wouldn't have thought you the sort for rustication."

"Technically, if one is at Oxford, one is doing anything but rusticating."

"Ah, right, when in Rome and all that. You didn't answer my question." She kept her voice as even as she could.

"This and that. A bit of research. A bit of inquiry. I don't want you stepping on my toes." She could tell he was hiding something, the breezy way he said it. He knew she knew, of course.

"Do you think that's likely?" Vivian leaned back in her chair, which gave a rather querulous creak.

"I have a variety of interests. Are you working with any museums while you're here? Historical collections."

Vivian peered at him, shifting the glasses she wore largely for show down her nose. "Historical items?" It was not precisely in her usual line of work, though she'd taken a few cases related to artifacts in museums over the years. Robin, though, had been making a bit of a wave for himself in antiques, last she'd heard.

"You know what I mean."

Vivian did know, but the fact he was being that vague did not suggest he was up to anything good. "My current project is related to this house, which may include its history, collections, and so on."

She watched him closely, and he let out a small breath, relaxing minutely. It was the angle in his shoulders that gave him away. Interesting. Uninformative, but interesting. "And you? I can't avoid stepping on your toes if I don't know where they are."

"A historical thing. Not your preferred period."

Vivian considered that. She wouldn't trust him to know her preferred periods, for a start. Certainly he didn't know about the interest in folklore. "And local."

"I do rather prefer London, yes. But the greater world does sometimes entice."

Vivian snorted again. "Not your usual mode, trees and hills." She considered. "And why'd you pick this house?" Caelano's line tended to be drawn to the hidden and secret, and while the landscape held many secrets, Robin had always preferred his creature comforts. A soft bed, a warm fire, good food. Vivian was not so drawn to the wild as her cousins in the line of Taygate, who had a particular call to the wild places beloved by Artemis, but she could hold her own in a campsite.

"I could ask you the same thing."

Vivian waved a hand. "I told you."

"Not nearly enough, dear coz, not nearly enough." He considered. "It is convenient to my needs. Both Oxford itself, and other points. I keep a rented horse in the stable. Rather a nag, but with an exceedingly smooth trot."

That suggested a fair bit of travel. Robin's family line dealt with things like trains about as well as Vivian did - which was to say, not a favourite mode, but a manageable one. But the horse suggested he was going to places the rails didn't run. "What will it take for you to stay out of my way, then?"

"You must define your terms, coz, you know that. Being so much my elder, and so properly one." That much was true. Robin was a good twenty years younger, just coming up on forty, though everyone assumed he was in his early thirties. He passed for an established young man, where Vivian was settling into amiable middle-age, as far as appearance went. She wondered, and not for the first time, what answer he gave when someone asked about his War service.

"My particular interest is investigating the curious goings-on in the house. As a favour to young Farran Michaels, who is friends with my assistant's brother."

"I was going to say, I'm quite sure they can't afford your fee."

Vivian hesitated for just a moment, then decided to ask. "What makes you say that in particular?"

"A dozen things. The menu is heavy on stew meats, eggs, and dairy - they've a cow or two, out in the back pasturage, and chickens. Quite a few chickens. Someone local makes quite a good farm cheese, thankfully. I noticed we'd had more chicken the last two days. Is that your doing then?"

Vivian nodded minutely. Robin hadn't seemed to have the same issue with red meat she and her line had. There were so many unexplained differences between the descendents of the seven sisters, and no one was inclined to talk about them with people from other families.

"Can't say I mind. Stew meat isn't my favourite, and she kept trying to feed me liver and onions, though that's a bit hearty for the older ladies here."

Vivian arched an eyebrow. "You implied there were other signs."

"Oh, the usual upkeep issues. The signs they're prioritising oddly. I did have a wander through the family wing when I knew everyone was out one day, and it's all quite dingy. Comfortable enough, especially that study Cadmus is using."

"You didn't." Vivian didn't bother to keep the shock out of her voice. She might be an investigator, but she had scruples about how far she pried. At least not without well-defined cause.

"Tsk, coz. Given what you do..." He let his voice trail off, and Vivian raised her chin at the implied threat.

"You know perfectly well I give as good as I get. If you make this difficult for me, I will do the same to you."

There was a terribly long pause. She did hope Robin wasn't going to be an idiot, in the entirely Greek sense of acting on his own behalf rather than that of the community.

"Fair enough. I won't tell on you, if you leave me be."

There was something entirely too pat about that. She looked at him. "You won't tell on me, and I will leave you be so long as you act within the laws."

"Both laws?"

"Plural, yes. Theirs and ours."

"On our foremothers, I suppose."

"Swearing on the Silence is not sufficiently binding for us, no." It was for those without their bloodlines, quite effective, and if she made an oath by the Silence in a formal court, it would act sufficiently the same as to fool anyone who didn't know better. But this was no formal court, with the additional magics binding intent as well as speech.

Robin took a deep breath, and then nodded. By custom, the younger went first. "By the line of my mother, by lightning-struck Celaeno," he began. "With the fire in my blood binding this oath, I swear on my magic and my foremothers not to reveal the true names, roles, or lineage of the one known as Vivian Porter. I likewise swear not to reveal her business here, save to those who are already aware of it."

Vivian nodded. "By the line of my mother, by dark-faced Electra. With my blood holding my magic and binding this oath, I swear on blood and tears and the powers that fill me not to interfere with the actions of this man, known by some as Robin Aelfdane of the line of Celaeno, unless he contravenes the laws of the Fatae or the laws of the Anthropoi."

"So made." As he spoke, she felt the slight faint ping, like a clockwork spring moving in the back of her mind, that made her sure that he had not yet broken those laws, but that he fully intended to if given the chance.

She barely heard his echo, but she felt the oath settle in place, and then she pulled up her sleeve, revealing a new dark freckle in the constellation of them on her arms that had not been there a minute before. Properly done, then, the oaths, that was something.

"Fair enough. Is there anything else?" Brisk no-nonsense practicality, that was the way to deal with Robin, she felt.

"We know where we both stand. That's enough to be going on with. Will you be eating dinner downstairs regularly?" He moved to stand up, not bothering to put the chair back in place.

"Oh, yes. Best way to learn about what's going on. You don't have any theories, do you?"

She caught, just for the briefest moment, a hint of something. Nothing she could call out, nothing she could pin down, but that whisper that here was something to note.

He didn't answer. Of course, he wouldn't. That would be entirely too helpful of him, and Robin was never helpful. She didn't know how that had gone wrong, but Robin had always felt disconnected from their customs, their codes of conduct. Solitary, where with most of her cousins, they may not have much else in common, but they upheld the traditions and commitments without complaint. Well, without much complaint.

TEN

C admus felt unsettled, all the way from teatime to supper. He couldn't put a finger on it.

His current translation was going along better, finally. It was complex, figuring out the ways to turn the Greek into English, but not just into English, but something that carried the appropriate connotations. He had turned his pen to it, two years ago. Someone in the Owlery had pointed out that with all his travels in Afghanistan and the surrounding lands, surely he might be better positioned to do a translation of the travels of Herodotus than many others. Certainly he might stand a better chance of glossing the names of animals and plants than many editions had done.

Cadmus hadn't been sure what he thought of that, but he had been casting around for a project, and it at least presented some amusing challenges. It was difficult to figure out what Herodotus had meant in the first place. More than a few of the creatures he described seemed entirely fantastical, even for someone who knew about magical creatures.

The second challenge was whether he could avoid

unintentional insults in the text. There were certainly plenty of intentional ones - Herodotus had thought the Greeks the pinnacle of the world, naturally. If he did this right, it would be a grand fit for a new line of teaching editions of classic texts that was in the planning stages. A bit more money, but better, the possibility of being included in other projects down the road. That was no small thing.

He had got into the second section, named for Euterpe. It had him thinking not only about Egypt, the topic of the moment, but about how Herodotus had structured the work in the first place. Each section was named after one of the Muses. The divisions of the muses and their realms had always baffled him. He had no extensive experience with women, not outside of his immediate family and the conversations with the residents, but he had always assumed they were as individual as men were, and as varied in their interests.

Classicists, at least those of his generation and older, did not spend overmuch time actually talking to women. And especially not about matters of translation. Cadmus had always rather thought you might get a lot further by consulting them about some of the metaphors - weaving, braiding, and so on. Or that a woman might shed rather a lot of light on Penelope, or Circe. Even Medea, for all she had done monstrous things.

He was deep in thought by the time the others filed in for supper, leaving space for Ann up near his end of the table. Andromache and Emma were deep in some debate about a modern play, and they had drawn Richard into the conversation. Robin came in, but sidled over to listen to them, rather than settle further up the table.

When Ann came in, shawl draped around her, she was carrying herself rather like a queen in exile. Regal, potent, but not quite in her native land. She glanced around the table with a tiny hitch of her shoulders. Then she dropped gracefully into her seat next to Cadmus just as Mrs Cooper brought the soup in.

"Pleasant day?" he asked, for lack of anywhere else to start.

"Oh, settling in, still. I didn't get as much done as I hoped."

"Do you have a usual routine?" Cadmus was, in fact, curious. They'd had several dozen researchers and writers and artists of various types through the house, and he was beginning to form a classification system.

Ann considered, eating several spoonfuls of her soup then setting the spoon down, before she replied. "This is excellent."

He nodded. "Mrs Cooper is a wonderful cook." He wondered if she was going to answer.

Ann took her time. "I don't have a rigid schedule, you understand."

Some people did, he could understand why she would make the distinction. "I am a man of rather settled habits myself, given the opportunity."

She tilted her head, considering. "Do you prefer your detailed work in the morning or evening?"

"That depends a bit on how you count." He considered, he'd never actually spelled this out before, not in detail. No one had asked, really. About his work, what he was doing, yes, but not how he did it.

"How do you count it?"

He tapped his fingers on the table, thinking. "At the end of the day, I read through the next passage - a page or two, usually, to a reasonable stopping point. I make note of words I want to look into more closely. Translation has a great many words that are easily managed. But some are more complex, the nuance. One in ten, perhaps, in Herodotus. Much more than that in Homer. The playwrights are somewhere in the middle."

Ann's eyes danced. "And the poets?" She was focused entirely on him, but Cadmus noticed the conversation at the other end of the table had dropped away.

"I find the poets rather more of a challenge, admittedly." He considered. "I worry I miss their nuances." He was startled by how much she'd drawn him out, but she was asking quite reasonable questions, on the face of it. Perhaps it was startling principally because she was asking, rather than turning the conversation to herself.

"Do you have a favourite challenge to set yourself against?"

Cadmus looked up, meeting Ann's eyes, then he looked away, flushing, and he didn't know why. "Do you?"

"I've an admiration for both Sappho's brazenness and her breadth of phrasing." Ann's voice had turned warmer, a velvety tone. He heard one of the other women laugh, something full-throated and not a sound he'd heard before. "And there's a rather glorious description about her, wasn't it 'violet haired, pure, honey-smiling Sappho'?"

From the end of the table, Andromache called out, "Do you have a favourite line?"

"Oh, yes, because it is a puzzle to me. I am not a woman made for a grand passion, you understand. The one that begins 'Love shook my heart.'"

Andromache nodded, and quoted. "Love shook my heart like the wind on the mountain, troubling the oak-trees." She asked, "Never married?"

"Marriage and passion fit to trouble the oak-trees do not go hand in hand, not among my kin." There was a little quirk of her lips, and Cadmus noticed that Robin had gone particularly quiet. "But I do sometimes wonder what that would be like to live."

Cadmus wondered, for a moment, what she meant by that. He supposed there were plenty of families who taught their children by tutors and apprenticeships, not sending them away to school. And many of those were known for matching their children off, by some arcane system or another.

Emma said, calmly. "I'm rather fond of that one about the Pleiades." She quoted, her eyes half closed. "The moon is down. The Pleiades. Midnight. Time flows on. I lie, alone." She added, after a moment's silence. "Not cheerful, that one, but - I've felt that more than once. Not so much recently, thankfully. It did not agree with me."

Ann nodded slightly. "The War, or something else?" Her posture had shifted, becoming slightly more guarded.

"The War did not help, no." There was something there that Cadmus couldn't begin to translate. The three women were having a conversation in a language he thought he knew, but there were layers of nuance there that made no sense to him. It was as if someone had introduced an entirely new voice, like middle voice in the Greek, that made implications cascade down like waterfalls. He missed at least half a sentence.

When he could pay attention to the words again, Ann was saying, "Do you have a preferred way to work, Andromache?"

"Oh, I'm curious about Cadmus. He hadn't finished, we did distract." And then, as if she was a queen offering a welcome, Andromache added, "Perhaps you might join us after supper, for some further conversation?"

Emma nodded. "My room has a lovely view of the

garden, and we like a little conversation before we read and sleep."

Ann inclined her head, and again, there were layers there Cadmus could not make sense of at all. "I would be honoured." She inhaled, her entire body shifted, aligning on him again, and she said, evenly, "I'm sorry, we did interrupt your explanation."

Cadmus did his best to gather himself. After a moment, he said, "In the morning, I start by looking over the words I'd listed out, going through the lexicon and all that."

"Liddell and Scott, I assume?"

"And various other sources, yes. You are familiar?"

"Modestly. I have some familiarity, though not as much as my mother would prefer."

That made Cadmus lean forward. "Schola?"

Ann shook her head. "I was privately tutored, then apprenticed. I do envy those who had a chance to go away to school, really." She waved a hand, then added, quoting, "Remembering those things we did in our youth, beautiful things. My beautiful things were rather solitary." Which answered his thought from earlier rather conveniently. It was rather nice when people were so obliging, and also rare.

Cadmus caught Emma making some gesture to Andromache, but then turned back to Ann, uncertain where to go. She smiled at him, almost beatific, and said. "After you consult the lexicon?"

"Then I will settle into the work. Greek has quite complex sentences, often, so I review the text, then go sentence by sentence, to begin. Once I have the meanings down - rather like scratchmarks - I work on the nuance."

"How much do you do in an hour? Or is that a terribly impolite thing to ask?"

"It is rather." Some people bragged about how long it

took them to finish a page, or a dozen lines. "In the current project? Half a page in an hour, if it's not too complex, but I can only do two pages in a day, usually. I'm working on a section about Egypt, and many of the terms he uses, I need to check in other sources, to make sure I'm translating them correctly."

"I have some connections to people working on the Egyptological digs, if that would be of interest."

"Petrie and that lot? I thought they weren't magical."

"There's a movement to get someone with proper language skills and sufficient magical skills to have a good look at the collection."

That was most intriguing. And it suggested a rather more far-reaching interest in research than Ann's comments had implied, so far. It was certainly more than folklore of plants, though he supposed she hadn't confessed a personal interest, just that she knew people. And Professor Murray wrote about both Egypt and the British Isles, even if he was not at all sure about her conclusions, given that she was clearly not of magical stock as Albion counted such things.

ELEVEN

FRIDAY EVENING

"Do come in, here, these chairs. Em, grab the desk chair, I'll take that." Andromache had a proprietary air about her, for all they were in fact in Emma's rooms. They were a mirror image to Vivian's. Emma had the rooms at the end of the hallway, like Vivian's, but with a better view out over the garden because of being a floor higher up .

The colours, though, were rather different. Where Vivian's rooms were muted blues and greens, Emma's rooms were in muted neutrals, shades of brown and beige. It would have been boring, almost tedious, except that there were splashes of bright jewel-toned embroidery on the bedlinens and curtains. And the colours were echoed by radiant glass vases and bowls, the vases themselves bursting with colour. Silk flowers, Vivian thought, given the time of year. It made her feel as if she were in a quiet wood, on the edge of a flower-filled meadow, and there was something decidedly peaceful about it.

"There you go." Vivian had settled into a comfortable brown velveteen chair, which fit her surprisingly well. She found most chairs a trifle too tall, but this one was sized to be comfortable and let her rest her feet solidly on the ground.

"Have you lived here long, Emma?"

"Oh, since the War, though I've worked at various places during that time. All in Oxford, of course. It's a pleasant walk to the station and a short train ride."

"And you, Andromache?"

"Andie, please, in private? So much more congenial." It was rather hail-fellow-well-met, but then she went on, her tone getting softer. "After the War for me. A year and a half ago. And Em and I found we suit rather nicely."

Vivian glanced from one to the other. "I am a trifle surprised you're still here, and didn't get a flat together somewhere in town. People would tut about spinsters, but that's not so uncommon these days."

Andie laughed, loudly. "How obvious were we, then?"

"Well, the Sappho rather confirmed things." Vivian grinned. "But I suspected the first night. Nothing obvious, you aren't giving it away to everyone. But the way you were with each other. You leaned over to mention something quietly to Emma. Something in the angle."

"Are you inclined our way yourself?" That was Emma, and it had a sharper tone.

"I've a rather odd background." Vivian shrugged. "I have little tolerance for most men, beyond specific intellectual projects we might collaborate on for a set period of time. I'm not at all sure I'd want to keep one around the house. I get along better with women, but I don't necessarily want to live with one either, and I'm not - mmm. Particularly inclined to a more sapphic sort of partnership."

"As you said, nothing to trouble the oak-trees in your past. And you're - mid-forties?"

Vivian considered. She hated lying outright to people, and age was one of those things most people didn't ask a woman, so it was easy to duck. Most of the time. "Older than that - my family doesn't look our age."

"Including your cousin?" The question was amiable enough, but Vivian could hear the interest.

"Distant cousin, but he's near enough the age he looks to make no real difference. Early thirties." She gave the age he used, not the one he was, as was their firm custom. "Has he been a bother? I can set a terrible aunt on him or something."

Andie laughed. "Oh, you have a terrible aunt too?"

"My aunts mostly think I'm the responsible sort." Vivian said. "But Robin? Oh, he's got terrible aunts."

"He's been very polite, really." That was Emma, who was settling in her desk chair, leaning back with a soft creak. "The sort of very polite that makes a sensible woman suspicious."

"Quite right." Vivian considered. "I've been wondering what he's up to, but he hasn't told me."

Andie tapped her fingers on the chair, then got up, and went to go make tea properly, from a small kettle on a side table. "Honey? Sugar? I'm afraid Em's out of cream." It was clear to Vivian that Andie wanted time to think before venturing something further about Robin.

"Honey is excellent." Vivian considered. "I assume the others don't know."

"Goodness, no. I don't think Cadmus would throw us out, but it would be awkward, and that kind of awkward is so terribly exhausting. The expectations. I wouldn't be surprised if a couple of them had guessed. Danae, for example. But your distant cousin keeps flirting with both of us, unrepentantly, or trying to. I can only assume he's either stupider than he looks, or we're doing well enough at obscuring our affections." Emma picked up easily.

"It is perhaps useful he wasn't around for the discussion of Sappho." Andie pointed out. "It was a bit less subtle."

"Quite. Though I don't think he's much of a reader of women's writing, classical or otherwise." Vivian didn't bother keeping the dry amusement out of her voice. These women would certainly appreciate it.

"Oh, that sort. Did he go up to Oxford? Or, no, he looks more like a Cambridge man, if he went to either." Andie brought a cup over, setting it in front of Vivian.

"Neither, actually - nor Schola. I think he was rather put out by that, actually. I remember someone telling me he'd got very into that set of Victorian school stories, all about the escapades and midnight feasts, and the mermaids in the hidden cove, and all that. Most of which I assume aren't that true. But he was certainly quite interested in the mermaids."

"Well, not the way they come up in stories. Not so much midnight feasts, no - the kitchen was across the court-yard, and rather well guarded. My house mistress used to have biscuits and cocoa out sometimes at curfew. But that's not the same thing as sneaking around at midnight to get it." Emma sounded very amused. "I was in Owl, mind, and we did have a couple of late night raids on the library, but one of the librarians always caught us at it."

"You too, Andie?"

Andie was busying herself with the tea, still. "I was in Seal, actually." She paused, then said, "The mermaids aren't something to joke about."

Vivian tilted her head. "May I ask more about that?"

Andie glanced over. "You may ask, but that's a bit outside your line of interest, isn't it?"

"We do live on an island. And I've always been interested in the liminal, I suppose you might say. The coastline,
the places things meet." It was a deflection from her memories of Scotland, going down among the cousins there, and
seeing to their needs, the things that people on land had to
bring to them. Gold that would not tarnish, volcanic glass
for tools, all manner of other things.

"Huh." It did not convince Andie, clearly, but she then
gestured. "Ask, and I'll see if I have answers."

Vivian nodded, to acknowledge the boundary. "So there
are mermaids there? I've heard stories of them in other
places. Cousins in Scotland, more to my taste than Robin is,
for one, they have a whole set of stories."

Andie picked up her tea, but when she set it down she
seemed more willing to speak. "The houses, at Schola, they
select for a whole set of things, but for those in Seal, liminal
is a good enough word. We were encouraged to go talk to
them, but never forget that while we have a great deal in
common, we are not the same kinds of beings. That there
was etiquette and politeness to be followed, on both sides,
but we shouldn't assume we wanted the same things, or to
do them the same way."

"That seems fair enough, really." Vivian considered. "A
good teacher, then, to make that lesson clear. Along with
your other studies?"

"Oh, yes. I focused on the Quadrivium, actually. Less
common than some of the other areas, like ritual magics or
alchemy or materia, but more useful for my purpose, since
those four arts - mathematics, geometry, music, and
astronomy - form the basis for so many of the early
sciences."

"A much broader education than I got. Or rather, much
of mine was either following the interests of whoever was

teaching me that week or that month, or going off on my own and learning about something, until I could demonstrate my knowledge to whoever I was reporting to."

"Aunts, again, I assume?" Emma cleared her throat. "Not uncles?"

"In our extended family, mostly aunts doing that sort of thing. Not always, just often."

Emma considered, then something sharpened in her gaze. Vivian could see the point where she decided to ask directly. "Why are you here?" Emma leaned forward, and added, "And it's not just about the folklore, I know better."

"The odd things that have been happening. Farran Michaels, he was at school with my assistant's younger brother. Schola. He's a polite and observant young man, so if he said there was something odd going on, I was inclined to take a look." Vivian saw no reason to deflect on that point, not with people who might be allies if needed.

"You don't think it's anything to do with the Pact?" Andie was more hesitant.

"Why do you say that?" Vivian was quite practiced in not sounding too keenly interested.

"That house they found, not too far from here. The one that reappeared after centuries. There was a paper, the latest issue of *De Magia*, the main journal for magical history and theory, about how they were fairly sure it disappeared right after the Pact. It has every historian of the era I know completely up in arms, the idea of having a perfectly preserved space."

"I heard a bit about it. I run an inquiry agency, by the by. People with interesting problems."

"Mermaid kinds of problems?" That was rather light-hearted, at least.

"As a rule, no." It might well be better if the mermaid

question settled into a comfortable sort of shared joke. "Investigations that take discretion, or a long view. I have a variety of staff, different kinds of skills. Many of them are clever women, some younger, some older. They take on positions as assistants or what have you, and can use that to figure out what's actually going on."

"Your usual clients?"

"People with sufficient coin to pay the fees - and I don't generally come cheap. This is a favour to Eleanor, my assistant. To be fair, I was a trifle bored, and it seemed an intriguing sort of problem. About a third of my work is for the Ministry, situations they can't resolve internally for some reason. A third are clients who need discretion, a business need, or family complexity. The last third are often Guard related. Art theft and forgery, for example, where they don't have specialists to spare, or need more evidence to use the formal legal oaths."

"Can't arrest people without cause, no." Emma's voice was sharper. "I'm none too fond of the Guard as a whole."

Vivian cocked her head. "Oh?"

Andie shifted and patted her hand. "Emma's a bit of a radical at times. Had a few run-ins with protests about suffrage. That sort of thing."

"Thank you for putting yourself there." Vivian was clear on how much that mattered. While she qualified herself, under the post-war expansion, as a householder, she felt everyone ought to have a say in their own government. In the magical community, it wasn't a bother, their elections ran differently and everyone of age could place their votes, but the non-magical community spilled over onto them far too often. Especially for anyone who lived and worked among the non-magical, whether in Oxford or elsewhere.

"I qualify due to being a university graduate, naturally."

Andie's mouth quirked in something that was not at all a smile.

"It is ridiculous, isn't it?" Vivian shook her head.

Emma came out with, "These things that have been happening. Do you know why?"

"Not yet, but I've only been here two days. I agree, though, there's something very odd about them." She considered. "You asked if it might have some relationship to the Pact, or that house that reappeared, and I can't say it's inconsistent with some of the things I've seen of the Fatae, but I certainly wouldn't lay it at their feet without a great deal more evidence."

"The ghostly figure, last night? How does that compare, then?"

"Unlike anything I've seen. Certainly not the common or less common illusion methods I know. I don't believe it was mechanical, though with a table turner, I suppose one can't be sure."

"You are not a fan of our spiritualist, then?"

Vivian considered. "I think that spiritualism fills an emotional need for many people. The tremendous losses so many families suffered. People wanting any hope of a last word, a last moment. And I've met spiritualists who handle that well. But there's no denying there are far too many who take advantage, or worse, are entirely fraudulent."

It earned her a small smile from Emma. "Quite."

"So, what can we do to be of help?"

"Tell me if there are events you see that I am not around for? Or if you notice anything else out of the ordinary, even if it doesn't seem connected? You've lived here longer, especially you, Emma. You must know the way the house normally sounds, the creaks and shifts." Vivian asked, "When did you first start noticing something odd?"

"The obvious things - you must have a list from Farran? Such a thoughtful young man, but I don't think he's at all happy in his apprenticeship. Of course, he'd never say anything to his uncle." Emma was clearly talking while she was thinking about the details. "But I think I first felt something odd a week or two before the first of those, the greenhouse. The orchid, specifically."

Vivian nodded. "Can you figure out when? It might be a help?"

"I'll go through my diary, and see if there's any note. There might be something in my work log, I make note if I'm not feeling the usual thing."

"I appreciate any details. I've long ago learned that you can't tell what's relevant early on. Or often later, for that matter."

Emma laughed, and that allowed them to shift to a more general discussion of some of her research problems. From there, they went on to some of Andie's difficulties with fellow scholars, and a few of the cases Vivian could talk about freely. It was far more productive an evening than she'd expected at the start of supper.

C admus settled down at the table for lunch not certain what to expect. Mrs Cooper had mentioned, when he checked in with her that morning, that Ann had asked for a packed lunch to take with her. He supposed it must be something related to investigating some of the folklore she was researching. She'd spent the past few weeks settling in, taking walks around the grounds, and investigating the library, but he supposed she must need to go further astray sometime. There certainly wasn't too much of interest to a researcher of folklore here.

He'd heard Ann talking with Emma at lunch yesterday about possibly going into the Bodleian for research sometime soon. But that would have involved lunch with them, in some cafe or pub or restaurant, not a packed lunch. Or so he assumed, since he knew the two working in Oxford often lunched together, and he rather thought Ann was not terribly miserly about her finances.

It was at least a pleasant day, perhaps why Ann had picked it. The weather was clear, with that briskness of the approaching winter. Plenty of sun, and no prospect of rain or damp until late that evening. He did wonder where she was going to, if it were nearby or if she'd caught the train somewhere further away, into the countryside.

Cadmus set that aside, reminding himself to nod pleasantly to those already there. As usual for lunches, it was a small crowd. The three elder women, Madam Etna, Mistress Cole, and Madam Gregson were all down at the end of the table they usually claimed, chatting among themselves. They rarely made space for him, and he had no intention of forcing himself into their conversation. It was often about loss and memory, and he did not need to encourage that in himself.

He dealt with the seances because he wanted to make sure Madam Etna was not causing harm, and because a small exposure to that torrent of loss was something of a help to him. He couldn't describe why, and he didn't like what it did, but it released something that cramped and tangled his magic.

He was glad Mistress Cole found the company congenial. She had a niece who visited her occasionally, taking her out to the shops and making sure she had what she needed. The niece had confided that retiring had been difficult for her aunt, and more so after her sense of the practical began to slip. She had been glad to find her aunt somewhere with people around, who would notice if she didn't come down for meals.

Mistress Cole didn't need a care home, nothing like that, but she had needed a change from the things that reminded her of her former routines. And perhaps also less access to an oven or stove that could be left on accidentally. He'd arranged to fit up her rooms with one of the new magical fire grates, much safer with small children or those who might otherwise be at greater risk.

Cadmus did worry a bit about whether Madam Etna took advantage. He didn't think so, he kept an eye out, but he worried about what he missed. Because he knew he missed things, the little hints of emotion or manipulation or hidden goals beneath the surface went right by him. They always had, and probably always would. It had been something of a gift, actually, in the Colonial Service. People all around him would be jostling for position and notice, and he just went along steadily, ignoring it.

One of his friends, there, had sat him down and explained it, not long before things happened. About how he might just be doing it naturally, but that it made him a stable point for others around him. That he wasn't changing what he was doing to adapt to the changing winds of fortune and politics every three minutes. He just got his work done, went on the outings he wanted, and got on with life.

Cadmus, for his part, couldn't imagine how people survived being the more changeable sort, reacting to all those things he couldn't see or sort out. Oh, that lack had got him into muck a few times, thinking people were his friends who weren't, not noticing when people treated him poorly until it was far too late to solve. On the other hand, the sort who wanted political advantage had usually moved on relatively quickly when given the chance, while Cadmus had been pleased to stay put.

Mrs Cooper began to sort out the meal, bowls of creamy white bisque dotted with parsley and a simple quiche with spinach and ham. As she was setting out the bowls, Robin and Danae came in, in a fluster of noise and colour. Mostly, Robin, on both counts, though Danae was doing her best to uphold her side of it. He was wearing another of his startling coloured coats, this one in a deep purple only a shade or two lighter than a ripe aubergine. It made the green of his eyes particularly bright and more than a little unsettling. His hair was loose, not held back in a queue at the back of his head, and he was gesturing. Exuberantly.

"You know, that's just making me the more eager to see how you're getting on. Do, please, may I enter your bower today? If not today, tomorrow?"

Danae laughed, her head back. "Don't rush excellence, Robin. You want the thing done right, you can't rush me." She then settled in her chair, after he made a show of pulling it out for her.

Cadmus hadn't thought Danae the sort who liked being flirted with. She'd kept to herself before Robin, pleasant enough at meals, but neither lingering nor drawing other people out.

When Robin arrived, though, he'd taken an immediate interest in her. Danae was quite skilled at her work, of course. Cadmus had had a pleasant time talking about her approach, when she'd realised he did some of his own work with hammer and anvil and forge. They had different interests, of course, she favoured decorative work most of the time, and he tended toward the utilitarian. Mrs Cooper's pots, for example, at least mending them or smoothing out a dent. It had been some time since he'd turned his hand to anything more complex, but nothing had caught at his mind to make or shape.

Mrs Cooper set a bowl in front of him, and made the little encouraging movements. "Eat, Eat." He inhaled the scent of the soup, parsnips and turnips, and cream and salt. Robin was teasing Danae back, still, when Cadmus turned his attention back to them.

"I've got the gems, you need to see those."

"Yes, I do, but not beforetimes. I've got things on the workbench, I don't want to fiddle with them. And I don't want to risk you messing with them, either."

"Me?" Cadmus couldn't make sense of the tone. He suspected it was what other people would refer to as mock-offense. Certainly, Danae wasn't offended. Becoming a bit worn down by his repeated requests, perhaps, but not offended. "I would never."

"You know you can't wander past something without wanting to pick up and handle it. Some art specialist you are. You know things are delicate."

Robin laughed, and it was loud and clear and startling enough to dislodge the trio of older women at the other end of the table from their conversation to peer at him over the rims of their glasses, in a curious unison. It didn't appear to bother him. Honestly, he didn't look like he was paying attention to anything other than Danae.

"Art speaks through the fingers, as well as the eyes, Danae. You've told me more than once, that's how you do your work so well. Listening to the metal, the song of it, the ring of it." He was leaning forward now, and Cadmus suddenly realised what Paris visiting the courts of Menelaus might have looked like, before he and Helen fled into the night. Robin was certainly extending his charm and flattery.

She shrugged, and again Cadmus couldn't be sure if she meant what she said next, or was dancing with him. "Art does. But that doesn't mean your fingers are good for the art." She considered, then offered. "Tomorrow. Before lunch. Eleven. I should be able to clear some of the benches by then, and I can look at your stones."

It was Mrs Gregson who inquired. "Stones, Danae?"

Danae glanced up, and there was a shift, too sudden for

Cadmus to follow or begin to name, something like a cloud before the sun. "Robin has a commission for me. A few family stones, to be set in something new, he says. I of course can't commit without seeing them. People do such awful things when cutting stones, some of them are awfully hard to work with. And I'm not a jeweller, either."

Cadmus considered, focusing on his soup, to avoid staring at them, as that would not be taken well. Robin had been quite an enigma, and he had not become less of one the longer he'd stayed. He had clothing that seemed like he was well off, and he had no obvious form of income. But here he was at a boarding house with water stains and sagging staircases, never mind the current difficulties, in the middle of nowhere. And now he had family jewels to set, which only made the curious matter of his family - and Ann's, of course - seem a little more significant.

Cadmus had the impression that men about town were normally found in town, after all, where they could talk to other people with money, property, artifacts, or all three of the above. And surely, even if Robin had to work for a living, if he dealt in art or items or something like that, he was not likely to find either artifacts or buyers here. Bar a few paintings, but he hadn't noticed Robin paying much attention to the paintings, even the Turner.

Now that he thought about it, that was a bit curious. Certainly, one had areas of interest. He, for example, was largely disinterested in much between the Wars of the Roses and Waterloo. Except as it had directly affected the family or the property, of course. But he was still quite capable of noticing that they existed, and might be of interest to someone else.

It was puzzling, and not in a way that would yield to translation. Perhaps, at some point in the future, Ann might unbend enough to say more about her distant cousin than the few sparse words she'd offered so far. He appreciated her skills with language, but he wished she were more prone to a dramatic chorus, explaining the current action, than a cryptic epigram.

He was distracted enough by his thoughts that he did not realise the others had departed from the dining room until he looked up and the room was quiet. That was awkward, then, but he'd done worse in the past. At least no one would be lurking, waiting for him, on his return to his desk, and the challenges of Persian flora and fauna.

THIRTEEN

SATURDAY, NOVEMBER 4TH, LATE AFTERNOON

Cadmus was not at all happy. There had been an itch between his shoulder blades for the last half hour, a vague sense that something was not right. He had not been able to settle to properly begin his work. Something had got tangled, somewhere, on the grounds, like a verb in the wrong place in a sentence.

He had stuck his head out into the hallway, but he heard nothing. No footsteps in the hallway, no voices, not even the sounds of people out in the gardens. Cadmus went back to his desk, and sat down, but five minutes later, he had not managed to pick up his pen again.

Walking around the property wouldn't do any harm. It might even get him past this sticky bit of translation. Discussing animals was always complicated, because one never quite knew how animals matched up. He was not at all sure he was describing the various snakes and serpents at all accurately. He suspected he was going to need to make a trip to the London Zoological Society, and consult one of the herpetologists. He did not care for the snake house, even if they were all behind glass enclosures, but he didn't want to get this wrong.

Pushing back from the desk, he stood, making his way out of his study, through the hallway, and down the stairs. There were no sounds. The cleaners must be having their tea break, or something of the kind. It was about that point in the afternoon. Most of the residents were out, or occupied, as they should be in the afternoon. He didn't much approve of people hanging around the place. It was one of the challenges that Robin Aelfdane presented, being a man of some leisure without many obvious appointments. Though then the man disappeared without much notice other than saying he wouldn't be at a meal or two, and without comment afterwards.

No one was in the library, nor in the parlour, and he made his way out the front steps, and around to the side of the house. The light was golden, the late afternoon beautiful. Heading for the greenhouses, he spotted a few rustles in the garden, but those were likely rabbits. They'd been rather a difficulty this year, and the kitchen gardens had suffered a larger loss of vegetables than usual. It was still quite warm out for late October, pleasant with only the light cardigan he had on. It had been a relatively mild autumn, and the roses were still going along well, and their kitchen squashes.

The greenhouse door was closed, as it should be, when he got there. He stopped and listened with his hand on the handle, then pushed it open. If he were going to check the property, he should walk through the greenhouse. Besides, the problem with the orchid had been bothering him since it happened. If that could happen to one flower, what about others? So many plants could be quite dangerous, with only slight variations.

The front of the greenhouse was exactly as it should be, but as he walked toward the back, he frowned. Something felt off. He couldn't even begin to put a word to it for a moment, but he felt as if he had fallen into one of his translations. Greek had dozens of complexities, but one of the ones he found most interesting was how they talked about colour, or didn't, as the case might be.

He'd read a theory, when he was at university, about how they valued different things, so talked about them more. How, what was the word. Saliency. How noticeable the colour was, that was it. The greenhouse made him think of it, the flashes of colour, the way the different shades of the petals and leaves came across.

Cadmus caught a glimpse of something, almost out of the corner of his eye. But every time he looked straight on at the flowers at the far end of the greenhouse, that flicker of light disappeared. He opened the back door, turning left toward the rose garden and some of the outbuildings, none in much use at the moment.

It wasn't until he was well into the centre of the garden that he realised the problem. He cast a charm light, to see better in the sunset, cupping it in his hand. The roses were shimmering, that curious shift of colour that led to people fussing about translating Homer's infamous wine-dark sea or gleaming-eyed Athena. One part of his mind thought it a fascinating demonstration, giving him a clarity of understanding that he'd never had before. The roses had gone dark, to the depths of a purple balanced between blue and red, a curious colour for them. They had that shine to them, curious and alien and not at all of this world, that the ancients had referred to as porphureos.

Cadmus was glad he had a word to explain it, a word to help him grasp what had changed. It did not help with the larger problem, however, which was that the vines were growing across the entrances to the garden, slowly but visibly. Already, he thought he did not dare risk pushing through them, there was a gleam to the thorns that made him realise blood had that unsettling glimmer too.

It was then that he felt the fear leap down his spine, like a lightning bolt, his body reacting before his brain could catch up. This was too like that moment in the mountains of Afghanistan, the moments before everything had gone completely to hell and back. He had to swallow hard, tasting the bile in the back of his throat, looking around to find somewhere he could retreat to.

There was the fountain in the centre, the water still flowing. He could see a vine or two beginning to drift away from the edges, toward the fountain, but for the moment that seemed the best choice. He climbed onto the rim of the fountain, balancing uneasily, to give him enough height to see if there was anyone nearby. He caught a rustle of something, a half-shadow against a building, before he turned, watching the vines again.

They were definitely advancing, and none too slowly. He looked around, trying to remember his training from his time in the Colonial Service. What were his tools? There was rope, he had a bit of height here, standing on the fountain. No shears, and he wasn't sure what he thought about trying to cut those vines. He suspected they'd object.

He patted his pockets, and then found his pocket square. It was a pale golden yellow, which meant it would stand out in the twilight, well enough. If it came to that. He looked around, then sent up a little pulse of magic, partly as a test. The vines recoiled for a second, then surged in growth, visibly. No more magic, then. But he set the spinning globe of light above his head.

Cadmus could see a figure coming across the field, aiming at the formal garden, and he called out towards it. "Hello the field."

The shape turned, and he could see now that it must be Ann. She dressed differently than the other women. More formal than Andromache and Danae, but less old-fashioned than the older female residents. She turned, and came across, but he held up his hand. "Don't come close. Can you get help?"

She tilted her head, in the unmistakable sign of someone thinking. The light was largely behind her, so he couldn't really see her expression, just her silhouette. Then she took a step closer, and another one.

"No, go get help." If she could hear him, she wasn't listening. There was another step, and then another. She came closer and closer until she was about ten feet from the other side of the garden wall. She was close enough now he could see her focusing on the vines. He couldn't quite hear her, but he could see her mouth move, and then her hands. She was making some sort of gesture that wasn't sign language, at least not any he knew, and then she walked forward again.

He could see light now, coming from her hands, small trailing sparkles. He thought he could see her mouth moving, but it wasn't words, it was some sort of music. Not sung, but rather hummed,which would explain why he couldn't hear it. There was a shift of her feet on the grass, a pattern of some kind, as if she were dancing, only it was far less active. The movement was, perhaps, in the same relationship to a dance that whispering was to speech. Her movements were small, but there was a precise kick with her right foot, a particular angle, as if she would normally have been shaking something, a fold of cloth, perhaps.

Whatever she was doing, it made the vines and roses take notice. They stopped twining across the gates, and there was a rustle of the leaves, then everything fell still.

It put her comments that she was interested in the folk-lore of plants in a rather different context.

FOURTEEN

TWILIGHT

Vivian had almost ignored the shimmer at the back of her mind. It was easy to miss, the brush of the magic of her foremothers, like a breeze across her skin. But then she realised what it must be, and had to trail around the property, playing Hunt The Thimble.

It felt ridiculous, like playing any children's game as a grown adult often did, but it was the only way to figure out where she was supposed to be. At the front gates, she almost couldn't feel the brush of the magic at all. It grew stronger as she walked toward the greenhouses, and then beyond them to the gardens.

Of course, by the time she got to the rose garden, she could see as well as feel that something was not right. It was not the usual sort of thing for adults - at least those over university age - to be seen climbing the centrepiece of a fountain. As she drew closer, she could see the roses twining, and she finally began to realise precisely what was going on.

He called out to her, and she ignored it. Vivian knew he was there, just as she knew what needed to be done. His additional comments would likely not add any useful information. Instead, she focused on her hands. First she drew her gloves off her fingers. The First Gesture, the Second, and then she cupped her hands, making a small space between them. Just enough for a sphere to form. She whispered the Second Word, the one that would let whatever magic was at play here know what and who she was.

She let out a single sharp breath, into her cupped hands, and then opened them, watching the sparks of her magic spread like fireflies. Then she began the tune, the one that would give her the rhythm for the other portion of this.

Vivian had learned the dances well, it had always been one of her better skills, her mother and aunts had said. Left toes pointed, then right, toe, heel, bend the knee, feel the rhythm. She was using the least obvious of the forms. That was not only because she knew Cadmus could see her, at least somewhat, in the fading light. It was more because she was old enough that the hops and skips and flourishes of the full form of the dance were not a thing she wanted to attempt in an uneven field in walking shoes, and certainly not in the deepening twilight.

If the modified form didn't work, they had a much larger problem on their hands anyway.

Step, step, rise on the toes, touch behind, cross, point the toes, step, step, repeat. She could hear the faint shrill of the pipes in her mind, too, setting up the harmonies she needed. And then the smile. Smiling was key.

It was a form of dance and magic that had begun as a battle magic. There was nothing so terrifying as a group of people advancing on you, smiles on their faces and wild magics swirling around them, the heart-drums keeping time.

Not that she needed that here. No, she adjusted the width of her steps slightly, to encourage the evenness she wanted, smoothing out the demands of the vines, easing them into compliance. They slowed, and stilled. She waited for a moment, shifting from foot to foot as she traced a half circle on the grass on the right, then the left. Then she coughed once.

The rose vines parted, melting away like ice brought in by a warm fire. They shrank back from her, coiling back where they should be, properly. She nodded at them once, then looked up at Cadmus. "Come down?"

He didn't move, and she repeated, "Please. Come down."

The second time, he came, landing on his feet deftly enough, then walking through the gap, glancing side to side. She tsked at the vines one more time, and said "Behave," and they bent away, shifting to coil against the stonework again.

When she turned around, Cadmus was half way back to the house, in the open grass. He had stopped to look at her, but she couldn't see his expression with the light behind him. She did hope he wasn't going to be difficult, but she suspected he would be. He did not seem like a man who could let a bit of native magic be.

"What did you do?" His voice rang out, sharper than she expected.

"I have a way with plants. Well, some plants." It wouldn't do to brag. That led to trouble.

"That was not just having a green thumb. Your hands. The way you were moving." He waved his hand, visibly unsure how to explain it. "Folklore, you said." What she had done didn't make sense, and he did not like that at all.

She shrugged, slightly, with just one shoulder. Past time to let Ann's body language fall into place again, like putting on a cloak. As long as he was spluttering, it was easy enough to dodge the implied questions. "Come along, we should get you some tea."

"You were one of those terrifying women staffing offices in the War, weren't you." The mutter amused her.

"Not quite, no." Something about that assumption amused her. "But I do know how to make a nice strong cup of tea. I am English, after all."

"Not Welsh? You live in Trellech."

"My people are from Wiltshire. And right now, we're in England." A little idle talk wouldn't hurt as a distraction.

"Is that where you learned the... " He waved his hands. No, he was going to be stubborn.

"I'd ask if you had family traditions, but I know perfectly well you do. What was it you were saying about your great-aunt Ivanhoe at dinner?" He did have one, though who'd name a defenceless young girl Ivanhoe, she had no idea. Even if the Victorians could be quite odd sometimes.

"She married in, that's different." But he was now sounding defensive, which was better for her.

"Your great-uncle... Thersander?"

"You were paying attention!" He sounded delighted, and, more importantly, diverted. "Almost no one does."

"I do like knowing the history of the place I'm living. And you have rather a lot of stories."

"I should show you the portrait gallery, properly. We have some rather fine works up there. Though they could all use a bit of conservation, I suppose."

There, now he was suitably distracted, and talking about the portrait of his great-grandmother and great-grandfather. Vivian could guide him along, nodding and offering a quiet "Mmmhmm," of agreement at intervals.

Somewhat to her surprise, he went straight up to the

family wing, opening a door on the near end of the hallway. She hesitated. He blinked owlishly at her, his hand on the doorknob. "Well, come in."

Inside was about what she had expected. Wood panelling, in decent shape. An older leather desk chair, a large wooden desk that must have been his grandfather's from the age.

He gestured. "There's a kettle on the table, there." He went around the desk, sitting down heavily in the chair, and rubbing his face.

If there were to be tea, she was clearly going to have to make the tea. At least she had implied she might, rather than him.. She examined the kettle - a decent model about two decades old, she'd passed down the same sort to Eleanor for her house.

"Your preferences for tea?"

"At the moment, strong, black, and there should still be a lemon."

Of course he was the sort of man who drank strong tea. She had a preference for something much lighter. Jasmine green tea, or a white tea, or at least something that did not beat you about the head with the fact it was tea.

Fiddling with the necessities took a good few minutes, long enough that the kettle had come to a boil and let off its chime. Much better than the non-magical whistling she'd been subjected to occasionally on her travels. She set up a small tray, and once the water had boiled, she brought it over. Teapot, mugs, and lemon slices on a plate.

"Thank you." He didn't make a move to pour, letting it steep further. She sat on the other side of the desk, and looked at him, squarely. "What were you doing in the rose garden?"

"Getting on the wrong side of the roses." He grimaced as he said it.

"Did you get scratched?" That might be a problem, especially if they'd actually drawn blood.

"I wasn't that foolish." But he shrugged off his cardigan, unbuttoned his shirt cuffs, and rolled up the shirt, to check. She looked his arms over closely, then he flipped his palms up, so she could see the underside. No scratches. "None on my ankles, either. Do you need to supervise that?"

Vivian settled back in her chair. "I trust your word. You spotted nothing unusual?"

"Something felt off. Enough that I went to walk the property, the feeling got stronger in the greenhouses, and then in the garden. Everything moved very quickly." He did not approve.

"Far more quickly than plants ought," she agreed.

He tapped his fingers on the desk, and then moved to pour the tea, and a cup for her, then he slid it across the desk. "You still haven't explained what you did."

Despite his narrow escape, he was proving quite tenacious. Or perhaps it was because of the narrowness of the escape, that he was pursuing understanding rather like a terrier who had found a rat hole. "I am still good with plants. Even difficult ones."

"If that is the level of your skill, I am sure you win first prize at every garden show."

She flicked her fingers lightly. "Are you going to be difficult about it?" She had tried disengaging, since that hadn't worked, she might as well try bluntness.

"I am still getting over the shock of it, honestly." He lifted his cup, took a drink, and she realised there was something else going on for him than just the roses. Not that the roses weren't complex enough.

"Some other experience?" The way he'd responded, she suspected there was something else there.

He nodded once, precisely. He was not going to talk about it, clearly. Men of his background almost never did.

She took her time drinking a little of her tea, then set the cup in the saucer and said, "I'm glad I came along when I did. I'd also be glad to go have a good look around tomorrow when the light is good. Is there any risk anyone else will go out there this late in the day?"

"Oh, no, I don't think so. I hope not. Do you think we should put up a sign?"

"If there's an easy barrier, perhaps that? Or a notice on the board?"

Cadmus raised an eyebrow. "No one actually reads the board reliably. It is there as a thing to point to when people don't." His tone seemed a bit odd to her, but then he offered an uncertain smile, and she realised it was something of a joke.

FIFTEEN

SUPPER

A n hour later, Cadmus was alone in his rooms again. Ann had utterly evaded any attempts at further questions. She had refused to respond to his query about why a scratch from the roses might be a problem, never mind anything else he tried to ask. His tongue felt clumsy, as if he were working in some dialect he barely had a grasp of.

He had the sense she had waited a particular length of time, and then determined he could be left alone safely, but what criteria she used, he could not begin to say. Presumably it had to do with folklore. Once she left, he did go and check his ankles, carefully, even getting out the hand mirror that had been his mother's to make sure.

Cadmus could not decide whether to be grateful or infuriated. She had done something to his roses, that was inarguable. But his roses had attacked him, and that was terrifying in a way that made him shy away from further thoughts. Whatever she had done had put them back where they ought to be, at least, for now.

He could not settle in the half hour remaining before

supper, picking up a book and putting it down a dozen times before he washed his face and changed his cardigan for his favourite smoking jacket. He preferred it to something more formal and tailored for supper. The fabric felt good against his skin, with more give than a more tailored jacket. This one was a deep green that made him think of holly bushes in winter.

When they gathered for supper, Ann had changed her clothes into a sedate grey frock, with a deep cobalt blue shawl over her shoulders against the evening's chill. Her dress hadn't seemed soiled, and he wondered for a moment why she'd changed, before he realised he must be staring, and looked away.

Cadmus had, however, forgotten that Madam Etna was intending to do the seance that night. Of all nights. There was a storm coming on, but he supposed the full moon wasn't something one could reschedule. One part of him couldn't help wondering if something she'd done had been what made the roses dangerous. That, however, would require assuming that anything she did was particularly effective.

Oh, he knew that spiritualism had a place, somewhere. If it brought some small comfort to those, that was no bad thing. Not for those who had lost sons and husbands and brothers and friends to the Great War, or the wars before that. So long as the spiritualist wasn't an out and out fraud, or looking to get elderly fragile men and women to give up their last coins.

Madam Etna had boundaries, better than most of her sort, and she had been a good and kind friend to Madam Gregson, who was very alone in the world. And she was, when not about to do a seance, very patient with Mistress Cole. Boarding houses tended to acquire spiritualists and tablerappers and all of their kin whether you wanted them to or not. He much preferred someone who did not do harm, and sometimes improved the place.

Dinner was thankfully quiet. Ann did not mention their difficulties with the roses. In fact, she said very little at all. She encouraged Richard in telling a story about a conversation he'd had on his lunch break, something long and rambling about a cat and a bird. Robin was gone again. Cadmus rather suspected he was avoiding Ann, at this point. They seemed to be civil about it, at least, no screaming fights or unfortunate nonsense. It did make him wonder what sort of family they were, to track admittedly distant cousins closely enough to have some sort of gentle feud.

When they had sorted out the pudding, Madam Etna excused herself. "I must go and prepare. You will all join me in half an hour. You will make sure Ann knows where to come, will you not?"

It was no use arguing, but Ann nodded. "I look forward to it, Madam Etna."

Neither Emma nor Andromache usually took part in the seances, but this time they both said, "Set a place for us, please," at the same time. Madam Etna looked quite pleased, and once she swept out of the room, Cadmus stood to see about tea and after dinner drinks.

Stirring her tea, Ann said, "So, what should I expect?"

"You've been to seances before, you mentioned. We've set up a room with a round table and chairs, adaptable to the number of sitters. The room has curtains that can make it entirely dark, of course, and there is a screen for Madam Etna to prepare. We enter, take our places, join hands, put our feet on top of each other lightly. The usual precautions."

Ann nodded. "I'm quite familiar with them, yes." Her voice was even and quiet. "And of course, I know not to disturb Madam Etna, or make sudden noises or any of those things."

"I laughed, at my first one. Though to be fair, it was a joking spirit. Born under the same star as Beatrice, I'm sure." He made the Shakespearean reference mostly to amuse Emma, who chuckled appreciatively.

"And then?" Ann leaned back, and she seemed to be waiting for something.

"Then a lamp is lit, the lights are dimmed, and we see what happens."

"May I ask the usual range here?"

"Oh, faint lights, moving, the shapes that might be faces or tricks of the light. A few times she has said something quite specific, a personal phrasing or example meaningful to someone." That was Emma, tapping her fingers on the table thoughtfully. "Is there anyone you would expect to hear from?"

"A loved one who died in the War?" Ann shook her head. "Not I, no. Not that. My parents died some time ago, I was a late child. I have aunts and uncles and so on, but no one I would think especially interested in me at this point, not from beyond death's veil."

The way she phrased that made Cadmus take note, something in it very precise. He thought that it seemed she expected words from somewhere else to be much more likely.

"Ah, pity. That makes it harder to evaluate the quality of information. It's very difficult to do a rigorous examination of material from a seance. You'd think there'd be proper studies about it."

Ann smiled for a moment. "I'm sure you've looked, then."

Cadmus considered. Something had shifted, in how she talked to Emma and Andromache, beyond even supper a few nights. They kept making references to conversations he hadn't been around for. He was certain he was missing things, missing dozens of things, signals he'd never been able to read correctly. It was what he hated about being the responsible one, here. And about Farran being gone. Farran was so much better at this than he was, spotting things.

He coughed. "One last round of tea, anyone? Before we go along to the seance room?"

No one had any need of tea. Or further conversation, apparently, as there was quiet until they trooped along the hallway to the small room they'd set aside for Madam Etna when she moved in. Madam Gregson and Mistress Cole immediately took up their usual places at either side of her. After a moment, Cadmus moved to take his, the chair directly across from Madam Etna. Ann hung back, he noticed, seeing where people usually sat, until she was directed to sit next to Cadmus, at his right.

That was curious. It took him a moment to realise that Andromache and Emma had settled next to each other, with Andromache next to him. They were, no, he paused to count again. They were eight tonight, a larger group than most. Madam Etna, Mistress Cole, Richard, Ann, Cadmus himself, Andromache, Emma, and Madam Gregson.

No Danae, however. She'd mentioned something the other night about having a current commission, something she was eager to be working on. No Robin, but he was not expected, and of course no sign of Herr Professor Bolsano, who thought the whole thing ridiculous.

"No assistant, Madam Etna?" That was Ann, her voice polite, but very curious.

"Ah, no, not here, I have a fine girl who helps with clients. But that is different, this is my home, the spirits know how to come here, where to be. Please, sit, and I will dim the lights. We are all ready?"

Cadmus settled his hands on the table, as he had been trained to do. It meant the ladies on either side could decide how to rest theirs, not forcing a closeness they did not wish. Andromache rested her fingers lightly on his wrist, and a moment later he felt her shoe on top of his toes.

Ann, on the other hand, set her hand across his, skin to skin, and then her foot next to his, which somehow felt more intimate. He could say nothing, of course, even if he could think what to say. Was it that their adventure of the afternoon made her feel bolder? It was not how he'd expected her to respond. Proper translation was entirely impossible, which made it the more frustrating.

He made no comment, simply nodded at Madam Etna that they were settled.

"They have explained, Mistress Porter?" That was Madam Etna. "How we do things?"

"Yes, Madam Etna. This is, as I said, not my first sitting. Please, do continue as you normally do, I will keep quiet and listen."

It was a specific sort of promise, really, one that made it clear that she did not promise belief, or support of belief, just a lack of disruption.

"So." Madam Etna's voice was not quite approving, but agreeing, something in the tone. "I will dim the lights." She shifted in her seat, freeing her hands for a moment to wave them, and the light charms faded.

Cadmus took a breath. He found himself more

distracted by having Ann there, touching him, than he thought. Certainly her presence had a different quality than Andromache, on the other side. It made him begin to wonder if there was a language that had terms for the quality of presence, the way two people were with each other, the way there were terms for colour or taste or the sounds of the world.

Something about Ann had a vibration to it, something of the same quality as the saliency of colour. It wasn't about what she was doing, it was present even when she was sitting there, quietly, barely moving. She didn't fidget, either, and that was rather more common.

SIXTEEN

SATURDAY EVENING

Vivian settled into her chair, leaning slightly to see if the wood made any noises. Though, she supposed, if she were a spiritualist setting up a seance and intending to fake noises, she would make certain only one chair triggered them, and only on demand.

She was familiar, of course, with the theoretical precautions of a seance. Hand on hand to prevent anyone there - including Madam Etna - using their hands to fake an apparition. And resting shoe or slipper against shoe, to prevent people using their feet the same way. It seemed scarcely adequate. Any half-competent magical practitioner could in fact come up with a dozen ways to make a particular noise without moving so much as a hair on their head. A little flex of the elbow, a twitch of their knee, a slightly deeper breath.

What was Madam Etna up to? She had asked for no money. Andromache and Emma had made it clear that she did not, though on occasion people left her something, if the reading was moving and powerful.

Vivian grimaced, then transmuted it into chewing on

her lip. Undignified, but less suspicious. She still did not have a good sense of Madam Gregson. Mistress Cole, she'd talked with, but the poor woman did not run as deep as she'd used to. Nor, for that matter, did she have much sense of Madam Etna beyond the show she put on.

She tried to sort through the options one more time in her head. It was possible this had nothing to do with the odd and dangerous magics swirling around the property. Hundreds, even thousands, of people participated in seances most nights, and most of the time nothing particularly dire happened. There might be something different here, or there might not be. She would need more information.

Eleanor was working on proper research about Madam Etna, in case there were any particular concerns there. Since they had not turned up anything obvious before Vivian turned up with her bags, she suspected that if Madam Etna was the cause, it was not because of her day to day spiritualism.

It might be one of the other participants, someone using it as a cover for their own purposes. That, she thought, was perhaps more likely. Not Robin, or one could assume so, he was not here. Unless he was using the excuse of everyone else being occupied to do whatever it was he was up to. And he was certainly up to something. Cadmus had said he regularly attended the seances, but he was quite likely avoiding her.

Logic suggested it might be Cadmus, but she thought not. The terror in the rose garden had been real, and if he had been behind whatever caused it, she rather thought his reactions would have been different. She prided herself on reading a person's thoughts in their expression, the twitches of tiny muscles, the way the eyes widened or narrowed.

Cadmus had been afraid, and he had not known why he was afraid. Having seen him, seen his office, he was too much a man of precision and structure to have a working go out of kilter quite that way. If he had been doing a working and it failed, he would... She could not put her thumb on it, but it would be different.

Madam Etna dimmed the lights, and Vivian turned her attention to the circle. She could barely see the shapes of those across the table, just a faint shift of shadow. There was a sharp inhale, and then Madam Etna's voice came, sharp and clear. The medium had stage training, that was immediately apparent.

"We call to you, spirits. We call to those who have words of wisdom for us, words of knowledge, words of comfort and compassion. Come to us, come join us at the table, in peace and friendship." They were a better invocation than might be. Far too many failed to specify what they wanted, or the acceptable etiquette of the occasion. Peace and friendship was not a bad start.

There was a shiver from someone on her right, the kind of movement that shifted through the circle. Then Vivian heard a voice, much lower pitched than Madam Etna's, but within the range of what a woman might comfortably manage. "Who disturbs me?"

Someone inhaled audibly, and then Madam Etna's voice came out of the darkness, across the table. "Good evening, spirit. Is the Grey Dancer near? She is the one who normally comes to bring us messages."

The voice turned gruff. "No dancing here." Vivian felt Cadmus's fingers twitch under hers.

"Who are you, kind spirit?"

Vivian did not think this spirit particularly kind, but she supposed flattery was a safer choice than anger.

"Aurangzeb."

"Aurangzeb." Madam Etna repeated it, carefully. "Welcome, Aurangzeb."

Something tickled Vivian's memory, that it was a name, however uncommon, that she had come across before. It may have meant something more to Cadmus, because she felt his fingers twitch under hers, just once. He'd mentioned Afghanistan before, that might at least be the right part of the world. At least, the sounds did not seem implausible.

"Masks, masks I see, masks dancing, people laughing. All different kinds of masks, some with feathers, some sparkling, some of comedy and others of tragedy."

When the voice began, Vivian wondered if it meant her. She was certainly keeping secrets from those here. As it went on, she relaxed. Masked balls were common enough in some circles, there was nothing terribly specific there. There was a long silence, then Madam Etna said, carefully, "Is that a message for one here, Aurangzeb?"

"Oh, no, no." The voice laughed, a long laugh that rolled on and on. "None here. But known to one who is." It chortled again, as if there was some great joke. "A gentleman, falling over his own two feet, a dance, feathers and masks, ridiculous preening of foolish young men, and gold, oh, plenty of gold." Then the voice shifted. "Hands singed by magics they should not meddle in."

"Is someone in danger, Aurangzeb?"

"No more danger than last week, and no less than next week."

That was utterly unhelpful. Madam Etna apparently thought so too, because her next question was more pointed, "Do you have a message for one who is here?"

A long silence, an inhale - how did something that had

no body inhale? Then the voice said, rattling the glass on the table slightly. "There are strange magics afoot."

"Yes, yes, kind spirit. That is why we have called out, reached out for help, from all friendly spirits who would aid us."

"The Shining Ones dance. A dance of power. Do not anger them further."

"The Shining Ones?"

"There are those who know them." The voice sounded deeply amused now.

It was not possible to shrink back in her seat, but all of a sudden Vivian wanted none of that attention anywhere near her. Why could her thrice-tangled cousin not be here as well? He would be a far better target for this sort of thing than she was.

"Do you have another message for us, Aurangzeb?"

There was a vast sound, like mighty wings or a wave crashing, something her mind could not sort out correctly. It was followed by a faint pop, like something draining out of a basin.

"Good evening?" It was a completely different voice now, younger, female, a bit hesitant.

"My Grey Dancer. Did something keep you from us? Are you well?" Madam Etna almost stumbled over the words, in her eagerness. Not a planned conversation, then.

"Oh, quite all right, yes, thank you." The voice was quite unlike Madam Etna's, though that could be done with a trick of the voice, pitching it higher.

"Do you have messages for us, dear dancer?"

"For Madam Gregson, yes, the comforts of memory."

Vivian listened with half an ear, but the following commentary was more or less what she'd expected. Sweet, largely harmless greetings and reassurances of happiness on the far side of the veil, from Madam Gregson's beloved dead, and Mistress Cole's. The notable point that evening appeared to be a contact from Mistress Cole's apprenticeship mistress. That woman sounded like one of the grand Victorian dames of her field, some kind of refined tincture making for magical work. Skilled work, certainly, and necessary for the healers to do their duty, but not intellectually stimulating for others.

There was a point where the conversation turned. Vivian had become lost in her own thoughts, trying to feel the larger energies of the room and the house, and failing utterly, like something was blocking her. She was better with people, and with plants, than with houses, but that was no excuse. In her distraction, though, she missed the beginning, in all the innocuous and unremarkable routine of what had become quite the pedestrian seance.

It meant the words hit her, half way through a sentence. "... have a care about the other people around you. You know the value of hard work, you always have, and you're not doing your best right now, are you?" It seemed directed at Mistress Cole, the kind of scolding an apprentice mistress might offer. But surely, the older woman had done plenty, in her life.

There was a faint protest, from that side of the table.

"Reach out, Cole. See what help you can be, to those who passed through your workroom." Perhaps an attempt by Madam Etna, in collaboration with a former employee or apprentice of Mistress Cole's? Vivian could not decide if it was an actual worry.

In the end, the comments from the Grey Dancer tailed off, until Madam Etna said gently, "Thank you, dear, for your help tonight. Until next we call."

"Next time." The voice sounded brighter, and then it

went silent. A minute passed before Madam Etna spoke in her normal voice. "Natalie, please, the lights." That was apparently Madam Gregson, who moved to turn them on again, the glow casting shadows in sharp relief for a moment.

"That was a long session. Thank you, everyone."

They had got no closer to any meaningful answer to the problem, and Vivian was willing to admit it even if no one else was. "You have no interpretation of the reason, Madam Etna? For the disturbances here?"

"I am sure the words will make sense in time, my dear. Perhaps sleep will knit the ravelled...." Her voice trailed off, as if she had entirely forgotten what she was half-quoting.

There was a cough at her shoulder. "Ann, anyone else - a drink somewhere else, so Madam Etna might rest?"

Vivian nodded slightly. No good would come of pressing the issue here and now. A drink would at least give her time to think about what that first entity had meant. Or rather, if it had meant more than the obvious.

SEVENTEEN

SATURDAY EVENING

Cadmus had led the way back to the library, as a well-lit space. Something about the seances always disconcerted him, and this one rather more than most. He could not quite place a finger on it. Certainly the unexpected spirit, and with a name that sounded Persian, did not help. He fussed slightly over pouring out drinks.

Someone had been at the brandy again, it had been watered down, but it would do for the moment. He'd have to sort out some sort of sufficiently subtle way to stop that. Perhaps the unsubtle approach of moving it to his private office, with its better locks.

When he turned around, Ann was settled on one of the side chairs. Andromache and Emma together were standing by the door and he frowned slightly.

"I think we'll go upstairs, thank you, Cadmus." That was Emma, her voice clipped.

"Are you both all right?"

"Oh, nothing wrong at all, just a trifle tired." It rung false, even to him, and he almost never managed to sense that kind of thing, but he also knew it was exceedingly rude to argue. Cadmus simply nodded, and said "Of course. Tomorrow, ladies."

Once they had left, Richard came in, closing the door behind them. "Most curious, Cadmus." And then he nodded. "Ann. You must think us quite queer."

Ann shook her head, though she waited until Cadmus handed her a drink to say anything. "Not the usual sort of thing, no, but I do not think that is particularly to be laid at your feet."

"Nor yours?" Richard was leaning forward, and Cadmus wasn't sure he liked the implications.

"I was a simple observer." Ann pointed this out evenly.

"But you were our newcomer. And the spirit, the first one, was unusual. Did nothing in that make sense to you?"

"I suppose people do go to masked balls, from time to time. Not generally in my immediate circles, mind. And it does not seem an immediate danger, if there is no more next week than last week." One shoulder shrugged, but Ann seemed not to be offended or upset, at least. "He seemed more interested in whatever that was supposed to be than our concerns."

Cadmus lifted his glass. "It did not answer the questions we actually had."

"There was that mention..." Richard spoke, though he didn't look up this time. "The Shining Ones."

It was one of the names for the Fatae, and Cadmus did not like that prospect at all, but surely they wouldn't be interested in something here. And why now, it was not like the estate had changed substantially in decades. Arguably in centuries.

Ann shrugged slightly. "Given the stories," she said. "If they were present, I suspect it would be more than a fleeting phantasm, or plants with a mind of their own." But she tapped her finger on her glass, a move that seemed unusual for her.

Richard pressed on. "You study folklore, you said? Surely you must have stories?"

"Oh, I'd be considered a biased audience on that count, don't you think?" Ann was leaning back now, glancing once at Cadmus before returning her attention to Richard. She responded differently to Richard than she did to Cadmus, he realised. Here, she leaned back, one arm crossing over her lap, the other holding her glass. If she'd been wearing riding gear, he'd have taken her for a slim young man at a hunt breakfast, taking his ease. That is, until he looked at her face, which was not at all a man's.

"I prefer my biases well-informed, it's rather a tendency in my field. I know we're known for taking a look at someone and diagnosing them off the bat. But a trained eye does spot all manner of things not obvious to the casual observer." Richard was parrying the conversation quite well, Cadmus thought, and enjoying the challenge.

"Let us start there, then." Ann turned the tables rather neatly. "What did you think of Madam Etna and our other sitters?"

Richard frowned now. "There was more strain than usual. In Madam Etna, but also the others."

"Andromache and Emma?" Cadmus offered.

"Oh, I think their fatigue is reasonably legitimate, but they seemed a bit strained. No, I was thinking our Madam Gregson and Mistress Cole."

Ann arched an eyebrow. "Your?"

"Well, we do try to look out for each other, here."

"You do." It was not a question, it had a curious tone

that Cadmus couldn't quite decipher. Except that Richard had responded to it like someone had almost slapped him.

"You doubt that, then?" Richard responded with a challenge, but instead of folding, Ann smiled.

"You heard how the seance went. Those questions, pressing Mistress Cole." She rummaged for the right word. "Suggesting a dependency. You don't have a difficulty with that?"

"What do you mean?"

Ann shrugged, a small movement. "What I saw was how Madam Etna set up a - wove a story in which the only way to connect to the pleasant memories, the joyful ones, was through her. Connecting, giving the woman a place to remember her loved ones, that's a kindness. But increasing guilt, in a woman who surely has done plenty in her life to help others, that's unkind. And setting up as the only one with the key to the lock - well. My aunts would call that a deliberate spreading of miasma."

Richard looked like he'd had a pitcher of cold water dumped on his head. Cadmus wasn't sure what to do, whether to defend his friend, or his resident, or - or admit that Ann might have a point.

The silence stretched out for a good minute, then two, and finally, Richard said, "You think it that serious?"

"I do not think Mistress Cole will give Madam Etna all her money. And I am not even sure Madam Etna is doing some of this, maybe even all of it, consciously. But the poison in a snake is no less deadly if the snake didn't really mean to bite, is it?"

"A slow poison, then." Richard was slowly recovering his wits. "Or an unintentional one."

"Something like. There's certainly plenty of folklore about that, people wasting away."

Richard blinked at her. "I'd never heard it quite put like that. But you're right. There's a similarity there."

Ann just smiled, raised her glass slightly in toast, and settled back. Cadmus could not help realising that she'd diverted them both tidily from any questions about her own experiences. Or motives. He didn't know how to begin to ask, and Richard certainly didn't seem to be.

Finally, he said, "Do you think it is an immediate danger? Madam Etna?"

That got Ann's full attention on him. "Oh, no. And I'm not suggesting you turn her out of the house. But I am suggesting it might be a kindness to pay attention, rather than treating the seances as a pleasant amusement. Perhaps encouraging Mistress Cole to spend time with other friends, or relatives, or ..."

"I think it's Madam Gregson encouraging her to take everything Madam Etna says as oracular truth." Cadmus felt somehow disloyal, but it was true.

"Well, that's no good. Perhaps I'll see about having a chat with her, seeing if there are other people she might talk to."

"Why?" Cadmus couldn't restrain his question now.

Ann looked at him, eyes wide and even. "It is a puzzle. I do not like letting those - remain tangled. Madam Gregson has seemed like a kind woman, if dealt a bad hand by fate and war. And Mistress Cole seems like she had a good life, and has earned her rest. There's no reason to leave her at risk of further hurt if I can help, and perhaps I can. Or someone else here, now you know what you're looking at."

"Is that how you do your folklore? Look at things differently?" It came out of him suddenly, and far more like a challenge than he'd expected. He cursed himself, for not having a better grasp on his words.

It was not a question she expected, he could tell that, the way her eyes widened and she stopped talking. Then she took a breath, and another, the little markers his brother had explained were someone figuring out how to go on. How pushing then got you in trouble, if it was Father or Mother, so don't do that.

"Sometimes." Her voice was even, measured, perhaps a bit flat in tone. When she was more relaxed, it danced, and now it plodded. Something like the difference between Greek and English, only not about metre, but instead pitch or inflection or some word he didn't know. He didn't like it, anyway, in Ann.

She went on, "I believe that if you notice a thing that is off, you have some responsibility to see if it needs changing. Many things don't. They are choices adults are making, and they may be foolish choices, or small-minded ones, or awkward, or a dozen other things you'd prefer not to do yourself. But adults can do that. But if someone is taking advantage, skewing things, out of the natural flow, that, that bothers me." Her voice got softer at the end.

"Huh." Cadmus breathed it out, as nearly as saying it. "Thank you."

EIGHTEEN

SUNDAY MORNING

The next morning, Vivian came downstairs to find Madam Gregson alone in the breakfast room. She'd been hoping for Mistress Cole, but Madam Gregson would do, she supposed.

"Madam Gregson, I do hope you're all right, last night was a tad unexpected, I gather?"

The older woman lifted her tea cup, took a drink. "Oh, quite well. I don't sleep much, had I mentioned that to you, dear?"

Vivian shook her head. "No, Madam Gregson, I don't think you had. But Mistress Cole mentioned something of the kind herself, and I know my older aunts often find sleep a fragile thing. I did worry a little bit, since it seemed there were some new spirits at the seance."

"Oh, Madam Etna is very talented, dear, and she has such a relationship with her dear Grey Dancer, I'm sure you heard that for yourself last night."

Vivian made up a plate for herself, eggs and toast with a bit of butter and jam. She took her time before she sat down at the table, opposite Madam Gregson's place. "You do regular sittings with her, don't you? Just here, or at her place in town?"

"Oh, just here, dear. Going there would be rather a lot of fuss and bother. I mean, I do occasionally, for more embroidery thread, or small things, but only if I feel up to. I'm not so young as I was, you know. Not at all."

Vivian nodded. "None of us are. And I am - your losses must be so hard."

That got her a sharp and intense look. "And yours?" The assumption that everyone must have some.

"None so close. My parents were dead, I have only cousins, no brothers or sisters. Some closer than others."

"No husband, no beau?"

Vivian shook her head. "I was handling some family needs, during the War, largely." Keeping an eye on the selkie communities of Scotland, and keeping them safe from invading forces and troublesome submarines. It had been no small occupation.

"Hmph." Madam Gregson disapproved. "I did War work, proper War work, in a hospital."

"Thank you for your service." It was both the proper thing to say and the correct thing to say. Vivian was glad other people had taken that up, she would have been horrific at it. Beyond all the other issues, she did not deal well with human blood. Or most blood. Nor half a dozen chemicals used for sterilisation, nor noise and clatter.

"Not even rolling bandages?" Madam Gregson was trying to find some acceptable action.

"I'm afraid I'm rather hopeless at knitting, too."

"You said you knew that..." Madam Gregson waved her fingers, faking sign language.

"Sign language, yes. That's different, there's no yarn to get tangled." Women of a certain generation did tend to be shocked that Vivian couldn't knit and couldn't sew. Vivian considered it an entirely reasonable cultural preference. But explaining that did not go well. She took a breath, then tried again. "Talking to Madam Etna, the seances, they help? What are they usually like, may I ask?"

That at least softened the moon. "Oh, Madam Etna is so kind. She never rushes me with my dear Douglas and Montgomery. Some people did, you know. I was living in another boarding house, in Skegness, for a while, on the ocean, you know, for my health. And the woman there, she always rushed through things, like she wanted to get back for the nine o'clock radio drama. Not at all the thing, she cut off dear Douglas when he was telling me the most important things about the old garden."

Vivian was sure this was going nowhere useful. "Oh, dear. The garden?"

"Oh, yes. He'd buried something there, something important, he said."

Vivian tsked. "And the other medium cut you off?"

"Very rude. But when I mentioned it to Madam Etna, why she spent hours, talking through things, letting Douglas talk to me, about where it was."

"Did you go look, afterwards?"

"Oh, I did, but there wasn't anything there, the lot had been all dug up for someone else, such a pity. It was ... it was a flower he'd grown, for me, specially. Nothing that would mean anything to anyone else, only I hadn't known he was working on it. You don't really, do you, when a man has a project like that, so sweet of him."

Vivian nodded. "That does seem very kind. You like flowers, then?"

"Oh, yes, we had a grand garden. Before."

"Do you do much with the greenhouses here?"

"Oh, oh, no. I'm not much for growing the plants myself, that was always my Douglas. He was very particular about it, fussing about the soil and the water and the sunlight. I could never keep it all straight, and of course I was busy with our Montgomery, and with getting the supper, and all that." Madam Gregson eyed Vivian. "No children, I suppose you wouldn't understand that."

"Not the same at all, but I helped with some of my younger cousins, several summers running, when their mothers were busy with other things. There's so much to keep track of, isn't there? Shoes and socks and who's eaten enough for the day, and whether that silence - well, the silence in the background usually means they've got into something they shouldn't, doesn't it?"

Madam Gregson's face changed completely. "Oh, good- ness, you do understand, you're not one of those people who claims they know. Right, then." It was clear Vivian had passed some sort of test.

Vivian ducked her head. "Enough, as I said. And I'm sure raising children, being the one responsible for them all the time, that's such an important thing. It shapes every- thing else you do, Madam Gregson."

Madam Gregson nodded, making a decision. "Please call me Natalie, if you'd like, Ann." She had decidedly passed a test.

"Natalie." Vivian gave it the proper weight. "Thank you. It's a beautiful name. So you were very busy with your son."

"Oh, yes. Until he got older and went away to school. He was apprenticed at one of the banks. Not one of the roles they kept for family, of course, we didn't have that kind of connection, but very respectable, room to move up to a more responsible position. Only...."

Vivian let her voice drop, all the things she had learned would feel right to the person she was talking to, when it came around to this conversation. "It changed everything, didn't it?"

Natalie nodded. "First Montgomery, he was twenty, then, and he wasn't an essential worker, if he'd been family to the bank, he'd have been needed, there are specific things that require the bloodline? But he wasn't, and so he got called up. And then Douglas, six months later. And for a long time I was sure well. We thought the War would be over by Christmas, or not too long after."

"Only it wasn't."

"No. I got to see them, on leave, once each. But then." She patted her side, and drew out a handkerchief, clearly still regularly needed, dabbing at her eyes. "The telegrams came. Two weeks apart, Montgomery first, and then Douglas."

"Oh, I am so sorry. And of course - you had so much you hadn't had a chance to say. Or time with them, not nearly as much time as you wanted."

"I never had as much time with Douglas as I wanted. He would putter in his shed, dear man, but he'd be out there, or the garden, or down the pub with his friends, and I'd be... Well, no use crying over spilt milk."

Vivian tilted her head, and said, after a moment. "And that's why you want to be in the seances now. So you could say the things you didn't then."

Natalie looked up, sharply, all honed intensity now. Then, very slowly, she said, "You are sharp, aren't you. So sharp you might cut yourself if you're not careful."

Vivian said, softly. "Pardon. I shouldn't intrude. You have your reasons, and I'm sure they're good ones."

The pacification eased things, but Natalie took a long

drink from her tea cup, setting it down again precisely, with a tiny clink. "You had a question."

"I did." Vivian set down her own cup. "About last night. The unexpected parts."

Madam Gregson had no particular ideas about who Aurangzeb might be. Nothing quite like that had happened at other seances, though a few times other spirits had come through. All of them had been somewhat vague about their origins, though one, two or three weeks ago, had claimed to be an ancestor of the house.

Before Vivian could ask too much more about it, Mistress Cole came in, harried and upset about a dream she'd had, something unusually vivid. Vivian tried to offer her help, but Madam Gregson immediately suggested a walk in the garden, just the two of them. Vivian found herself sitting alone at the table for a minute before she gave up the effort and went back to her room to ready herself further for the day.

NINETEEN

C admus looked up at the knock at his door. "Come."

It came out terser than he wanted, but he had the twinge of an unwanted headache at the back of his skull. He was still worried about that seance, and more to the point what Ann had said afterwards. It hadn't eased up entirely, even though it had been days.

The door opened, and Farran, his nephew, stuck his head around, his hair untidy as it often was. "Uncle, thought I'd let you know I was here."

"I thought you were in town until at least next week?"

"Delicate conjunction, something about refined energies. He wasn't very specific. Anyway, he sent me off until Monday."

Cadmus shook his head. "Well. Settle in. I've a few chores that could use two sets of hands, or someone to steady things. Let me work up a list."

He expected Farran to go off at that, they'd said the necessary things, surely, but there Farran was, waiting.

When Cadmus looked up again, Farran cleared his throat. "Uncle, there's something wrong here. This house."

"You've said that before."

"Mrs Cooper said there's been more things. Something with the paintings, and the way people were after the seance, no one explained it to her, not yet." Farran clearly disapproved of that.

Cadmus shook his head. "Most of it's been - odd, but not dangerous." Then he remembered the roses, and his hands stilled for a moment.

Farran caught it. "There was something else." His voice was sharper. He sounded so much like his father, like a fox snaring a hare. Part of Cadmus was proud and delighted at how the young man was growing up, even while he wanted no part of that sharpness aimed at him.

Cadmus looked away.

"Uncle." The voice was firm, now. "Please tell me."

It was the please that made him look up. Farran had taken two steps closer, to the other side of the desk, just far enough away Cadmus didn't feel crowded.

"There was something with the rose garden. It - was unsettling."

"That's what you say about your Colonial Service time."

Farran was right. It was. It had the same sort of feel to it, of magics that were not meant for him, not safe for him, circling and flowing. It felt somehow like a drenching rain that reshaped the land beneath it, everything it touched, washing away moss and dead leaves and revealing something new. He had no idea how to talk about it, he never had. Cadmus just knew such things were something to get away from.

As opposed to the cave and the forge, where there were

risks, but he had a much better sense of them. And some choices about the angle he took with them. Where and how he used his hammer or his other tools.

"Uncle?"

Cadmus could tell Farran was not going to let this drop. And by law - and his apprentice contract - Farran was an adult now, all the ways that mattered except his inheritance.

"Tell me why you're here." Which was suspicious, and they both knew it.

Farran met his eyes, evenly, and Cadmus looked away first. "If you tell me what happened with the roses."

Entirely too much like his father. Finally Cadmus nodded. "Fair." It was. He didn't like it, but it was fair. "You first."

"I dropped something again. The talisman he was preparing. He had to start over, polishing it. I didn't mean to." That came rushing out. "I had it in both my hands, a silk cloth so I wasn't touching it directly. But it did something, it felt - it felt hollow and like a spark, all at once, and I couldn't keep hold of it."

"Did he have to redo a lot of work?"

"A day's worth. And the conjunction is Friday, so he .. there isn't much time left. That's why he sent me away."

Cadmus leaned back. "Has this happened before?"

Farran had the grace to look embarrassed. "Not this badly. But - five or six times now. Six."

"Why didn't you tell me?" Cadmus wasn't sure whether to be angry or worried or nervous.

"Master Tambleton wasn't certain whether it was a problem. He still isn't. He said we can talk to some people at Schola, when he gets a chance. Next week, the week after. Maybe one of them will have an idea."

"Did anything like this happen there?"

"No. It was different there, we were doing different pieces of the work. It's the - slower thing, the things that are intricate to make, mostly. The inscriptions, those were all right."

Cadmus stood, moving to look out the window over the grounds, running his hands through his hair. Then he turned back, to see Farran standing there, just waiting. "Did you think I'd be angry?"

Farran chose his words carefully. "Disappointed, uncle. I know you called in favours, the distant relatives did, for this. And I want to do well, I promise. I've been studying hard, doing everything I can."

Cadmus shook his head. "I'm worried, honestly. Not disappointed."

"Worried?"

"When did this start? Was it about the same time as the problems here?"

"Oh, no, earlier. Nearly at the beginning, as soon as he had me working with some of the prepared blanks."

Cadmus shook his head. "Any chance it's a particular material? Or the fact he prepared the blanks or - someone else?"

"His previous journeyman. We thought about that, but it's hard to test. It would take time he didn't want to give up."

"So he sent you away."

Farran looked down, twisting slightly, away from Cadmus. "Yes." It came out muffled.

"Let me have another look at your contract."

"What? Why? Uncle, please." That came out nearly panicked, and that made Cadmus intensely curious.

"Sit." The instruction came out with all the weight of an order, all the authority Cadmus had once held and then set aside again. To his relief, Farran sat, ramrod straight, in the chair by the desk. It gave Cadmus time to go and open the safe in the back corner, where the family papers were locked away. He drew out a shallow fabric covered box, labelled with Farran's name, the green-black cloth still shining, not dusty at all.

He brought it back to the table and undid the ribbon ties, then lifted the lid off. The top folder was the one with the formal seals, he eased that out, and set it aside. Then he pulled out the working copy, with its much smaller stamped seal confirming that it fully matched the final copy. When he glanced up, Farran was watching him, steadily, but with a hint of something else behind his eyes.

"What do you not want me to notice, then?" Cadmus asked the question calmly.

Farran flinched, and broke eye contact, which made Cadmus feel rather more comfortable. "How did you know?"

Cadmus waves a hand. "Some things are very obvious to me." Not many, when it came to people's emotions, but Farran had always been different for him. When Farran was ducking something, it made everything in the room feel wrong, like it was vibrating too loudly.

Cadmus didn't press for an answer. He sat down, and looked through the copy, reading carefully and attentively. The first part was the usual language, they hadn't changed anything there. It laid out the structure of the apprenticeship, when it would start, and under what means it might be ended.

He kept going, running his finger down the margin, turning the page over, and then he hit the section he suspected was the issue. "The clause about termination for cause. How if you can't complete the apprenticeship, due to an irreconcilable problem, that he keeps the apprentice fee."

"Yes, uncle." It sounded resigned.

"We can see about that. He wanted that clause, pushed for it, and I did some research before we signed, about what that involves on his part. To meet the criteria."

Farran looked up, suddenly, "You did?"

"You are my best nephew, of course I did."

"Only nephew." The old and faded joke made them both smile.

"Still best. Measured among the range of possible nephews. I do know a number of other people's." Cadmus kept reading, his finger moving down the page, then to the next.

"You mean it might not be awful?"

"Look, if we lost the fee, it would be difficult. At least until you inherit. But there might be someone who'd be willing to take it on trust. Or a connection we haven't tried yet." That seemed unlikely, they'd reached out during Farran's last year of school, without much luck. Master Tambleton had been a stretch, given the resources they'd had. There weren't that many people willing to take on a young man for a modest fee, without family connections or particular talent to draw on.

"How does he treat you?" The question came out before Cadmus could think about it more carefully.

Farran flinched. "I don't know how to explain it, uncle."

"Try." Cadmus did his best to keep his voice even and steady.

"You treat me like an adult. You have since I was thirteen and off to school. You told me why you were making the choices you were, what they meant. You asked for my opinion."

"The choices affected you and your future. That seemed only fair."

"Other people aren't like that. Parents, I mean. Uncles and aunts too."

Cadmus shrugged. "Back when, you'd have had adult responsibilities from early on. And we were sending men not much older than you off to die. The least I could do was let you know what the choices were. The costs."

Farran shook his head, and leaned back in the chair. "Master Tambleton treats me like I'm tutoring age. Barely old enough to remember to wash my hands reliably. He's always pecking away. And some of it's, some of it's reasonable? There are plenty of things I don't know, that I'm there to learn. But some of it is ordinary things. How to organise my notes, where things go that he's told me and that I've been doing reliably."

Cadmus nodded. "Look, let me review the notes, see what the options are. We can talk them through."

Farran nodded, and stood. "I should unpack. Thank you, uncle."

It wasn't until the door closed that Cadmus let out a long breath of relief at not having to explain the rose garden. Yet.

TWENTY

Vivian rather thought it was time to talk to Mrs Cooper again, and perhaps more privately. She waited until just after lunch time, since there might be a break before doing the preparations for supper. She came down, standing in the doorway before she remembered the little charmed panel that triggered the light.

Mrs Cooper swung around, then blinked, then signed "Madam Porter?"

"Ann, please call me Ann." It took a moment to remember how to put that, the way the sentences were structured differently. Then she remembered to add her namesign, which was a gesture of one hand diving under the other, a reference both to her profession and where she'd learned to sign. Thankfully, not a direct reference to her full name.

That got a nod, then "May I help you?"

"Have you heard about the seance?"

Mrs Cooper grimaced at that. "The older women worry me. Last night, they slept badly." The sentences were short, precise, but the gestures themselves were expressive, and her expression was serious and earnest.

"Both of them?" Vivian did her best to match the style of the signing, for all she was quite rusty.

"Both." That got an energetic nod.

"And Cadmus?" Vivian had to spell the name, she was sure Mrs Cooper had a name sign for him, but she wasn't sure what it might be.

"Working." That ended with a movement pointing upstairs.

That made Vivian laugh. She was fairly sure that the world could be ending, and Cadmus would be at his desk during his chosen hours. If nothing else, she had to commend his work ethic.

"Something has happened."

She almost missed it, glancing away for a moment, then she nodded. "The garden. The roses." She had to spell that too, they were not a thing much used in her previous vocabulary. Cold-water coral, yes, various fish, yes, commentary about creatures in lochs, yes. Roses, no.

"Hurt?"

Vivian shook her head no, immediately. "Scared, I think." And then she carefully fingerspelled "Betrayed."

That earned her raised eyebrows, and a "Cadmus belongs to the land." And then a sign she didn't know at all. His name sign, oh, that was interesting, the sign for earth, hands moving horizontally out, spreading, but then ending in the c shape. It had an elegance to it, like a conductor's gesture, and she only caught the difference when the sign for earth was repeated next, without that touch.

She repeated the sign she didn't understand, and the questioning face.

"Steward." Mrs Cooper spelled it out for her.

"Things turning on him." She put her hands together, fists, twisting them in opposite directions.

Mrs Cooper didn't move for a minute, then she nodded. "Frightened." She stopped, her hands just held in the air, then she signed something Vivian hadn't expected, carefully spelling out "Afghanistan," before shifting back to the broader signs. "Service. Something happened."

"Do you know what?"

That got an emphatic "No." A moment later, Mrs Cooper continued, her gestures becoming less sharp and agitated. "He is a good man. He was hurt. I would not ask. Not my place."

"Thank you for telling me."

"You will help?" It was a question, a bit of urgency coming through clearly at the end.

That made quite a bit of sense. Vivian had to stop and think, then signed, "Have you had problems? Here in the kitchen?"

Mrs Cooper shook her head, then she shared a bit more. "Not in the kitchen. The grounds."

Vivian nodded. "Dangerous?"

"Weird." Mrs Cooper's index finger flicked out, making the sign. The one that meant uncanny, a magical sort of queerness, not just an unusual occurrence.

"How?"

"Not the right places. The right times. Time out of season."

"Out of season?" This was another place Vivian's vocabulary didn't suffice, and she signed "Plants" and then spelled out "blooming" and hoped that would get her idea across.

Mrs Cooper nodded, energetically. "Flowers."

Vivian nodded, and let her hands rest on the table. Mrs

Cooper got up, signing "Tea?" briefly, and Vivian nodded. They had a quiet few minutes before the kettle was ready. It made no noise, which didn't surprise her, but did have some sort of feature that lit up with a green light.

Vivian wasn't even sure how to ask half her questions, and the other half were rather pushy. She liked Mrs Cooper, so far. And certainly the housekeeper had not signed up for someone coming and prying in her life.

Once the tea was poured, Mrs Cooper sat down. "You sign well."

"Cousins up north."

Mrs Cooper just looked at her for a moment, and then her hands moved. "Ocean?"

Vivian considered before she realised she'd given it away, the way Mrs Cooper's eyebrows went up. "Yes."

"Some signs, making them." It got an eloquent little shrug at the end. "Not around here."

"Not on land." Then she added. "Don't tell, please?" with a hopeful twist to her hand, almost cupping.

It earned her a long look from Mrs Cooper. "Why are you here?"

Vivian gave what she felt was the most honest answer. "Farran asked me." She spelled his name carefully.

Mrs Cooper beamed. "Lena, me." She spelled it, and then shared her name sign, which was an L stirring a pot. "Farran is a good man." Farran's name sign was not what she'd expected. It was the sign for 'art' two fingers together, in a wave downward like a paintbrush then tapped into the other hand.

She echoed the sign, then asked "Farran likes art?"

"Not a good painter, but yes. He enjoys art."

Vivian considered. "He asked for my help. He knows my assistant's brother."

That got an energetic nod. "Good man." Then "You - help people?"

"I explore things." It was the explanation she'd come up with originally in Scotland. It made more sense to them than explaining investigations that were often about finances as much as people.

"For money?"

"Usually. Not this time. This is a favour."

Lena nodded, and said, "Not Cadmus?"

"I don't think so. He does not know."

"Keep an ear out. He comes down around now." It was shared amiably, putting them very much on the same side. Or rather, it put Vivian tidily on Lena Cooper's side.

She nodded, then asked the next question. "Is there more you'd like me to know?"

There was another long pause, both of them taking sips from their tea, and then Lena spread her hands. "It feels different. The light. Something here."

Vivian nodded. "When?"

Lena counted back. "Three months. Four months. Midsummer."

"Did anything happen then? Someone new?"

She stood, going and getting a notebook bound in faded blue cloth, clearly an accounts book of some kind. She thumbed back in the records, and said "People left. Not the problem?"

"The people who left aren't likely the problem."

Lena nodded, and bent her head again to read. Vivian waited, patiently.

Finally, her head came up, and her hands moved again. "Your cousin came in May." She consulted the book again. "First event I know of, 21st June."

"That is helpful, thank you." Vivian did her best to be as

earnest about it as possible, to let that show. This was the other part of signing she struggled with. Much of it relied on facial expressions for nuance and meaning, and she had trained herself, painstakingly, over years, not to let much of that show.

"Is your cousin..." Then her hands came down, as Lena reconsidered the question. "Do you care for your cousin?"

"We are not close." Now to try and explain this without giving too much away. Lena was top of the list of people in this house who deserved honesty, or at least as much as Vivian could offer. "Families are difficult. Distant cousins. Mother's mother's." Well, rather a lot more, back from there, but she was not getting into that.

"Not as children?" It was an abbreviated question.

"Only at big parties." It made Vivian smile for a moment, remembering what it was like running around in a mob with the cousins. The time before everyone grew up, and took on responsibilities and obligations, and the things that were customary even though they fit traditions that no longer functioned. The last part made her grimace.

"A problem?"

"I was thinking..." She let her hands float as she figured out how to sign what she wanted. "My cousin has not had a sense of doing things. I do not think it good for him." She didn't quite know how to put it into English, never mind sign.

Robin was one of the cousins who had always puzzled her. The assembled aunts thought, she believed, that he had been somewhat spoiled as a child. It wasn't just that he was an only child, that was fairly common in their family, but that his mother had travelled with him, widely and frequently. He didn't have the anchoring to the land or the steady customs that Vivian had.

As an adult, he'd done much the same. She rather thought he didn't have the habit of constancy. He always seemed, the times their paths had crossed, to be looking for something different, something other than family duty, or even art.

A hundred years ago, even twenty, he might have been a man about town, the eternal peripatetic existence. But since the War there was rather less of that. And rather more need for the cousins to step up, and keep things anchored.

It was then she heard the footsteps on the stairs behind her, and quickly signed. "Cadmus."

He came in in time to see her signing his name sign, and his eyebrows went up. "Chatting?" He said it out loud as well as signing.

C admus looked from Ann to Mrs Cooper. "I'm not interrupting?" He kept signing, trusting that it would work out.

Mrs Cooper shook her head. "Pleasant conversation." She was beaming as she signed it.

Cadmus knew far better than to get in the way of that. "Farran will be here until Monday morning. Can you add him to supper?"

"Easily." Then she added, "Ask him to come talk, please."

That was not so common a request, though Farran generally did. Cadmus nodded. "Of course. Should we let you get back to work?"

She waved a hand, but Ann moved to stand up. Cadmus felt suddenly embarrassed, that he'd walked in on something. For an instant, he felt an uncomfortable flare, a possessiveness about the kitchen and who could be there. That was quite unlike him. It was Mrs Cooper's kitchen, and she could have tea with whom she liked. To the extent it was his, he was stewarding it for Farran and whoever came after.

Before he could figure out what to do about the awkwardness, Ann was going back up the stairs. He watched her go, then looked back at Mrs Cooper, who had raised her eyebrow. She made the sign for "Go" at him, her fingers flicking at the end of it to shoo him out the door. It took him half a minute to gather himself, blinking like a rabbit at Mrs Cooper.

Then Cadmus went, pausing on the stairs to figure out if Ann were going up to her room or somewhere in one of the public rooms. The steps stopped at the ground floor, so he went along after them, into the main hallway. He could just see the flick of her skirt as she disappeared into the library.

By the time he got there, she had seated herself on one of the couches, and was drawing a book to her from one of the tables. One she'd been reading on and off, he realised, the bookmark was about a third of the way in. He stopped at the threshold, and cleared his throat.

She looked up, her movements slow and entirely at ease, like she'd never hurried anywhere in the world. "Yes?"

"I didn't mean to rush you out of the conversation. I'm sorry."

Ann blinked at him. "It is your kitchen."

"It's Mrs Cooper's kitchen." He was very clear on this. Everyone else should be, too.

"She's been with the family a long time, you'd said. But there's no Mr Cooper?"

He knew she didn't actually wrong-foot him three sentences into every conversation, but it certainly felt like that. "There was. She was married briefly in her twenties. He was a merchant seaman. He died at sea, and she came back here as cook, and then took over the housekeeping when our old housekeeper retired to a cottage on the property."

Ann tilted her head. "You take care of your people, then."

Cadmus found himself nodding and responding before he could think about it. "Of course." He then swallowed, and said. "Mrs Cooper doesn't - most people don't take an interest."

"It must be lonely for her? No other staff."

"We have the women from the village, but they - well, they're busy when they're here, and they don't sign well." He asked. "May I ask where you learned?"

She paused before answering. "Family, up north. Scotland. Extended family, not Robin's side. It was a pleasure to stretch my skills a bit, it's not something I get to use often."

"Do you - other times?"

"Oh, it's quite handy at parties, with people who know a few other signs. I'd love another drink, so and so is over there." She shrugged. "She was very patient with me, the signs I didn't know."

"She's a treasure." Cadmus said, loyally, then he sat down.

"You said your nephew was back?"

Cadmus nodded. "I'm a bit worried about him. I don't think the apprenticeship is going very well, but I don't know what to tell him. I went right into the Colonial Service, and that's more formal, like the Guard. You're an apprentice, but you're not just one person's particular apprentice with all their foibles. There are standard ways everyone does things. Or at least if they're not doing that, it's obvious they're not."

She tilted her head, and said, "You don't like it when something is not as it should be, do you?"

He shook his head. "Most people don't, really." He liked to remind himself of that, that his reactions might be a tad more insistent than most people's seemed to be. But in Albion, they were a people who understood queueing tidily and letting tea steep the proper amount, and the ancient sports traditions that must be followed in every detail.

Ann leaned back, watching him and taking her time. "And Mrs Cooper, pardon, I'm prying." She changed topics. "It's been just you and Farran for a while?"

Cadmus nodded. "His father was my brother. I'm the elder, I inherited the house and land, but not much money. I was in and out for a while, other projects. About a decade ago, I came back and set it up as a boarding house, when things started changing before the War. Six years ago - Farran was twelve - his parents were killed in an accident, out on the ocean. And I raised him. He was in tutoring school then, and got into Schola, and he had a good time there, I think."

Ann nodded. "It's hard to tell, that age, isn't it? We ask students to do so many things, some of which they're no earthly good at."

Cadmus nodded, his head bobbing up and down until he made himself stop. "Did you go to - no, you said at supper you hadn't."

She shook her head. "I read the stories about it, the novels. And I wish I could have been there."

"It's not much like the books. At least not the hearty boys books full of moral moments and lessons learned."

"That is not the genre I'm most familiar with, I admit." It had made her smile, which pleased him unreasonably.

"They're quite formulaic. I think most societies have

stories that they find - predictable is the wrong word. That play out the way everyone expects. Reliable."

"Folk tales. Once upon a time, a very long time ago," Ann's voice trailed off.

"Goddess, sing the anger of Achilles, son of Peleus, and the destruction it brought," he said, then echoed it in Greek, which as always sounded much better to him.

She smiles. "But there's other kinds of stories. School stories. What are the boys ones like?"

"Tell me about the ones for girls?" He wanted to gather himself, a little, for talking about stories he didn't fully understand. But more than that, he found himself curious, interested in her experiences rather than proclaiming his own.

She did not seem to mind he had put her off, at least, and he found himself feeling rather grateful. "Oh, there's some sort of improving story. A girl who is a bit bossy, doesn't listen to others. Someone from a difficult home situation who turns around when others treat her kindly. There's often some sort of animal, a lost cat, a hedgehog, a dog, something like that. Ponies, in one of them. A seal, but that was rather the exception."

"Schola is on an island, and I gather people do see seals from time to time. Besides the somewhat more metaphorical type of the house."

Ann considered, and peered at him. "What house were you?"

"Owl. I should have thought that obvious, given the classics."

She cocked her head. "I've known a fair number of people for whom the connection wasn't obvious, at least to an outsider. Do you think the stories depend on which house?"

"Oh, certainly, I think Horse tends to like a more domestic story, or at least a pastoral one. And I've known a fair number of Boar folks posted with the Army, who'd go charging off at things like their namesake. Owls are - well. Owls and seals are liminal, aren't they? The borderlands."

Something in that made her chuckle to herself, and he couldn't figure out why. "We've got away from the school stories?" Perhaps they could get back to something he at least had a framework for.

"Oh, indeed. Well, the girls' stories have midnight feasts - though I gather from Emma and Andromache that the kitchens were actually quite some distance away, across the courtyard."

"They are. But people sneak things out, or the head of house might have treats, or people get hampers from home. You store things up, and share them out with your friends."

"But it's not big rooms?" She was curious about that, she was leaning forward now.

"Only the first year. After that everyone moves into single rooms, mostly. Better for magical development, they said. And of course sometimes people have exercises and practices that would bother others. Study bedrooms, bed along a wall, desk and wardrobe, shared bathing room, some common spaces." He shrugged. "I didn't like the dormitories one bit, I'm sure that's no surprise."

"It must be quite a shock."

Cadmus nodded. "But I enjoyed the part about having people around. Nearby. Conversations at different times. I think that's why I wanted to open the house up to residents." He'd never actually thought about why, besides the fact it was a manageable way to bring in extra money, and the War effort needed housing. But he'd felt much more at home here with more people, like it had been in his childhood with at least a dozen family members in residence, plus the staff. Mostly older relatives, widowed aunts and great-aunts, and a few cousins, for the summers, especially. But somehow the family had fractured apart, as their elder generation died.

Ann nodded, then asked, as if she felt it was long past time for the conversation to go in an easier direction, "What do you enjoy reading? When you're not translating, that is." The discussion that followed carried them both through until it was time to change for the evening. If it didn't give him much more intimate a sense of it, it was at least pleasant to talk about a wide range of topics with someone who was well-read. She didn't lay her preferences out, but she didn't hide the fact she was curious about a great many things.

TWENTY-TWO

TUESDAY, NOVEMBER 21ST, AFTER SUPPER

After supper on the twenty-first, Vivian was already frazzled. She shouldn't be. She had done this ritual every year since she was seven. She had done it alone, in a tiny bedsit during the War. And she had done it with a hundred of her aunts and uncles and cousins dancing in the great field at the home grove, hearing the trees dance and seeing the light flaring through the first portal. There was the year she had been at a hotel, unavoidably detained by a Guard investigation. She had had to sneak up to the rooftop garden long enough to make the necessary gestures.

This time was proving to be decidedly awkward. She had to dodge three separate invitations after supper - from Andromache and Emma, Cadmus, and then Natalie Gregson. Turning her down had been the hardest, the woman had an excellent range of skill in puppy-dog eyes. Vivian had pleaded a headache, but that only complicated things.

First she needed to prepare herself. This was why she'd refused a room with the bath across the hall. She had known that she would need hours to prepare, if she were still here when time for the ritual came. She had steeped the water for the cleansing bath for the full hour required, in a small portable cauldron from her trunk, then poured it into a steaming hot bath.

Some lines, her aunts had told her, had particular incantations for the cleansing. She was grateful as she often was that in her line, she simply had to fully immerse her head three times, and as much of the rest of her body as could be arranged. Awkward, in some settings, but pouring water over the head would do in a pinch.

The cleansing had the same sharp herbal smell it always did, though the thyme from her garden this year had come out smelling sweeter than some. The rosemary was crisp, more evergreen than citrus, more than bright enough to cut across the almost honeyed scent of the elderflower. Part of Vivian thought it made the room smell like a roast for Saturday supper, but there you were. It was traditional.

Vivian dried herself off with the pure white cloth, taking time to make sure all of her was dry. She applied the infused oil, olive oil brought from the cousins in Greece with great pomp and fuss, then infused with herbs. It too, smelled bright and sharp and proper. She shrugged into the dress, loose undyed linen that fell just to her ankles, leaving it unbelted for now. Finally, she pinned up her hair, letting one long curl fall over each shoulder. The jewellery was already packed. She checked her basket one last time, making sure she had everything.

She'd been worried especially about Robin, but he'd made excuses to be away for a day or two. If he was going to the Grove, she might end up in trouble. Probably not. It's not as if they didn't know him and the way he made decisions as well as she did. And his charm didn't work on any of his cousins nearly as well as it worked on people without their blood. Still, she couldn't keep herself from looking over her shoulder as she made her way out across the gardens.

Three days ago, she'd finally found a spot she deemed suitable. There was a small meadow with a pond and a folly, quite picturesque. Not too far from the house, but well away from any of the areas where there had been trouble. More to the point, she'd spotted half a dozen elder trees, doing their duty as protectors, ringing the space.

Vivian was glad she'd walked this way several times in the daylight. The moon was a barely new crescent, not enough light to see her hand a foot in front of her face in the shadow of the trees.

She made her way along the path, pulling her cloak around her. She had the basket in her arms with everything she needed, the cloak - and a small enchantment - to hide her from passing eyes. It was dark and cold enough she suspected even the poachers weren't out tonight. Certainly she didn't hear anything large moving about in the brush.

The folly, when she found it, was open to the sky above on the top floor, and she could see the stars through one of the sets of pillars there. There was no moon in the sky, but even if there had been, it would not have been a problem tonight. The moon was the barest thread of a crescent past new. Once she was inside the ring of trees, she bowed to the bushes at the entrance, then to the folly's silhouette, then to the pool of water. The living land, the human made, and the liminal.

She set up the lantern, first, the sides carefully adjusted to cast the light where she needed it, toward the pool. Once she had that set up, she could withdraw the flat wooden altar panel she had brought with her, in the bottom of her basket. Just enough room for wine and honey and cream. And the cakes that Luned had sent along when it became clear it was that or figuring out how to bake on the hearth in her bedroom.

That had seemed likely to end in utter failure and possibly fire. And honestly, no one commented about the exchange of packages of baked goods. She could set the basket aside, at the edge of the clearing now, to keep her shoes and cloak dry, at least.

She measured out enough space around it to dance, and scattered the flower petals, soaked in the potion that would illuminate them when the time came. Careful not to step inside the circle once she formed it, she left just enough space open to take a careful step through. At last, she turned to make the last preparations. At least she had space for the full proper radius for a personal dance this time, which was a pleasure. She hated adapting to a cramped space. The magic worked as well if you did it standing in place, but it was rather harder on the ankles.

Finally, she needed to undo her cloak and put on her final adornments. There was the comb for her hair. She ran her thumb over the stars of the Pleiades picked out in silver, and the small sapphire set in Electra's place. Then she reached up, settling it in place in the coiled hair on the arch of her skull, making sure it would stay there through the dance.

Next came the cord belt, spun from fine silk, layer on layer of colour plied together from far thinner threads. Here was indigo's deep blue, for the family, then the rich blue green of copper and logwood for humanity, and madder's dark red. They twined around each other, all the little charms and beads she'd braided in carefully, years ago.

Finally, the necklace, the metal pendant, set with a large smooth piece of amber, painstakingly carved to collect and hold the light. She held it in her hand, before she reached behind her neck to do the clasp, looking forward to how it would feel when she was finished.

She slipped off her boots, and on sandals, wishing yet again that someone in the past millennia had adapted the ritual. Albion was not the same climate as Greece at all. But sandals it had always been, and sandals it would probably always be. She shivered, just once, before forcing her mind to focus, making the last checks of the ritual.

And then it was time to begin. She felt the magic in her blood shift. None of them needed a watch. Not for this, not for the ceremonies in the spring when their foremothers disappeared below the horizon for weeks and then returned, dancing back and bringing the spring. All of it was rubbish, if you looked at it with a scientific eye. The world would continue to spin, come what may, and the seasons change.

None of them dared give up the ritual.

That wasn't the point, not for Vivian. It was a chance to thank and honour her foremothers. That moment of numinous connection, the places where memory and magic and the sacrifices of their family over the centuries all were intertwined. She kept doing it because it mattered, not because she was told to. She suspected that was some of Robin's problem, actually, now she thought about it from that angle. All the things he was expected to do, that weren't what he was choosing himself. Somehow, he'd also got no grounding in why those things mattered, what they did, the substance of the magic.

Glancing up through the trees, she saw she could begin. The seven sisters were high in the sky. It was a matter now of entering the circle, and of dancing. Ancient steps, passed down from aunt to niece, cousin to cousin. She had originally planned a different kind of dance, practised the flourishes and touches that would set it apart. But this place, this night, this puzzle, they had called for something else, and she would be improvising more than she usually did. Art must yield to necessity, and there would be other years for creative flourishes.

She hoped.

TWENTY-THREE

AFTER MIDNIGHT

There was something wrong. Or at least, there was some reason Cadmus had woken up, just at midnight, with a sound in his ears.

For a moment, a startling terrifying moment, he thought he was back in Afghanistan. Back in the mountains, when everything went wrong. Then he felt the bed underneath him, and knew that whatever the problem was, he was in England. Fewer scorpions, fewer poisonous snakes. He would cling to that.

Sitting up did not change the tug he felt, of something off. It was like one of the great bells gone out of tune, a clang where there should be resonance. He closed his eyes, prayed to the Smith for strength, and stood, shrugging on outdoor clothes, then jamming his feet into shoes. Whatever was off was outside. He didn't know how he knew that, just that it had water in it and soft earth. That was not in the building itself unless the wood rot had got much worse this week than he hoped.

He heard no one else moving in the house as he ducked through the side door, but the grounds were immense. He

had no idea where to begin. Cadmus eyed the direction of
the rose garden. He decided to give it and the greenhouses a
wide berth, and turned towards the other side of the main
gardens. There were paths there, the folly, a pond. He
couldn't get the faint taste of dampness out of the back of
his throat.

Cadmus saw no signs of anything wrong, but as he took
the path along the edge of the woods, he thought he saw a
flicker of movement. It could have been a deer, or even a
poacher, but a poacher was not the thing that would wake
him. And so he turned, down toward the pond and the folly,
moving more slowly now, carefully.

It was a good thing, because when he came over the
slight rise in the hill there was a glow from the lake. It was
distressingly like the glow there had been in the Hindu
Kush mountains, north of Kabul. It was clear but gleaming.
It was not wine-dark, but star-light, with a shimmer that
compelled him to look, to come closer, despite the fact the
rest of his heart and mind wanted to run. Part of him
wanted to look away, but the rest of him knew he needed to
investigate.

There was enough logic left in him to take a deep
breath, to force himself to take slow steps, to stay in the
shadows of the trees. When he was perhaps forty feet away,
he could make out more details. There was a woman, or at
least he assumed a woman. He could see the flare of her
skirt and the curve of her breasts and hips as she turned,
silhouetted by the light. She was wearing more clothing
than a flapper might, but not by much, certainly not as
much as the women of his acquaintance wore.

She was dancing.

It was not like other dances he knew, the more sedate
ones. There were a whole class of dances suitable to middle-

aged men with no real sense of rhythm and too much
dignity to make a fool of themselves. It was not like the
modern dances he saw sometimes, done by other people,
kicking and shimmying, arms swinging high and low. It
wasn't the demanding passion of a tango, or the intimacy of
a waltz.

He stopped, transfixed. In another time and place, it
might have been seductive. He recognised elements he'd
seen before, in tribal dances, in performances put on for the
military officers and Colonial Service staff, a little bit of
local colour. He had no names for what this dancer was
doing, and he could tell that many things were different. He
could hear faint bells, but softly. No finger cymbals, no
drum to guide the beat. Just this woman, dancing, strands of
hair loose behind her, flowing down to her waist when
gravity pulled them down at last.

Step, step, pause, step, a twist of her head, as if it was
some silent challenge. Then she made a graceful bow.
Toward the pond, he thought, before she stepped back and
he could see some low table or bench set on the ground, ten
feet before her. Then there were a series of delicate steps
backwards, precisely measured, each marked with a precise
kick of her ankle and chime of gathered bells as she began
moving in a circle. She reached down to the things on the
ground, then up, then down again.

If she knew he was there, she gave no sign. And he was
not close enough to see her face, or any other detail that
might help.

Part of him, now there was quiet to think, wondered if
this had happened here before. If somehow, there was a
woman who came to dance in his woods every night, or
certain nights. He could not decide if he wanted there to be.
Or if, instead, he was terrified - again, still - that there were

layers under his notice, things he had no idea about, close enough to touch.

He had no idea how long she continued, or how long he stood there. He became slowly aware that that glow, from the pond, or from in front of her was no longer just in front of her. Something, a necklace, perhaps, something on her chest, it was beginning to shine. And this time, golden, rather than silver. He blinked, trying to make his eyes focus, and he couldn't for a minute.

When he could look back, it was because the dance had changed. Her movements were faster, sharper, precise, cutting like a weapon. There was something that it reminded him of, the little quick movements with the feet, while her hips stayed still. Then a sharp jerk, building up the energy and tension with controlled, refined movements.

She was forging something, he realised. Each movement was a hammer blow, forging metal into shape. Probably cold forging. That light was brighter, though he could feel no warmth, but it was building and building. It was coiling, tighter and tighter, then there was one last shimmy, a chaos of chimes from the bells she wore, and then everything was silent. She stood there, facing the lake. He could not see her hands, just the straight perfect line of her body, fully intent on something he could not see, only feel.

When it came, it came with a clap of thunder, the kind that would shake everyone in bed awake, and a flash of light. But there was no storm, no ordinary storm. The figure inhaled, he could see her shoulders lift, and then there was a curious motion he could not begin to describe. It was not a curtsey, for she did not lower herself, but it was a gesture of reverence, done fluidly and gracefully.

Finally, the light began to fade, first from whatever she wore that was glowing, then from the pond, like a sunset, only it left the sky dark rather than turning it brilliant shades of pink and orange. There was a curious kind of processional dance, now, slow and tight. It was if she were unwinding something with each step, setting the stars back in their place with a resolute precision. He watched closely, so closely he could see the moment her hand shook, then her ankle almost gave way, before she gathered herself again, and continued.

Part of him wanted to slink away home. Part wanted to rush up to her and demand to know who she was, and what she was doing. Most of him was terrified now that that bright glowing presence would come back, because he knew that awe. The last time he had trespassed on mysteries that were not his, his world had exploded.

He could not retreat, the chances were excellent she would hear him. And in his more rational mind, he thought that this woman, whoever she was, had the blessing of her god or goddess. The light had not had a form, not to him, but who knew what the woman had seen or heard or felt. He could not intrude. He could only stay where he was, and hope she didn't notice him. Or if she did notice him, that she was not inclined to make an Actaeon of him.

In the faint light of what must be a lantern, she finally came to a rest, and she knelt for a minute on the ground. It must be cold and even damp. This was November, in England, when sensible people would be tucked in with a hot water bottle or a warming charm. Then, finally, she made the small movements of someone pouring a final libation, then standing to claim a basket from nearby, and fill it, extinguishing the lantern last.

It left them both in the dark. Cadmus held his breath as he heard soft footsteps come up the path, the faint rustling of fallen leaves, a swish of fabric. She passed close enough to him he could smell herbs and a floral note, a mixture he'd never been close to before. He waited, wondering if she knew or sensed he was there, but she moved evenly, as if every step were still part of her precise and measured dance.

Then she moved well past him, and she was gone, moving up the path, out of the woods and toward the open ground. He waited until she was back toward the gardens, and turned down the path, toward the pond. Finally, he was able to cast a light cantrip, breathing "Fiat lux" in the ancient words that he'd learned at school, cupping the light in his hands. He could see a ring of flower petals, demarking the space she had been in, impressions of her little altar, a few gleaming drops of her libation. But there was nothing left to show what gods she had been calling upon, and they were none that he knew.

Finally, he turned back, to return to the house. Whatever had woken him had faded. He had no idea if it was this mysterious dance, or if that dance had driven off some great evil. There were stories of that, in parts of Italy, he knew, and in eastern Europe, and other places, as well. Not here. He had thought that left elsewhere.

The garden fields were quiet. He could see no sign of movement, beyond the slight comforting sounds of small animals and birds rustling in the leaves. He realised now that those sounds had been entirely missing earlier. In a minute he would be back in the relative safety and normalcy of the house, and all would be well.

TWENTY-FOUR

AFTER MIDNIGHT

Vivian walked back in a daze, the magic coursing in her blood. Her heartbeat was drumming in her ears, and she forced herself to take careful slow steps. She needed them, not only to preserve the dance as long as she could, but because she had no wish to fall on her face.

The offerings had not been like that for her for years. The last half of the dance had been transcendent. She had that moment when her foremother reached down, and stars danced in her blood. Even more so, something in her blood had sung out to the heavens. She'd had that once before, when she was twenty one and considering a commitment to a pleasant young man who flattered and pleased her. Richmond, of all the ridiculous names.

After that night, he'd seen something in her change, and he hadn't liked it. He certainly hadn't wanted her to have something he didn't understand and couldn't control. She was glad then, had been glad since, that she'd had that moment when she did, not a few years later. It was part of what had got her into her line of work. She might keep up the beautiful offices and the necessary staff by jobs for the Ministry and others who would pay handsomely for discretion and competence. That that enabled her to help people who needed it. Richmond's later wife, for example.

There had been no clear message tonight, not like there had been then. Then it had been a flood of images of what would happen if she kept her road. They had come too fast and became too chaotic for her to make any single image stick. But together, they were clear, leave this man, get away from this man, he does not mean you well. She had listened, and her foremothers had been right, as they reliably were for those who had ears to hear or eyes to see.

This time, though, it was different. Whatever message there was was a sweeping instruction to be open, to flow, to dance, to keep dancing. There had been an outpouring of magic, with the taste and scent of the line of her mother's magic, all the way back to Electra. There was the faint snap of ozone, the buzz in the air before a lightning strike or in the silence after a thunder clap. Then, under that, the hints of flowers, long past their proper season. She inhaled, breathing in the roses and the orchids, and something else she couldn't name.

Modern English didn't have words for this, because this magic was almost unknown among mortals now. Just her kin. And only if they were blessed with it. She was fairly sure Robin had never felt that touch, or he'd be a different sort of man. It wasn't a religious conversion, as the missionary faiths hoped for, a lightning bolt from the sky. It was more like a river being set back in its proper course after a flood, or a pond flowing free after the silt had been dredged. Not gentle, but a fluid sort of transformation.

She was so caught up in what the right metaphor might be that she was back at the house before she realised it, by the side door. She had left it slightly ajar. Otherwise she would have had to sign out, and get the latchkey from Cadmus, and that would involve either explaining or lying to him. She had not wanted to explain, and she wanted even less to lie to him. The fibs she'd told so far were bad enough.

She reached for the latch, moved to open it - and it did not budge. She tried again, as if that would fix the problem. With a sense of growing alarm, she rattled the latch.

Of course nothing changed. Vivian took a deep breath, and another. She had left this door open, she was sure of it. But now it was locked. And she had no key. It was well after the household curfew, of course, and she could see no lights on other than the dim charm light in the main hall.

She had been in difficult situations requiring ingenuity before, though admittedly not when she was more than half-drunk on magic and power and the world reshaping itself around her. If worst came to worst, surely there was some outbuilding that would be safe enough. There was a carriage house, empty now except for storage but it had walls and probably not too many pests. The back kitchen entry had a little shelter, even if it might disturb Lena in the morning.

She grimaced and took a step back, then heard something behind her and whirled around, nearly dropping the basket.

It was Cadmus. The look on his face was somewhere between awe and fear and confusion, and he took a step back, then he bellowed, "You."

This was not going well. She could tell that, all her senses were jangling now, with uneasy worry, dropped out of the elation of the magic and the mystery and the ritual. It felt like a large jar, smashed on the ground, leaving nothing.

She stepped back, feeling the lintel of the door at her heels, and the wood at the back. "Cadmus?" She hoped calling his name would help.

He was watching her, like she'd gone through a magical transformation in front of his eyes, turned into a lion or an adder. Then, no, he stood back, and he said, "What are you. Tell me the truth." His voice was rough and raw. "Who are you." It was all order and command, and he wasn't lord of the land, but this was his domain, and she felt all the old powers that came with that. An Englishman's home was his castle. Cadmus belonged to the land, Lena had said, and it answered him.

She closed her eyes, taking a deep breath. He didn't seem likely to hurt her, she could have read that in an instant. This was something more complex, about trust and treachery, about knowledge and lies.

"Vivian Porter." She said her name, carefully, evenly.

"Not Ann."

"Vivian." She repeated it, as carefully as she could. "Ann is the name I use sometimes."

"What are you doing in my home? Was it Farran?"

She considered how to answer that, and she saw him spot the hesitation instantly. "Tell me, tell me now. What do you mean to do with him?"

"I don't intend him any harm." Vivian kept her voice even. "These problems you've been having, with the orchids, and the roses, and the spirit."

He cut her off, abruptly. "Go upstairs, pack an overnight case, and I will send the rest of your things on." It was a flat dismissal.

"It is well past midnight. If you want me to leave first thing in the morning, I will."

"I can't trust you. I apparently can't trust anything you say. Even your name."

Vivian took a deep breath. "Farran asked for my help. Talk to him, please. About why. He was worried about you. About the house."

"Farran." It wasn't dismissive, precisely, more about an ongoing problem. "Farran is a young man who has no experience of the world." Cadmus shook his head. "I should harness the cart and take you to town. Some inn or pub would take you. They're used to university students."

"Farran worries about you. About the house." She had no idea what repeating it would do, but she was chasing that thread of magic on pure intuition.

"Who are you. Not why you're here. Who. Are. You." His voice was a low growl now. He was keeping his distance, still, like he thought she might be able to slip away, glamour him, do something, if he got closer.

"That's a long story. An old one. Millenia, and centuries, depending." Keep her voice even, don't give any more threat, nothing to scare him.

"We have time." There was a little flick of his hand, forming a charm light. "Sit."

She sat on the lintel of the door, perching on it, her knees up, almost against her chest. It felt undignified and vulnerable, and the stone she was sitting on was cold, even with the cloak beneath her. "I am of the line of Electra. The Fatae, the shining sisters."

Cadmus watched her, visibly dubious, glaring at her like she had done something wrong, or shameful. "And what does that mean to me?"

This was always a delicate part of the explanations. The

few times Vivian had had to do it, it had never been this fragile. "When Richard made the Pact," She didn't have to explain which Richard, it was always the Third, always 1483, the date around which their world pivoted. "Someone had to stay, to make sure the rules were observed. My foremothers."

His eyes narrowed. "Matrilineal."

"Yes. The responsibilities."

"And your cousin? Same side of the family?" Oh, Cadmus, for all his absent-minded classicist self was sharp.

"Not mine to tell." Which was as good as telling, given what he'd said so far, but she couldn't help that.

Cadmus shook his head. "Why shouldn't I throw you out? You can fend for yourself, I assume."

Vivian said, softly. "Because I think I can help. With whatever's going on. If you let me."

"I can't trust you. You snuck out of the house, you did - something - in the woods. And you're not telling me any more than you absolutely have to."

He had a point. And she was arguing from a weak position, at best. "Look." She tried again. "It's late. We've had a long night. Nothing in this will change if we go inside, warm up, have some tea, and go to bed."

"And in the morning, there'll be a handful of leaves instead of your week's fee?"

Vivian drew herself up as best she could. "I am not that kind of woman. I pay my debts."

Cadmus glowered at her, and then he spread his hands. "Tomorrow. Do you promise you will tell me what I ask?"

"Within my other promises, yes."

Cadmus eyed her. "That is not at all satisfying." It wasn't, but it was what she could offer. Then he stood. "Come here, so I can unlock the door." He gestured at a spot on the path. She got up, brushing her cloak out behind her, and waited until he unlatched the door, then stepped back, letting her go first. Not holding it, as he would for a lady, but watching to see what she did.

"Tomorrow." And with that, she picked up her shattered dignity and took herself to the stairs, walking quietly.

TWENTY-FIVE

THREE IN THE MORNING

Cadmus paced, in his office. Clearly, sleep would not touch him. He had no idea how that, that woman had been able to turn on her heel, and walk up to her room as if nothing was wrong. There had been something in how she'd done it, deliberate, as if she were certain, in a bone-deep way, that she had been in the right. He never felt like that, except about the house. He never had.

He wanted to go yell at her. He never yelled, he was not a person who yelled, he was certainly not a person who thought yelling fixed anything. But here he was, pacing in his office, fuming, wanting to go yell.

Most of all, at the moment, he wanted to know what Farran had been thinking, to invite someone like that, someone twisting and complicated into their house. He felt very much as if the world had changed around him, without asking his permission. He'd been thrust from Sophocles to Euripides, into one of those plays where things pivoted, and you saw things in a whole new way, and all the old rules got twisted up. He'd barely managed those stories when he was translating them, words fixed on a page, so he could certainly not manage being dropped in the midst of one.

He felt like Baucis and Philemon must have, realising that Zeus and Hermes stood before them, and he wondered, suddenly, and with a rush of fear, whether that was what had happened. Was Ann, Vivian, whatever her name was, some goddess he had now offended? Or would the gods feel he had broken hospitality by questioning?

Cadmus stopped, dead, on the rough spot in the carpet, and then turned to the door. He might not be able to go continue the confrontation with Ann. Vivian. Whatever she was calling herself going forward. But he could, in fact, go and talk to Farran.

He glanced at the clock. It was three in the morning, now. If he wasn't going to sleep, Farran shouldn't sleep. Besides, young men could bounce back. The family quarters were thoroughly warded for sound, they had been for ages. And those charms at least had been solidly done in the first place. Not like some of the weatherproofing. They could have an out and out screaming match if required, and the residents wouldn't hear more than a whisper.

Cadmus shook his head. He didn't want to yell at Farran. Not precisely. But he needed to understand, needed to know why this woman was here, and what she wanted, and what it was going to cost them. All of them. He was not the folklore specialist. Hah, he was sure she wasn't either, or at least not at all the way she'd implied. But he did know that being close to one of the Fatae was dangerous, and Afghanistan had taught him that there were reasons for those rules.

And now he had one in his home. Well. Not one of the Fatae directly. That was forbidden by the Pact, any child of twelve knew that. But that only made it worse. The Fatae were bound by the Pact, not to interfere, to withdraw, and he'd thought England was safe from that kind of thing. Warping the magics around them. And the light and the dancing and the way whatever it was, whoever it was, seemed to reach down. The god-touched.

That made him pause. He had his own moments of that, of having felt The Smith's hand on his shoulder, the warmth of it. He'd certainly smelt the tang of the metal and the iron in the roast meat. He'd had his own chance to be touched by the gods, even if he didn't know what to do with it now, when he'd fled in Afghanistan, been a coward.

Well. Whatever he was, he would take care of his land. He would always take care of his land. And his people. Not that there might not be a bit of well-earned scolding coming up shortly for one of them. Figuring out what Mrs Cooper knew, if anything, also was likely necessary.

With that, he turned, shrugging on the cardigan again, and went along to go and knock at Farran's door. Once, twice, then three times in rapid succession.

He waited, and after a minute without any response, he knocked again, louder. From inside the room, he heard a sleepy, "Uncle? Is there something wrong?"

"I need to talk to you." It was more of a demand than he'd ever made of Farran, beyond the necessary requirements of raising someone for several years.

"Um." The voice sounded uncertain. "Come - come in?" He could see the light appear under the door, and then footsteps, and Farran opened the door, rubbing his eyes. His dressing gown was draped loosely around him, the belt dangling. He could see there were spots wearing through at the cuffs, and that the legs of his pyjamas had got too short again. He must have grown another inch since the last time Cadmus thought to check.

"Uncle?" Farran was uncertain.

"We need to talk. Now. It can't wait. Put the sound charms up." His voice came quick and sharp.

His nephew nodded, and gestured at the chair by the window, the one with the repaired leg that was much newer and lighter wood than the other three. He touched his hand to the panel that triggered the sound warding, then pulled his desk chair over and sat on it uncertainly, arms akimbo. "Uncle?"

"Tell me what you know about Vivian Porter." Emphasis strongly on her full name.

Farran opened his mouth, then snapped it closed.

"She came here under false pretences. And she said, earlier tonight, that you asked for her help."

Farran wrinkled his nose, but then straightened up. Some part of Cadmus was proud to see him acting more like an adult than an uncertain youth. "I did."

"Why?" Cadmus did his best to keep his voice even and mild. "From the beginning, please."

Farran's eyes widened, but then he nodded. "My friend, Anthony Sturgis, his older sister - she's Mrs Norton, but she's a widow, now - raised him and their other brothers and sisters. She works for Madam Porter."

"In what capacity?"

"Mrs Norton runs the office."

Cadmus managed not to roll his eyes. "What sort of office, Farran, don't play the fool."

Farran swallowed. "An investigation office. I don't know many details, but Anthony said she does things for the Ministry, sometimes. There was a case she did for an art museum that apparently got a lot of press a while back. But that it's mostly work that takes discretion, Anthony said. I was worrying over the things here, the strange things, the uncanny things. Anthony said I should ask his sister, and she said she'd see if Madam Porter would talk to me."

Cadmus considered. That chain of events was better than it might be. Someone wishing to set up the family might use the connection, but it was a fairly slender chance. Farran had talked about Anthony for years, on and off, as one of his better friends. So unless Madam Porter were routinely a great deal better informed about the life of an employee than most people, and a great deal more inclined to meddle over the course of years, it might be as Farran said.

"What did you tell her? In as much detail as you remember."

Farran lifted his chin. "I can do better than that." He got up, went to his desk, and pulled out a small journal, flipping through pages, then handing it over. "To the end of the facing page." He handed the volume over. There, in the tidy readable handwriting Cadmus had painstakingly taught him, was an admirable summary of the conversation. Cadmus read to the end, frowning at it.

"You're not paying her?"

"I didn't have anything I could offer. No money, and - I knew you'd be angry about other things. Commitments. Promises. Or that they weren't sensible, whether or not you'd be angry."

Cadmus had to smile slightly at that, despite that. "What did you think of her?"

"It's there." Farran leaned over and pointed to a word along the margin, in Greek letters. Polytropon. Many turning, the word applied to Odysseus, complicated, twisting. Probably not many-travelling, though how Cadmus might know, he had no idea.

"That's not wrong, no." Cadmus considered. "And you asked her for help anyway?"

"Well. I wrote that down after we talked. Because of the bit about owing her or not owing her. I think she didn't want to take advantage?" Farran flicked his fingers at the book. "I - sort of wondered if something I said made her want to be here? But that's ridiculous, isn't it?" Much more quietly, he asked, "Are you upset?"

"I ought to be." Cadmus had to think it through. "You asked someone into our home, without checking with me, about something I've been very worried about. It looks like she didn't take advantage, but you gave her every opportunity if she'd wanted."

"Mrs Cooper likes her. A lot. Called her by first name. And her name sign."

"Did she?" Cadmus peered at Farran again. "They were talking earlier, when I came downstairs, a day or two ago."

"And Mrs Cooper is good at spotting people who don't mean us well. She likes Madam Porter. Like she likes Mistress Price." Which led to the question of who Mrs Cooper didn't care for. Cadmus wasn't sure he was brave enough to ask that directly.

Cadmus shook his head. "She's done it at least - what, four times now?" He tapped the book, then handed it back. "I am upset with you. But I will, I'm not going to do anything hasty. I won't be around tomorrow, you can see to everyone, tell them I went into town."

"Are you going into town?"

"I'd like a better library than the one here, honestly. And I don't trust myself to be civil to Madam Porter in public, possibly anyone else."

Farran nodded. "So I should see to things. Do we have any deliveries, or is it just the meals?"

"Just the meals. I've got that list of tasks for you, and you can demonstrate your earnest desire to make up for not telling me by getting a decent number of them done."

Farran ducked his chin. "Fair." Then, as Cadmus stood to go get at least some rest, he added, "Thank you, uncle. For not. For taking me seriously."

The way he said it made Cadmus scowl, but he nodded. "Leave me a note if there's anything I need to know. I'll be back after supper sometime." And then he did stand, and make his way back down the silent dark hallway to his own rooms.

Vivian had been unable to settle to anything, all morning. She had woken mid-morning, that part was unsurprising. All her kin tended to sleep soundly after that particular kind of ritual, even without the fact they rarely saw their beds until nearer dawn than midnight. But the mix of a curious lassitude and a relentless agitation was not at all normal for her. She couldn't settle to anything. Not tidying her room, not reading, not even to walking around the property.

At lunch, Andie and Emma had settled with one on either side of her. She had hoped her state of mind was not quite so obvious, but they had the way of a pack working together to peel off a particular target. They did not press her, mercifully, through lunch itself, a meal of soup and sandwiches, nothing difficult to manage. At the end, though, Andie stood come up. "I've something I'd quite like your opinion on, Ann. Come upstairs for a bit? We can give you some of the good tea stash."

Vivian thought about arguing, briefly. But she did not

have anywhere she had to be, and she was fairly certain that as good as her dissembling was, these sharp-eyed women would spot it. She gave in, as gracefully as she could. "Oh, the good tea, is it? I don't have anything pressing."

Once Emma's door was closed, and the kettle was on, Andie settled in her chair. "Something's wrong. Or at least different. Cadmus left the house early, and he went into Oxford, entirely outside his usual schedule. You weren't down for breakfast. And you look..."

Emma chimed in. "Different." She flicked her fingers at the pendant Vivian was wearing, which wasn't obvious. "Also, that seems to be glowing."

Vivian peered down, then drew the chain out and cursed silently. She'd forgotten that her pendant, similar to the apprenticeship pendants so many others wore, sometimes reacted to ritual that way. It was harder to tell with amber, which often had a glow or a gleam of reflected light, but at the moment, it was rather obvious.

"We'd like to help." Andie followed up on Emma's comment promptly, leaning forward. "So long as you don't mean any harm to Cadmus."

Emma snorted. "That's not going to make anyone tell you."

Andie waved her hand. "We like Cadmus. And we like living here. The grounds are lovely, the food is good, no one fusses."

Vivian took a breath, weighing her options. She knew this was her choice. So were the consequences of the choice. It wasn't forbidden to tell people who she was, what she was, but if they reacted badly, it would be her responsibility to deal with. And there was the complication of Robin.

In the end, she gave herself over to that whispering

thread of the numinous, trusting to that pulse of magic and potential to see her through. What came out wasn't at all what she'd expected. "I have not been honest about my origins. Though quite honest about being here to help Farran out." Then with a little quirk of her mouth. "Also, I quite agree with you about the complexities of mermaids. I've had the pleasure of talking with quite a few."

Emma made the connection first. "That's why you sign." Then, almost as quickly, she continued. "And there are reasons you didn't go to school with us. I don't know what to call you, though."

"Cousins, usually, is what we call ourselves. Descendants of the Fatae, through the maternal line, one way or another. Some more distant, some tighter in."

"And Robin as well." Andie had settled back, considering, like she was beginning to lay out her research plans. "You're both descended from the Shining Ones, then." It was a challenge, deliberately pushing at that line from the seance, bringing the pieces together. That was the danger of intelligent women. They caught you out.

"Robin is a bit more distantly branched from the tree than I am. Somewhat fewer responsibilities, and a different foremother."

"What happened last night, then?" They were withholding judgement, both of them. They'd become closed off, both of them, nearly in unison.

"There is a traditional ritual. Done yearly. I went out to do it, the pond, that way? And Cadmus saw me. We had rather a fight over it, though I told him the truth."

"Once you had to." Andie's voice was crisp. "No wonder he's upset." She was clearly taking his side.

Vivian thought of a dozen things she wanted to say, that they were all still nearly strangers, it's not like she knew all that much about any of them, that there were good reasons her family didn't tell people. But also, Andie - and Cadmus - had good reason to be upset. She'd misled them. Deliberately. Instead, she said, carefully, "I've told him I'm glad to talk further, when he wishes."

They looked back at her, as if that were somehow not at all enough. It made her flinch, and before she could think of something better, she knew she had to leave, to be elsewhere. She stood, abruptly, going without her tea.

It wasn't until she was out of their room, the door closed behind her, that she realised she wasn't sure where to go. Without a better solution, she went back to her room, only to find Mrs Cooper - Lena - coming toward her door, carrying a basket of her laundry.

"Let me take that." Vivian signed promptly, glad of the excuse of something to do. She took the basket, which had everything folded neatly, the unmentionables tucked out of sight, moving into her room.

Lena lingered in the doorway, waiting until she had Vivian's attention again before her fingers moved. "Are you all right?"

Vivian considered making the obligatory response. That she was fine, that there was nothing wrong. But she suspected the appropriate pleasantries weren't enough here, and lying to Lena seemed worse than lying to anyone else. "A complicated night." She made the sign, fingers arched, like two roundabouts spinning opposite directions from each other, many moving pieces. It felt a little bit like carding wool did, a chaos that promised some sort of resolution, if you were lucky enough.

"Cadmus is gone for the day. All day." Lena did not approve. "Did you argue?" Also, she was being remarkably blunt.

Vivian had no idea how to explain this in words, never mind signs. Language lessons did not exactly cover this situation. Tea, yes. Conversation, yes. Practicalities, yes. Esoteric and private mystery cults, followed by something that included righteous anger on his side, and frustration on hers, no. After a moment, she signed "Moment, please," to buy herself some more time.

Lena came and settled down in the chair, looking like a woman who had all the patience in the world. Vivian snorted, nudged the door closed, and then came and settled on the window seat, facing her. The light wasn't bad from this angle, at least.

"I did a ritual last night." Only of course, it didn't come out exactly like that. It was the sign for ritual, and the sign for stars, her hands placing multiple radiant stars in the sky of her signing space with little pops of motion unfurling. It meant something more like astrolatry. If that were a word anyone actually used routinely. Not even Vivian's aunts did that. "A family ritual."

Lena repeated the gesture, thinking through it. "Specific ritual."

The question was clear enough, and Vivian nodded. "Every year."

"He saw you?"

Again, Vivian nodded. She wasn't entirely sure where Lena was going with this, and she didn't want to put worries in the other woman's head if they didn't actually need to be there.

"Is it safe? For him to see that ritual?"

"He did not disturb me. And it is not forbidden." This was more complex. "Men forbid it. My foremothers do not."

Lena narrowed her eyes. "Cadmus tells me the stories of the Greeks, of the gods, of hubris." Or at least that must be hubris. It was not a word Vivian had ever imagined signing, a slow twist of the hand in a Y shape, then the rise and fall.

She copied it, then checked. "Pride? Hubris?" She spelled the latter out.

Lena nodded. "Cadmus studied that." Then, after a moment, she made it clear that was in the more distant past.

"And now?"

"Stories of going other places. He circles around them." That involved placing the stories firmly in the middle, and little versions of Cadmus, name sketched out with the index fingers, prowling around the stories in the centre. The image was honestly hilarious.

Vivian pulled herself back from that, then asked, "Is he all right?"

"It is not like him to be away."

"I'm sorry. I upset him. He found out that I was here, who I am. That Farran asked me."

That got a good natured wave, that was clearly not the problem. "Farran explained this morning. Farran is a good boy." Which explained why Lena was being so blunt.

That was especially useful information, that Farran had explained. "Explained to Cadmus, or just to you?"

"Cadmus as well." Then she added, "Farran has many things to work on today. Patching a roof."

Vivian nodded, then she asked, "What would help sort this out?"

Lena shrugged. "Truth. Cadmus listening. You can only make one of those happen."

It made Vivian laugh, despite herself, then she signed the laughter as well. Lena grinned at her.

There was one last question. Lena's hands moved, more relaxed. "Do all your folk sign?"

"More of us than humans. I learned when I was helping

the selkies and the merfolk in Scotland." She paused, then offered, cautiously, "You could visit, if you liked?"

Lena gave that due consideration, then she nodded once, and signed simply, "Perhaps." She flicked her hands once, as if cleaning something, changing the subject. "I will let you know when Cadmus comes back."

"I will be in the library. It looks like it will rain." It was November, after all, that did tend to happen. And it was grey and dreary today. She was still recovering from last night, too - she had more aches than she used to, and she suspected particularly so today since the euphoria had been so abruptly broken.

"The library. Tea?"

"Please. And I should let you get back to your own tasks."

"Persian chicken tonight. Cadmus does not care for it."

"And since he's not here..."

"Exactly." Lena stood up, brushing her skirts and apron smooth. "Talk to him when he comes back."

"As soon as he's willing."

That earned her a gleaming grin. "Oh, I'll make sure he's willing."

And with that, she disappeared back out the door, leaving Vivian to put her laundry away properly, then gather up her books and notes to bring downstairs. Lena brought a tea tray just after she got settled, and they parted with smiles.

It was quiet when she got there. It was as if the house had gone still, with its steward gone, waiting for the next thing. If the problem in the house were related to Cadmus, then nothing would happen. If it were something else, perhaps there would be more of a problem. She really should take a walk around the property.

But she was tired, and she had pulled a muscle in the dancing, she had no idea how. It was a dull but persistent ache that hadn't been soothed by a morning bath or the salve she kept for such things. After the fortification of supper, that would do.

Vivian spent the rest of the afternoon doing her best to lose herself in a book. She hadn't quite succeeded, but she had at least got a better look at the range of the library. Some of it was much like any other country house she'd been in, at least of the modestly literary sort. Her discoveries included some of the household records, though not the most critical ones. There were a series of journals about the gardens in the latter part of the last century with some charming sketches and plans.

She'd found two volumes, bound in good leather, the way people did about a project they were passionate about. That had been a history of the property. As she'd thumbed through it, she rather thought more than a bit of the history was fanciful, but the author had at least been forthright when she did not have proof of her claims. It half made her want to wander down the hall where the family portraits hung,

Supper itself was quiet. Farran had poked his head in briefly before the meal began to nod at everyone, and check they had everything they needed, but had gone back to whatever his necessary project was, still in rough canvas trousers and a smock. Something involving either paint or a hammer and nails, judging by his hands. Possibly it was the roof that Lena had mentioned.

Cadmus was gone, Richard was gone, Robin was thankfully gone. Andromache and Emma were apparently having supper in town, which at least meant Vivian did not have to deal with that particular awkwardness, but it did not ease any of her pain at fracturing a friendship she had come to enjoy. Danae was absorbed in a conversation with Madam Etna, and the two eldest women were talking quietly between themselves. It left Vivian alone at her end of the table, in a solitary splendour that felt quite queer.

The food, however, was excellent, and she signed to Lena, when she brought the pudding, "If there is any left, lunch tomorrow? I would prefer to eat in my room then."

Lena nodded her agreement, and whisked the trays away.

Danae looked up. "You sign?"

"Not as fluently as I'd like, but yes."

It earned her a long stare, as if Danae was trying to fit her into a particular mould, and failing. "Did you have plans for the evening?"

"I thought a walk, now it's cleared up a bit." The afternoon's rain had given way to a pleasant enough mist, not too chilly.

"Care to see my workshop? It's safe to visit again, I spent the morning cleaning up. Some of the materials I use can be rather dangerous."

"Copper work, yes?"

"Yes. I do some etching, some hammering, some

jewellery. It's the chemicals for the etching that get complicated, mostly, but the metal shavings have their own problems." Danae waved a hand, easily.

"Certainly, I'd be glad to see your work. After supper?"

Danae nodded. "You'll want a shawl, likely - meet me in
the entrance, and I'll show you where I am." The rest of the
meal was leisurely, no one in a rush to face the dark on their
own. It wasn't until nearly nine that Vivian was back down
in the front entry, shawl in hand and boots on her feet
against the evening's chill.

Danae led her out the door, into the gathering mist. It
was quite dark out, just lit by the charm-lantern Danae
carried. They went across the side of the house, away from
the rose garden, down a little lane. "There are quite a few
outbuildings. I gather this was a workshop, back when it
was a much larger estate."

Vivian nodded, following as they went further down the
lane, chatting pleasantly enough about the changes of
season, and the juried show Danae had submitted to. When
they got to a long low building to one side, Danae went
ahead of her to open the door and set the lights going.
When Vivian entered, she had to blink several times. The
place was full of metal that gleamed in the charm lights
overhead.

Danae - and Cadmus - had said she worked mostly in
jewellery, smaller pieces. But there were large ones here,
quite a lot of them, set out on broad rustic tables, gleaming
metal bowls and plates. There were copper wind chimes
and mobiles hung around the windows. And then a table of
the smaller pieces, set out on a black silk cloth. There were
plenty of jewellery pieces, set with large cabochon cut
stones of deep green, vibrant blue, and other colours that

stood out brilliantly against the copper. She had an archaic feel to much of her work, something of William Morris's sense of space and curve, but all angles and precise lines, playing with colour and form in a way that drew the eye and pleased it.

Danae gestured, and Vivian moved slowly around the tables where things were set up, as Danae moved to her workbench in the back. Vivian began at one end, being systematic, which meant she started with some of the jewellery pieces, letting the pleasure of the craftsmanship flow around her.

As Vivian got half way down the room, Danae said, her voice casual, "What do you have against Robin?"

Vivian looked up. "There's some family history." She kept her voice even. She wasn't at all sure how to read Danae, whether this was a change in mood.

"How much of it is about him? In particular?" There was a new tone in her voice, more clearly, now, pressing forward.

Vivian considered her options. "I think he's a dilettante." Honesty might serve, and even if it didn't that certainly wasn't the worst thing you could say about someone. "He thinks I'm stiff and stuck up."

"He says you're treating him badly. That you've been poisoning the house against him. Literally." There was an edge to her voice now, like a hound seeking during a hunt, getting close to a scent.

"Literally?" Vivian moved further down the table, and then looked up from a beautifully crafted bowl. An offering bowl, she realised. A particular set of offering bowls. There was something here that didn't fit.

"He had to get Richard to give him salve for burns.

From metal, he said. That's why I'm making these for him."
Danae sounded proud, delighted. "Why don't you like him?
He's lovely and charming and he makes so much sense."

There was a note to her voice now that was something
beyond lovely and charming. It rang the harmonies in her
mind that made her suddenly sure there was an enchantment at play. Robin had been doing rather a lot more than
she thought, and now Vivian would have to see how to
untangle it. She couldn't afford to provoke Danae further, it
would just make things worse.

Vivian frowned slightly, and said, as a gesture of goodwill. "You do beautiful work. You've got a wonderful sense
of proportion, and how to bring out the copper."

It did not improve things. Danae came out from behind
the workbench, a small hammer in her hands, and there was
a gleam in her eyes Vivian suddenly didn't like at all.

Danae took a step forward, but it was as if she was
moving under water, or fighting a compulsion. The expression on her face was fear and confusion, not anger. "I feel
queer, I feel..."

"Danae, something's wrong. Let me help. Let me..."
Vivian tried to keep her voice even and calm. "Or I can
bring someone else who can, if you'd rather not me."

"Robin, Robin said you'd try something like that." Danae
sucked in a breath, then took a step.

"You're not yourself, Danae. Please, I can help."

There was a screech, primal and raw, like a wild animal
in the night, and Danae took a staggering step forward, and
another. Then she gritted her teeth, gasped, and managed to
say "Get out. Get out or I'll...." The threat wasn't finished,
but it didn't need to be. Threat, or perhaps a warning, as she
struggled with herself.

Vivian could do no good here, at least not with more

resources at her disposal, and that hammer was small but wickedly angled. It would do no one any good if it were used on something other than metal. Discarding any dignity she had left, she edged around the last corner of the table, and bolted for the door.

TWENTY-EIGHT

WEDNESDAY EVENING

That had been a decidedly unsatisfactory day. Medieaval history was far past his era of academic interest, of course, but even so, he had found much less material than he thought should be there. He had been looking, naturally enough, for what kind of ritual Ann - no, Vivian - might have been using, and what it was meant to do. Or even if it was connected to the Pact in the first place, which was only a guess on his part, if, he thought, quite a well-founded one.

It was not until after lunch that he'd thought to check one of the major calendars of all the festivals, the great list that coordinated solar holidays and lunar cycles. Fixed days on an unyielding calendar, and those that migrated depending on factors beyond counting. And there, he had finally found a small notation, 'Call to the Pleiades: cele-brated privately in some family lines. Not discussed outside of blood kin and formally adopted family members'.

Now, granted, many families had that sort of thing. The Howard calendar had two dozen dates they commemorated that no one else did, his own family had half a dozen, the small festivals, the personal ones. But most of those, people knew something about. Family attended them, but so did friends, sometimes, or the family of someone who'd married in, without needing particular oaths and agreements.

He had spent the next hours in the main library in Trellech. Once it closed, he had moved to the Owlery library. That had all sorts of arcane tomes, but apparently not the useful sort of arcane tome.

There, Cadmus had found plenty about astrolatry, about star-based religions, but he rather thought this had not just been about stars, for all it clearly had some celestial offering. Or at least some celestial response. Cadmus could not get the image of that descending, encompassing light out of his head. In the end he had come out of the portal back near Oxford, hoping Mrs Cooper had put something aside for him.

He was starving, his neck ached, his hand was cramped from taking notes, and none of it had done any good. He was back to where he started, falling back on his own experience of the mysteries of The Smith. It seemed the only place to begin to try and make sense of what had happened last night. It was not as much help as he'd like: his experiences in the cave and the forge had not prepared him for something with a different rhythm. It was, he rather thought, like trying to translate a passage into English and Italian at the same time, utterly confusing.

Cadmus was coming up the main drive, toward the house, when he heard something to one side. A deer, perhaps a badger or a fox, that small scuffling, then suddenly he was bowled over by someone colliding with him, knocking them both flat on the ground.

"Get up, oh, do get up, there's...."

It was Vivian, and she sounded terrified. He pushed himself up on one elbow, simultaneously dubious of anything she might tell him, and certain she was not feigning fear.

"Ann?"

"Oh, bugger the elder tree." It came out like a very specific curse, one she meant, and much cruder than he'd ever heard her. "Just get up, it's not safe."

That was not at all promising, but he managed to lever himself sitting, then standing, as she did the same. She wobbled for a moment - it looked like she might have broken the heel on one of her boots - before she said "It's not safe. House, please, just..." And then she sounded earnest and complicated. "Please."

He peered into the dark she'd come from, seeing the lights. Danae was at work late, but surely she wasn't a problem. Finally, he shook his head. "House," he agreed, and half-offered his arm, rather hoping she didn't take it. To his surprise - and possibly to hers, he could read her expression even less than he could read most people - she set her arm through his. If the heel caused her problems, it was only a modest wobble, and she kept pace with him. He let them both into the side door with the latchkey. "I'm starving, let me see if Mrs Cooper has something."

She blinked up, and it was only now in the light he could see she seemed very pale. Where she had been confident and graceful last night, now she was all odd angles, like something was out of place in her particular universe. Her skin was pale, what he supposed people called ashy.

He stopped, not sure what to do. He was saved, a moment later, by Farran sticking his head into the library, with a "I thought I heard," Farran stopped. "Um. Is there, can I be of help?"

"Food, please. Dinner leftovers is fine. And bring the good brandy and glasses." It came out of his mouth quickly, almost snapping. "Pardon. One for you too, and something warm for..." He waved a hand at Ann. Vivian.

"Right. Um. On it. Might be a minute for the food, I'll come back with the drinks." Cadmus could hear the footsteps receding, and then he turned back. "What should I call you?"

She waved a hand. "Vivian. He knows that's my name. I'll answer to Ann." It had a distracted, distant sound to it.

"Are you - no, you're not all right. Do you need anything other than a bit of brandy and something warm?"

Vivian blinked up at him, then she shook her head, drawing her arms around herself. She sat there, looking resolutely at a point on the floor. Cadmus finally pulled one of the easy chairs over to be within reach of the table in front of her, and went to the library to flip the sign to "Reserved" that should keep other people out, if they wandered by. It seemed like there wouldn't be any sense out of her for a good bit.

They waited, in awkward silence marred only by the occasional shift of a foot on the floor or a creak of a spring in a chair. Finally, Farran came in, balancing a tray with the brandy snifter, three glasses, a bowl of soup, a bowl of something white with specks of nuts and fruit. He had a very embarrassed expression. "Mrs Cooper made the Persian chicken you don't care for, uncle. There's a cheese sandwich, too, in case you can't stomach it. Or the soup, if - um." He nodded at Vivian.

Cadmus nodded. "I'll manage." That recipe always

made him remember the particular experience that still haunted him. "Vivian, you should have some of the soup, at least."

The name made Farran blink, and some part of Cadmus took a bit of pleasure in that. Vivian peered slightly at both of them. But she took a reasonable sip from the brandy when Cadmus poured and Farran handed the glass over, and then took the bowl when Farran passed it over, cupping her hands around it. Cold, then.

The first bite didn't have the bitterness he'd come to expect, a tang of something that didn't have a name, but that he didn't like. Curious. He took another bite, and another, and it was only after he'd eaten half the bowl that he looked up, feeling a bit more grounded in reality. He set the bowl aside, and turned his attention to Vivian.

Cadmus was never sure about what other people meant, in how they moved their bodies, their faces, reading all that subtlety was painfully hard for him. Words were a lot easier to sort through, though honestly he preferred words that someone had written down centuries and centuries ago.

In this case, Vivian was looking back at him. She looked less, well, less wrong. That was something, at least. Farran was still sort of hovering, not quite sitting. That, at least, he could sort out.

"Farran, sit. Drink. Sensibly."

"Yes, uncle." There was a creak, and Farran took the other small chair, leaving Vivian in solitary splendour on the sofa. "What happened?"

"I had a less than entirely productive day in Trellech." That was unspecific enough, at least. He wasn't at all sure he wanted to discuss the details of his investigations with Vivian. Certainly not right now. "I was coming back down the lane, and Vivian ran smack into me. She was frightened, we came back here."

He kept watching her, and added, "I told Farran about last night, of course." It was a pleasure to see Farran's smile, and also to see Vivian's expression flicker. He couldn't read it well, but he was sure he'd found a sore spot somewhere.

TWENTY-NINE

WEDNESDAY EVENING

Vivian swallowed. There were many places she'd rather be than here in this room, called to account for herself. On the other hand, no one here had tried to physically attack her, even last night, when Cadmus had been so furious. She set the bowl of soup aside, took a sip of brandy, and steadied herself as best she could.

"Where would you like me to begin?"

"At the beginning, please."

That made her snort, despite herself. She took a breath. "You are both adults, in our society. You made your oath to the Silence when you turned twelve."

Cadmus raised an eyebrow, clearly somewhat dubious, but Farran nodded along.

"In the Pact, back in 1483, the agreement was that the Fatae would withdraw from Albion, not to step foot on its land, except under very specific conditions. Formal situations, best described as a diplomatic visit by a head of state, with all due pomp, circumstance, and limitation. Highly orchestrated and arranged in advance."

Cadmus cleared his throat. "How does that apply here?"

Vivian gestured. "I am increasingly convinced that someone tried something. Not me, I will swear on the Silence it is not. I think they are seeking to open a gate to the realm of m - to the Fatae, for some reason of their own. Out of season, and without the usual rituals that would make such a thing as sensible as it is going to be." Then she paused, considering, remembering something Emma had said in one of their conversations over tea. "A bit like bending two pages to touch, but folding others away to make it happen."

Cadmus caught the slight glitch. "And what do you know about it? What was that you were doing last night? Why should we believe you?"

"To be fair, I did save your life in the rose garden. By the old laws, that has some consequence."

Part of her was rather satisfied to see Cadmus wince, and Farran look baffled. After a moment, Cadmus said, "But didn't you just point out that the old laws are no longer in play?"

It made her smile. She did like a challenge. And, well, Cadmus was still not attacking her. "Point." she agreed. Then she took a breath. "Which of those do you want first?"

"What you know about it." He answered quickly.

Vivian nodded. "My name is Vivian Porter. Through my mother's line, I descend from one of the Fatae, known in Greek lore as Electra, and by other names in other places. The - the daughters and sons of the Fatae who took human partners, their children, and grandchildren, and umpteen great grandchildren, we still have duties. To maintain some of the magics that make the portals possible. There are seasonal rites, not unlike the Lords of the Land, but with a different focus. Half a dozen things."

"And how much of your life is that?"

That was an interesting question to start with. But she could see why he might ask. "It's a bit like asking you how much time you spend on the house, I suspect. It depends. The season, the person, who has the skills for a particular thing that needs doing." She tapped her fingers on her thigh. "For me, eight or ten hours of active work a month, as well as ongoing correspondence, research, and so on. And a couple of meetings a month, usually, which range from quite pleasant to as tedious as most meetings anywhere."

Farran said, in a rush, "Are you - pardon, ma'am, are you - human? Not human? Is there..."

"That, young man, is a trifle rude." But she smiled as she said it, and when he stopped, and leaned back, she considered. "Barring some fatal accident, I will likely live longer than a human with magic. If you and Cadmus might reasonably see your centennial, I will likely make it to a hundred and thirty, or a bit more. There are foods that do not agree with me - red meat, mostly, or other foods that depend on blood. There are specific things I do or avoid, but those are closer to line of skill and craft - much as your apprentice master does. Some magics do not twine well with others."

Farran nodded, and something in the last part of her comment seemed to catch his interest particularly.

Cadmus broke in, "How old are you, then?"

She arched her eyebrow, waited for him to look thoroughly embarrassed, and then took some pity on him. She wanted to keep him off balance, not upset him further. "Sixty-three. And I know I look two decades younger." She considered, then added. "Robin looks near enough the age he is. Our ageing seems to slow down a great deal once we hit full maturity. Probably a good thing, as I don't think any sensible adult wants a child on the cusp of full adulthood for a decade or more."

It made Cadmus laugh, despite himself, and he looked fondly over at Farran. "Ah, I'd not mind too much." Then the situation caught up with him again, and he said, "So what you know about it is... the family magic."

She nodded. "You have a framework for that. Not everyone does. We have what you'd call a whole cosmology of magic and rituals. Dances and arrangements of gardens, jewellry, and food - all sorts of things. They help us maintain the proper flow of the energies, and to... " She considered. She wasn't used to explaining this in English, and she never had to explain it in the family tongue, of course, even to the littlest nieces and nephews. "Much of what we do is rather like dredging a stream or a lake, so the water can flow clear."

That made Cadmus tilt his head, thinking about something he definitely wasn't going to explain. There was a set to his shoulders, a stubbornness coming through.

Farran asked, "There was something last night?"

Vivian nodded. "There is a ritual we do to honour a particular celestial event, the Pleiades, our foremothers. The stars that are our foremothers, or represent our foremothers, or - whatever way we see it. There is a ritual when the Pleiades are as high in the sky as they will be that year. That was last night, and something led your uncle to come to where I was, and watch."

"Did it hurt anything?"

Oh, that was interesting, that the question of harm was Farran's first thought. "What makes you ask that?"

Farran waved a hand. "When I asked for your help, I

said that things felt wrong. Started feeling more wrong. If you're doing a ritual to make things feel a certain way, interrupting, interfering, that would make a difference, wouldn't it?"

She nodded. "It would. This ritual is not something that usually has observers. If we do it with other people around, they are part of it, yes? Sometimes I go to one of the family estates to do it there. But we can do it wherever we happen to be so long as it has what we need. Someone watching, it's not one of those rituals where someone will get struck by lightning for seeing it."

"Fortunately for me." Cadmus broke in again, though he sounded more thoughtful than agitated. "Are there rituals like that, then?"

"Oh, all the best secret societies have something like that, don't you think?" It was a stab in the dark, but she saw him blink, rocked back by something in the comment. That was exceedingly useful information.

He gathered himself, and something in what he'd heard had changed something for him. "So the ritual last night was not connected to the various things that have been happening."

"No, not beyond the fact it has to do with my foremothers somehow. That flavour of magic. The roses, particularly, were a giveaway there."

"The roses? What about the orchid, in the greenhouse? Or the ghost? Or the paintings?"

Vivian shrugged slightly. "I do not have a perfect hypothesis for every event. But it did occur to me that many of them either involved growing things - a particular interest of the Fatae, after all, that is how humans have portals. Or they involved pigments - which in many cases come from plant materials. The apparition, I'm afraid I can't explain that way, but I have some theories."

Cadmus nodded. "And my obligations to you, for saving my life?"

"When Farran asked for my help, he - mmm. Gave me every opportunity to bind him to a much larger agreement than he realised. I was not inclined to do so, even leaving aside the point that Eleanor - my assistant, his friend's older sister - would disapprove. Likely at great length, and with much disarrangement to my filing system. I do try to save that only for occasions where nothing else will do."

It took Farran a moment to follow the line of thought, then he nodded. "You were very clear that there was no obligation on my end. That's a part of the Fatae lore, I remember that from school, there's a whole expectation around obligations, oaths, commitments."

Vivian nodded. "Some would lure you in, so watch out if it comes up again. It's far safer to negotiate clearly in advance, what the costs and commitments are. There are a few books I can recommend, accurate ones, about what to look for."

Cadmus cut in. "We'd both appreciate that. And me? We did not precisely sit down with a formal contract."

"No." She looked him up and down, considering her options. "I would like a conversation in private, when we are done with the larger questions, here. I will consider that my payment."

Cadmus frowned. "That seems rather small. I am not sure what I think of that."

"As you say, you had no chance to negotiate. And you did help me tonight."

"Tonight, yes." Both of them looked at her, expectantly.

THIRTY

WEDNESDAY EVENING

Cadmus leaned forward, wondering what she was going to say next. And what on earth she had been doing in the first place. He was not at all sure what he made of her explanations so far, but they were at least consistent with both his own experience and his observations. He might be slow to put pieces together, but he was solid once he'd had time to consider the chain of events.

What she'd said about being struck down, though, that had found a mark. There were at least two deaths he knew of, people who had intruded on the rites of The Smith. In both he knew about, there had been a thunder clap, they had fallen dead, in what looked to all the world like a heart attack. Was she threatening him or warning him? He couldn't begin to tell.

"Tonight," he agreed. "You were terrified."

Vivian - he would repeat that name until it became natural, though he supposed it had a certain mythic refer-ence - nodded. "Thank you." She seemed in earnest, though how he'd tell, he wasn't sure. He certainly had not guessed she was a decade older than he was, rather than a decade younger. "I was." She didn't continue.

Cadmus waited, giving her the space, because he certainly had plenty of questions still swirling in his head.

Finally, she looked up. "Danae invited me to come see her workshop. Supper had been a little awkward. You weren't there. Lena was - well, she made the chicken because you don't like it. I think she rather enjoyed the opportunity."

Cadmus glanced at the dish. "Huh." He wasn't sure how to respond to that, but he nodded. "Wait, Lena?"

"She invited me to use her first name." Vivian's hands made the name sign. Of course, Cadmus used that, but he'd never dream of disrespecting her by calling her anything other than her proper formal name out loud. There were customs to be observed.

"You don't have household staff." It wasn't a question.

Vivian shook her head. "No, I have a housekeeper who lives out, a distant cousin. I do understand the proper form. Of course, in public, I'd never dream of using her first name. She does a most impressive job here. But I will also not insult her by refusing the invitation." Vivian had a line in the sand, clearly.

Cadmus considered, and nodded. "Fair enough." It was an agreeable thing to say when he did not want to take the time to understand the nuances. It usually worked. "Supper. And then Danae invited you to her workshop? Was there any reason for it after supper? She usually finishes work for the day well before that. I gather she needs to wash the metal dust off carefully, something like that."

Vivian shook her head. "She said she'd been finishing up, and had cleaned things up so it was safe for me to come look. I thought it curious, but it was a brisk but otherwise pleasant night. She had a lantern, and it was just down the lane. And when I got inside, she has quite a lot in there, doesn't she? Have you seen it recently?"

Cadmus tried to remember the last time he'd actually been inside. "I do an inspection on the quarter days, so it would have been Michaelmas. Two months ago, give or take. She had her small workbench, a number of items, but there wasn't much out on the other tables. Why?"

"She's been rather busy then. Those tables were full, and with larger objects. Bowls and platters and such. Oh, there were smaller pieces, as well. She has a fine eye with colour, and the contrast of the copperwork with stones." Vivian's voice had turned brisk now, a bit of evaluation.

Farran coughed. "A bit reminiscent of Archibald Knox, but not so focused on the Art Nouveau lines, but rather the more Celtic or Roman decorative elements."

Vivian looked up at him, sharply, as if making note of something. Perhaps Cadmus could get her to tell him later why. Then she nodded, firmly. "Quite. She has an excellent eye, and a deft hand. She went behind her workbench, and she picked her hammer, and she started asking questions. Specifically, what I had against Robin. And why I was turning the house against him."

Cadmus frowned. "The people? You've barely mentioned him, at least where I could hear. Been quite civil, actually."

Vivian shook her head. "She meant the actual house. She said something about him having been burned by metal - his line of the family's more sensitive to iron as a metal than I am. She said she was making copper bowls for him."

"And you don't know why?"

"There are rituals with offerings. I need to do more research, to determine what - what he has in mind."

"Is Danae..." He stopped. "Someone should go see," Cadmus stood, feeling it should be him.

"She nearly attacked me. I don't think she wanted to, entirely? I suspect he's glamoured her a bit, and it was an effect of that. Wanting to defend him, and that meant attacking me. Left alone, she might come back to herself." Vivian held out a hand to stop him. "I think it might be better to check on her in the morning. Unless there's someone neutral."

Farran shifted. "When we're done here, I can go walk around the property, Uncle. She likes me, but she wouldn't think I'm a threat like you might be."

Cadmus settled back. "If you insist." He did not feel at all sure this was the right thing. But he also was not up to arguing with both of them. "What do you think is going on, then?"

Vivian tapped her fingers on her leg again, a habit he found mildly fascinating, the way her fingers shifted. The pattern meant something to her, he suspected, it had a beat like a measure or three of dance music, before stopping. "I don't think it's just Robin. Whatever Robin is doing." She waved a hand, her fingers flicking out. "It's more of a wave than a ripple. Robin, by himself, would be a pebble in a pond. This is more like a large boulder. Perhaps a tide. It has a weight to it."

Cadmus did not like that thought at all. "Why here, then?"

"That might be Robin. Or me, but I think Robin. You will have to take my word for it, but I have done no partic- ular magic other than the ritual last night. Not beyond the ordinary sort of warding and protection charms on my personal property. Nothing that causes difficulty to existing magics, as a rule. I do have manners." He wasn't sure he believed her, but the arch tone at the end, the indignation that she would be that kind of rude, did amuse slightly.

"You came into my home under false pretences." He felt obliged to point this out, it seemed to have got lost in the other chaos.

"And if I hadn't, you would have had an exceptionally bad time in the rose garden." She tilted her head, thinking. "Two incidents with flowers, one with roses. Other plant material. I wonder."

She didn't say anything further, and there was a long and awkward silence. Finally, he said, "Explain, please." He put some weight into it, feeling a draw on the land magic, the parts of it he could.

Vivian looked up, suddenly, and said "Mmm. There's a thing."

"Cryptic is for sphinxes, in our family mythology. And whatever else you are, you are not that." He was fairly certain, at least. No part of her seemed to have fur, or wings, or claws, for that matter.

She laughed, an honest laugh, like he hadn't heard from her before, but this was different. Then, her voice more fluid, "No, not that. I was just thinking that many of the events took place when you were there. And you are clear about your stewardship of the land." She gestured, then, her fingers delicately shaping his name sign, and he flushed.

"And you think that is relevant?" Farran, he was glad, was keeping quiet, though he was listening intently.

"Looking at this. The events started after Robin took up residence here. Tonight made it clear he is involved some-how. I don't think he means to hurt Danae, precisely, but he does not have a history of thinking ahead about conse-quences to others.."

"Why do you think he doesn't want to hurt her?"

"A number of aunts and cousins who would make his life miserable if he went beyond a certain point. His line has a greater deftness with glamour, enchanting the senses, than most. There are limits on how that should be used. He's right up to the edge of them, but not across them, I think."

Cadmus did not like the sound of that one bit. However, he suspected the digression into magical ethics and morals and the impositions inherent in the system would not help one bit. Also, it made him decidedly uncomfortable, given his own experiences in the past.

"So what is causing this?"

Vivian pursed her lips. "I am not certain, but I have a theory. I'm not sure how to prove it right, though."

"What is the theory?"

"Two years ago, a manor house reappeared after several hundred years... elsewhere. It was thoroughly investigated first by the Guard, then by a team of historians and other specialists. The house itself is being preserved for historical research. But some of the duplicate items have been sold off to raise funds for the long-term preservation, staff to investigate further. You know the sort of thing, twenty barrels down in the basement, sell off the most ordinary five after they've been fully reviewed."

Cadmus grimaced. "That seems like desecration. Is that the word?"

"It is not what I would have picked, but I was not consulted." Vivian sounded amused again at something, he couldn't tell what. "But I wonder." She was choosing her words with visible care. "It is not general knowledge, the Guard kept the initial inquiry tightly contained, but I understand that the reason the manor disappeared was the owner attempting to contact the Fatae. Not long after the Pact itself. The running theory is that the entire manor ended up in a liminal space, until - well. There are theories. Somewhat distasteful."

"How does that connect with this, here?" He would like an answer.

"I wonder if Robin - or someone, but Robin seems the most likely, really - has got his hands on one or more of the objects from the manor. More than one, I suspect, since the incidents are increasing, not decreasing. And if he intends to use them, somehow, for his own benefit."

THIRTY-ONE

WEDNESDAY EVENING

V ivian waited. Both men blinked at her, with nearly identical expressions on their faces. They then exchanged some wordless - and gestureless - communication, and Farran stood. "Good night, Madam Porter. I do hope you get some rest. Uncle, I'll come let you know immediately if there's anything to deal with, and otherwise check in in the morning. Nine on the dot."

"Be safe."

"Of course, uncle." Farran sounded amused, not mothered. He left the room, closing the door behind him, before Vivian could say anything. It left her staring at Cadmus, who stood, though in less of a rush. "Look, let's go upstairs. My study?" he suggested. "We still have a fair bit to talk about, and the brandy's better there."

"Not the bottles you keep for guests?"

He shook his head. "My father and grandfather actually put down a quite nice cellar. It would be hard to sell it off, it's all two or three bottles from a case left, so some we're keeping for Farran, and some we're enjoying now." He gestured with his hand. "And I do owe you a conversation in private."

Vivian smiled at that. "And you are the s..." She reconsidered. Saying he paid his debts, given the tenuous financial situation here, would not be kind. "You keep your word."

"I do." He watched her. "I don't understand people who don't." He added, "Folklore says, the Fatae twist promises."

"I don't have an easy answer for that." Vivian gave him the best truth she could. "But that's an upstairs conversation, I think."

He nodded, and then cleared things up enough to set them on the tray. "Let me take this to the back stairs, where someone can get it in the morning. Go on up to the family wing and wait by my door?"

She nodded, and then had an awkward few minutes of wondering if he had taken the excuse to slip away somewhere. She'd never know if he came up a back stairway into his bed room, or some back guest room.

But then she heard footsteps come up the stairs, and then his figure, shadowed with the light behind him, toward the family wing. She had settled out of the way, where she could be seen by someone coming across the long gallery at the top of the steps, but not someone coming up to the resident's wing.

He carried a different tray, with a few other things on it, small pastries of some sort. That was more hospitable than she'd expected. He set the tray down on a side table, passed his hand over the panel by the door to unlock it. Then he gestured for her to go inside as he held the door open. Maybe this would work, then.

She nodded, and then went in, glancing around. He followed, motioning. "The chairs, more comfortable." There were a shabby pair of chairs, clearly the sort of thing he'd use talking to Farran, with a decent sized table just behind them, looking out a large window.

"Not your desk?"

Cadmus shook his head. "I - you and I, we need to sort things out. For the good of the house."

"This is difficult for you. What part of it? That I didn't tell you the whole truth?"

"That is not a small thing."

Vivian opened her mouth, closed it. He had something of a point, and yet she did not owe him the entire truth of her life, she didn't owe anyone that. But then she shifted, all the little adjustments of openness. "Look. I had a thought earlier. May I start there?" It startled him, she could see that, but that was part of the point.

"Yes?" He sounded extremely cautious now.

"Tell me about your name. The name of this house. Tell me about the city of Thebes."

Again, it was clearly not anything he was expecting. "You know it, surely."

"You owe me a conversation. Humour me." She leaned forward to take a glass of the brandy from the tray, cupping her hand about it, leaning back in her chair with her ankles crossed.

"There are competing stories, but I have always been troubled by the dragon's teeth."

"Go on." She kept her voice gentle now. No need to scare him off.

He looked up at her, still baffled, but he obliged. "The story goes that Cadmus was a prince from the east, from Tyre, sent out to find his sister Europa back home, after she had been abducted by Zeus. He did not find her, but he came to Delphi. The oracle there told him to follow a cow, a particular cow, and build a town where she lay down. The cow went to Boetia, he followed, and there he founded Thebes."

"That does not get us to the dragon."

Cadmus, perhaps despite himself, smiled. He reached for his own glass and took a sip. "He travelled with companions, and a version of the story has them drawing water from a spring guarded by a water dragon. It killed them, and then he slew the dragon. Athena instructed him to take the teeth and sow them in the ground. Armed warriors sprouted, fully grown, attacking each other until only five were left, and he stopped them. They became the founders of the noblest houses of the city. But..." His voice trailed off.

"But?" There, this was promising, he was at least not fighting the direction she wanted the conversation to flow.

"There are stories about the consequences. And really, I think Thebes is all about consequences, the stories we have of it. The choices we make, with knowledge, and the choices we make in ignorance."

Vivian nodded. "There's a tale about a necklace, isn't there?" Her hand went to her own, as if thinking of something specific.

"There's a story that the gods gave Cadmus a wife, Harmonia, and they had a son and daughters. That Athena wove her a peplos to wear, and Hephaestus made her a necklace. But there were stories about the necklace being cursed, and how it cursed everyone who came too close to it. And stories about Cadmus having to serve Ares for years, because the dragon had been sacred to him."

He paused and reached for one of the pastries, as if gathering the rest of what he wanted to say. "One story - do you know that one? It has him saying if the serpent was so important, he might as well be one. In another version, he and his wife were changed into serpents after their deaths." He shook his head. "It seems unfair. And like ..." He waved his hand. "Like he'd touched things he had no business being near."

"If he'd just been a prince in Tyre, and not gone to Delphi. But he was travelling to find his sister, who had - rather literally - been touched by the Gods. Well, one god."

Cadmus nodded, leaning forward. "And I've - I've always had a, if I had a different life, I'd have liked to be a blacksmith. I know a little, but my life went other directions. I - it's a thing, the mystery, I find most fascinating. In the religious sense, I mean." He seemed to feel he'd revealed too much, as he finished the sentence, and shifted back, crossing his arms in his lap and closing himself off.

"It is curious, isn't it? There are so many gods in that story, far more than in most of the myths that aren't actually about them. But you have Zeus, at least as the catalyst for events, you have Ares, you have Hephaestus, you have Athena." She tilted her head. "Do you think the necklace was cursed?"

Cadmus shook his head. "I've mostly tried not to think about it, honestly." His voice got softer. "I didn't want to think the Smith so petty. Or so - underhanded, is that the right word? I suppose the Gods do things for their own reasons, but the idea of him cursing the necklace seemed so out of character."

Vivian smiled a little. He was going where she hoped. "And you didn't like to think that. You must have other theories." She could easily appeal to his classics interest, it was just getting him to go down the pathway she wanted.

"Oh, I suppose." He stopped, visibly trying to decide whether to say something. Then he let out a breath, and said. "The Fatae are real, then? And if they are, the Gods might be?"

Vivian nodded. "My foremothers are quite real. We do not, we do not have much direct interaction, you understand? But enough to be sure it is not some fantasy inside our heads."

"Last night?"

That was a complicated question. Finally, she said, "More direct than I've had in years. Decades."

He looked at her for a long moment, trying to decide on something. Then, his voice back to the measured and even beats of a man of his class and background. "Do you think I am cursed?"

"You personally? No. Only some of the events here have directly touched you. Even though it is your property, your home. You have a strong connection to the land, don't you?"

He seemed baffled by that question, but he nodded. "We're not Lords of the Land, of course not. But I make the offerings, planting and harvest, and walk the bounds, and tell the bees. The small steady things."

"And you've done that for years?"

Cadmus nodded. "Since, since I came back from overseas."

"What happened there?"

Now, he stared at her, wide-eyed, and there was fear there. He seemed unable to answer her.

THIRTY-TWO

WEDNESDAY EVENING

C admus could not stop himself from shivering, his hand clenching. The glass he was holding was solid, but he was suddenly worried the thick glass would shatter in his hands. He looked down, away from her, and how she kept watching him. He felt like a schoolboy being scolded, and like he'd disappointed his favourite uncle.

How could he tell Vivian what happened there? Either she wouldn't believe him or she would mock him for being scared. Being a coward. He dared a glance up at her, moving just his eyes, not his head. She was sitting there, steady and even and like she had no troubles in the world.

He had no doubt she would keep waiting until he said something. Something sufficient. And as she pointed out, he owed her this conversation. She could have asked for so much more. His indentured servitude for seven years or more, for starters. He knew those stories nearly as well as he knew the legends of Thebes.

It made him realise, though, when he thought about it, that it had been a series of catastrophes here, even before the recent problems. The kind of thing that might be a normal run of bad luck, other than Farran's parents dying, but added up, one after another, they came to an unsettling sum.

Finally, he looked up, properly. "What have you figured out?"

Vivian spread her hands, setting her own glass down as part of the flowing motion. "I know you spent several years there, in the Colonial Service. I know you were invalided home, for reasons unspecified. That since then, you have stayed here at Thebes, or very nearby. Your War service was unspecified, but not far away. One of the publishing projects." It was a guess, but an accurate one.

"Publishing and intelligence. They were much the same for a bit in there. That's where the original residents came from, people on those projects who needed a place."

She nodded, then asked. "And before that?" She would not let him duck it.

"I thought I would like the Colonial Service. The work was challenging enough to be interesting, keeping everything sorted. The land was beautiful, and there were interesting archaeological excavations and ruins. Kandahar was one of the cities much influenced by Alexander the Great. Ancient, amazing history."

She nodded. "Later than your usual period?"

"Oh, yes. But I'm not that narrowly focused, there's too much out there that's fascinating."

Something in that made her smile. He found himself liking her more when she did, when the professional mask dropped for a moment, and she indulged in pleasures and amusements.

"But we went up into the mountains." he said. "And I don't know what it was, I still don't. But there was something huge there, and it was - it was wrong for me to be there. A desecration, a wound, a tearing of something I didn't know could be torn." He said the words slowly, carefully.

When he looked at her again, when he dared to look at her, her head was tilted to the side, and her face and hands were still. He couldn't stand the silence, so he continued. "I couldn't - I couldn't be there, so I ran. When they found me, the next morning, I was..." He stopped. "If they hadn't found me, I'd have been dead inside an hour or two. Not enough water, no food, no cover from the sun."

Vivian tilted her head, and Cadmus couldn't begin to read her expression or make sense of it. Finally, she nodded. "What do you remember? Anything?" Her voice was very soft, now, the kind of voice you'd use so you didn't scare a skittish animal.

He shrugged, hating to think about it, but they were having this conversation now, clearly, there was no way around that. "The local guides were scared. We were supposed to be going to a ruined temple, I think. Temple. Palace. Something like that. And there are legends, in those mountains. Giants. Rocs. Spirits." He gestured, his fingers flicking helplessly. "I don't even know all the names, I tried asking, and the stories all tangle up in each other. Different people knowing different things."

Vivian nodded. "Trusting mythology is never easy." She was watching him again now.

"It was getting on to afternoon, maybe two hours from sunset, when the light started changing. We were high up, so it was brisk, there was a wind, and then there was a roaring, a buffeting, somehow, and that's where I ran."

"Were you hurt? Other than being on your own?"

"When they found me I had ... " He gestured across his

chest. "Three cuts, here. Like a roc might make, if it were a fairly small roc. But I don't - I don't think that was it."

Vivian peered at him. "And it felt - uncanny? Weird?" She made a quick sign with her hands, the same one Mrs Cooper used when odd things happened.

He nodded, repeating it, the little quirk of something being askew in the world.

"Like last night? Or different? Like other things you've been around?"

That was much more difficult to sort out. He'd been caught up in her dancing last night, tangled up in what she was doing, and the reflecting light, and the shift of feet to music he couldn't hear. That had been uncanny, but in a way that hadn't scared him, hadn't made him run. Last night had been like his nights in the cave of the Smith, feeling the clang of the hammer reverberate through him. He let out a breath. "Different."

She nodded, then asked. "Did last night scare you the same way?"

He shook his head, then ventured. "I - have some experience. Initiatory orders. Last night felt more like that. A different flavour. A different kind of wine, but still a wine, even if I'm..." He considered the options. "More used to, oh, something fortified. Port. And last night was a dry white."

That comparison made her throw back her head and laugh, something delighting her that he couldn't understand. He was glad he'd pleased her, that something had broken them both away from this careful awkwardness. Usually he could provide all the awkwardness a room needed by himself. When she finally caught her breath, she grinned at him, a fleeting moment of the young woman she'd been once right on the surface. Then she sobered, and settled back. "Fair enough description."

"What does that mean? Do you..." He hated to ask, if she knew, if she could shed any light on what had warped his life around that fixed point, something in him had to know. "Do you know what it was?"

She shook her head. "Not exactly. I don't know that region well. I've been to Greece once, and Italy, but - never further." Vivian considered. "The way the Fatae are, in other places, it varies. There's a reasons the stories say some are kind and some are petty, and some are wise and some are cruel. And some are wise and cruel, for that matter. Some of it is - that the Fatae are like people, that way. Some kind and helpful, others who aren't."

Something in this struck him suddenly. "You said the Fatae. Not just - people like you, descendants."

It made her drop her eyes, then look up, and they were damp, shimmering. "Our foremothers made agreements here. Albion. Some in Ireland, but a bit different. And the ones here, well, those carried over other places. The Commonwealth continued the agreements, even when they were not a fit for the local customs and agreements." She paused. "I gather in many places, the locals just kept on with what they were doing."

"And Afghanistan?"

"Certainly not the Commonwealth, for all there's a strong British presence there. I've never been quite sure what Russia was up to, but I do not think their Fatae are like ours, nor did they make the same agreements. Not entirely, anyway."

"So it could have been one of the Fatae. Someone, some-thing..." He looked up at her. "What is the word?"

"Someone has always seemed polite to me." Vivian said. "But some of the Fatae are not very human at all. You may have heard of the Belin?"

"Only very briefly. They're not, then?"

"No, they look like small piles of rocks. That move. Very particular about some things, the Belin." She waved a hand. "Those are not Fatae who left human descendants, mind. Or at least I'm told not. It makes the agreements different. No one can mistake them for human, for one thing. And for another, they mostly don't want to talk to us or interfere, anyway."

He looked away, focusing on his thoughts "So what I saw there...." He stopped. "That was one of the Fatae." It wasn't really a question anymore, he realised.

"Probably. I can't begin to tell you which one it might be without research."

"Because we were intruding? Doing something wrong?"

"Possibly. You know as well as I do that people tend to build holy sites on powerful sites, going back through the ages."

"England's churches built on hills with ancient temples and just as ancient yews. If we're lucky, the yews survive."

That made her look up. "Not a Christian, then."

He shook his head, and said. "The Smith."

Vivian tilted her head, considering him.

Vivian was not at all sure what to make of Cadmus. Last night, he had been angry, but where most men would bluster and threaten, he had confronted, but not - changed the nature of the thing from words into violence. She could, of course, protect herself if needed, but he had had no way of knowing that.

And now, tonight, he had listened, he had taken in new information, new ideas, remarkably quickly. She could not tell whether it was because of his education, his experiences in Afghanistan even if they'd clearly been traumatic, or something else. He had not seemed a man who took to change quickly, in her interactions so far, but he did well enough in the moment of crisis or concern.

She was glad she was able to be more honest with him, too. There was something intriguing in his openness, that made her want to respond to it in kind. She realised with a start that this must have been the first time he could talk out his experience in Afghanistan with someone who not only would not mock him, but who might have some explanation for him.

She could not give him all the answers he hoped for. She did not have them to give. But she wanted to help him learn what he could. And now here he was, and she was sitting in a chair in his study.

And he was watching her. She realised with a start that he had been watching her for more than a few moments. She nodded, picking up her glass for a last small sip, to cover. "I'd not have pegged you for the Smith," she said, finally.

He shrugged. "Most people couldn't see it. But I've been loyal, throughout."

It made Vivian smile. "Your loyalty, I don't doubt. But - even with the stories?"

"Because of the stories." he said, after a moment. "I wanted to understand."

Something clicked for her then. "That's why Afghanistan bothers you so much. Why you like translating. You want to understand."

He blinked at her, as if she'd suddenly bottled the sun and shone it into the darkest corners under the stairs of his mind. Into the places you never expected someone to see. Then he nodded. "The world, the current world, even before the world. It is - big and bright, and things move very fast. Oxford's not so bad, Oxford's been the same for centuries, give or take. And Trellech, well, Trellech doesn't even have automobiles. But London, London's chaos. It was even before the War."

She tilted her head. "I don't care for cities, but it's not the noise, it's the -" She wiggled her hand. "They buried the rivers, in London, most of them, and the Thames has been awful, and the fogs are worse. All the muck in the air. Factories and their vibrations and the way they make people miserable."

"But you live in Trellech?"

Vivian smiled. "It started out as a city to support mining and manufacture of arms. But that was over by, oh, the thirteenth century. When we moved in."

Cadmus considered. "You know, no one talks about that. Massive city, near the Severn, and then it goes away, changes."

"Power rises, power falls. The stars are eternal, and the gods, and everything else changes around them." It was one of the responses, more or less, from the call and response teachings she'd learned as a child, and taught others as a young woman. Not quite in those words, but taken out of their fancy rhymes and poetry and allusions, that was what it meant.

"And you see more change than I will. Have seen and will see."

She shrugged. "I will. But I'll have a bit longer to figure it out, too. And our work, my cousins and I, we mostly - some of us like Trellech. But a lot of us are out in some rural country house, with an elder tree to talk with, and bees to tell the news to, and all the old traditions, and what newer ones we find help us. But it's on our schedule, more or less, not anyone else's. It's why we don't go to Schola, or any of the other Five Schools. Most of us aren't ready at thirteen, our magic hasn't begun to settle. Those who are, certainly aren't ready to be shoved into a fixed timetable. Full of times when the lights have to be out or on, or when we need to be coherent and cheerful."

"Not morning people then, are you?"

The phrasing made her snort. "In some seasons, yes. In other seasons, less so. And it varies. The line, the intermarriages."

"Do you, then?" Then there was a slow dawning bafflement. "Do you have - is there a Mr Porter?"

"Oh, good grief. No. Nor any little Porters who are my children. Never had any. Never particularly wanted them? I mean, once thought about marrying, but he was..." She waved her hand. "You saw Electra touch me."

Cadmus blinked at her, several times in a row, looking very much like an owl. "Pardon?"

She gestured, and tried in different words. "Electra, my foremother. The ritual last night. One of them coming that close is rare. A few times in our lives, if we're lucky. Usually it's a more general feeling of goodwill." She had to smile. "Or if we're not doing our fair share, the sort of disapproving glare any grandmother worth her salt might give."

"That," Cadmus said, "I understand entirely." It sounded heartfelt indeed.

"It's happened for me one other time. I was twenty-one, and considering the courtship of a ridiculous young man. He didn't like who I was when I'd been that close to Electra's touch. And she disapproved of him."

Cadmus nodded, looking away, as if there were too many things to think about to look at her as well. "Did it hurt?" It sounded like he didn't mean to ask it.

"At the time, yes. I was young. And foolish." She shrugged. "I've had occasional company since, no one who wanted to stay. And now I'm older and settled, and I do love my work."

"Inquiry agency." He sounded a little dubious.

"Of a particular kind of problem, yes. The sort that's outside the scope of the Ministry or the Guard or anything more formal. I am quite good at what I do. Most people don't spot me at all. I'm impressed that you did."

"Seeing you dance in the moonlight was rather a tip off. Considering."

She glanced away, then smiled, before she looked at him more closely. "You feel shy about it."

"That was a, do you call her a goddess?"

"I call her Grandmother Electra, so I don't have to think about that, mostly, actually." Then she continued. "You watching, it's not, I said this, it's not a dangerous thing. But it's an intimate one."

He chewed on his lip as if thinking through something. "There's different kinds of intimacy. I don't invite residents in here. If we have private business, I use the little office off the library."

"When I signed the agreements, yes." She tilted her head. "Are you a confirmed bachelor?"

"Of the sort who, no." He let out a breath. Even he knew that code, the thing people generally didn't talk about except in hushed whispers. "I can't live with someone who puts me on edge. Mrs Cooper is grand, but she's like an aunt. A reasonably approving aunt, not a disapproving one. But everyone else, I need them on the other side of the house."

She considered that, watching him. "Everything's very complicated for you, isn't it? Figuring out how to make things run."

Cadmus nodded. "My brother said he had everything sorted out, if anything happened to them, and then he didn't. And if we can just keep things going for a few more years, it will be fine, but," He let out a breath. "And Farran's having a hard time with his apprenticeship. And he won't talk about it, and I don't know how to fix it, I don't know how that kind of thing works." It was as if she'd uncorked something all of a sudden.

She tilted her head. "I can help with the last part, if you'll permit me."

"You didn't apprentice." It was a bit accusatory, she felt. "Not like that."

"No, but I've helped people sort out issues before. And I know people who handle apprentice contracts, and all of that. That's what I do. I don't know everything, but I know people who are specialists in a great many areas."

Cadmus close his eyes again. "Why are you doing this?"

"Farran asked, and Eleanor wanted me to. She's my assistant, and her brother's fond of Farran as I said. It's an interesting problem. That we haven't actually got closer to solving."

"What is your theory, then?" He rubbed at his forehead.

"If I had to pick one, I would say that Robin has somehow got his hands on one or more Fatae-touched pieces from the house that reappeared. Something small, portable. That might not look particularly notable to someone who didn't have the background I do. More than one thing, I suspect. Two, maybe three."

"More?" Cadmus peered at her. "How did he get them?"

"The sale, I'd suspect. They do need the money. I tried to get one of my more reliable cousins on it. Actually, I think Robin tried to get on the team investigating the historical aspects of the house, and neither of them managed it. And if the things sold off had been ordinary, it would be fine. It's the small things that get you with my foremothers. It always has been."

"What do we do, then? We can't just go storming into his rooms, or Danae's. And I do hope she's all right."

"I think she will be, if I stay away from her. Until we can figure out what to do next. I can go back to Trellech, my more sensible cousins, round up some things that would - it's like dowsing, only it actually works."

That made him laugh. "Those are fighting words in some places. I've known some very fierce dowsers. But I do get the idea." he agreed. "Um. So. We do that."

She looked him up and down. "I should tell you it's me doing it. But you'd argue, wouldn't you?"

Cadmus nodded. "It is my home. My family."

It would make things difficult, but he was right. Vivian nodded, and let out a long breath. "Right. I'll be going into Trellech first thing tomorrow."

THIRTY-FOUR

FRIDAY EVENING AROUND NINE

"Where did you get this?" Cadmus was baffled by the things Vivian was unpacking. She had been gone all day, coming back only on the evening train, not making it up to his office until nearly nine the next night. Now she had taken over the table, removing a series of boxes of varying sizes.

He had spent the day trying not to fuss. Something continued to feel off to him, and he couldn't tell if it was his usual discomfort with new situations or something else. The usual discomfort would be entirely sensible. He'd had half a dozen sizable new situations dropped on him. His newest resident was not entirely human. His nephew, for whom he was responsible, was struggling in ways Cadmus had no idea how to solve. Someone was using his home, his land, to do a rite of magic that was hurting and scaring people.

Farran had at least told him that Danae White was all right. She seemed, Farran had said, very confused about what happened. He hadn't come out and asked directly about the attack, just about if she'd seen Madam Porter, he had a letter that had come for her. There had been no sign of antagonism or difficulty, but she also couldn't remember anything beyond walking out to the workshop with Vivian.

Cadmus had listened while Farran reported it, and then sent Farran off to walk the property, carefully, noticing anything that seemed out of place. He thought Farran might spot things he hadn't, and in fact over lunch, they compared lists. There were oddly-coloured flowers several places, plants besides the roses that shouldn't be blooming this late in the year, queer red berries on a few bushes that didn't bear that kind of fruit. Uncanny noises in the underbrush.

They had left their lunch half-unfinished, baffled by it. The patterns. It was all small things. But when you added them all up, along with the list of repairs that had needed doing out of season or sequence, it was clear things had been odd for a good four months, maybe longer. That this had been going on for so long, that they'd missed it, all of it made Cadmus antsy. He was unsettled enough he couldn't manage his usual translation work. He was fit only to reshelve books in his study, and downstairs in the library, entirely startling two people who came in during the afternoon.

Finally, he retreated back to his study, and hoped that Vivian would come and let him know as soon as she got back. When she had, however, he was not entirely reassured. "You found what you needed?"

"Oh, here and there. Attic storage is so terribly useful." She pulled out a series of copper bowls, nestled into each other, a few copper tubes on something that looked like wire handles. Then she pulled out a series of stones, rounded and smoothed, of different types.

"Is there a reason for the copper?"

"The theory is it's energetically conductive in useful

ways." The comment was sensible enough, but her tone was odd.

"You don't agree?" She was being confusing. Again. On the other hand, she didn't object when he asked her to explain, which was better than many people.

"I am inclined to think it is because copper is relatively inexpensive compared to many things, easier to shape by hand tools. And these days, available from a wide variety of people offering the finest of goods to home cooks."

That made him laugh, and he wondered if she'd meant to. She seemed more at ease with him, with Farran. "So we use copper."

"Yes. These things, here, you hold them, and the wires pivot toward the thing you're trying to find. I called in a favour to get something else from the house, something on loan."

"Loan? A favour?"

She shrugged. "I know someone who knows the Guard captain who oversaw the investigation. I promised we'd give it back, so be careful." The thing she took out of a silk-wrapped box was a small knob, as would be on a piece of furniture as decoration of some kind. "This should do well enough. It had rolled under a table, I gather, behind a shelf."

Cadmus leaned forward to look at it, without touching. "Is that - is that going to work?"

Vivian said, amiably. "It's what we have. And the theory is sound. We want to use it to find something else with the same resonance. Unless we're very mistaken, there are only so many objects which were tucked in a disused corner between the realms for a few hundred years. And most of them I'm sure are too far away for this to pick up."

Cadmus had to concede the point. "I suppose." Then he

peered at her hands again. "How do we do this? What do we need?"

"The knob goes here. I hold the handles, here. You open doors, as needed." She considered. "Chances are, it'll be in Robin's room, or a closet he's claimed or something. Is the lease you gave me the same one you gave him? Or are there changes?"

"Of course it's the same. Bar a slightly different rate for the room itself. Garden view is a bit more." Then he stopped. "Why do you ask?"

"Some places, the leases for men and women are rather different. If the place even leases to women at all."

Cadmus blinked, baffled. "That's not logical. Also not fair."

It made her smile, though it was a sort of sad smile, he thought, and even less possible for him to read than most expressions. "You do like your logic. No, it doesn't make sense, but a lot of landlords, agents, will charge women more. Or put extra limitations on them. So you have permission to enter if there is a significant safety need or need for repair. Even in his absence."

"It's an old house." Cadmus was defensive now. "We had a bad leak three years ago, and I couldn't get in to turn it off at the pipe, and it ruined a lot of things."

"In this case, it's very helpful." She reached out, and after a moment, touched his hand, the first time he could remember her touching him directly. He blinked at her, confused. "You're a very considerate sort, Cadmus. Thank you." Then she took her hand back. "Robin is next floor up?"

"Yes. Right side of the hallway, second door down."

"Do we know if he's in tonight?"

She hadn't been at supper of course. "He was out, but

he might have come in since. I don't know. He's not very informative." Cadmus tried not to sound plaintive, but he very much felt like that. Managing the house would be rather a lot easier if people had reliable schedules and came and went at predictable intervals.

"So we will go up. Is there some reason you might want to speak to him? Any small repair you'd said you'd think about?"

Cadmus wasn't sure he had anything that would fit what she wanted, it seemed absurd to make something up. "I suppose." He shook his head. "How do you do that? Come up with stories. Lies." He regretted it almost the moment he said it, he knew it was the sort of thing people took offence at.

She set down the device for a moment. "They're a particular kind of story. When I'm working, I think about the person I'm becoming. So do the people I hire. Usually that's not too far from the reality. It is much easier to tell the truth, and certainly much easier to keep it straight. There's a bit of a trick to it, but not much. I also remember what I'm presenting. It's a little like being on stage. There's no script, but I want that face to be consistent."

He frowned, watching her. "How do I know you're telling the truth now?"

"You don't. Barring an oath on the Silence."

That made him remember something else he'd been trying to figure out. "Does that even work on you? I mean."

"We take the same oaths, roughly. Just also some other ones. Because..." She wiggled her fingers. "When Richard III made the Pact, the agreement went both ways. We, the daughters, the cousins. Also the sons, but we always talk about daughters, it's a matrilineal tradition..."

There was a pause as she got herself back on track, he

felt she had got distracted. "We make the promises that humans make, not to reveal magic to people without it, the promises about which laws we bide under. But we also make promises on the other side. Later, usually, when we're adults, about caretaking. Watching specific spaces. Taking specific duties. Keeping people - human people - safe from the things in our magic that would hurt them."

"Is that very likely?" He was nervous now.

"It's the reason there's all that folklore."

There was an odd quality in her voice now, and he turned to look at her properly. "Explain." He did his best to sound authoritative, and it didn't work at all, but at least she didn't laugh at him. He liked that she hadn't. Not when he was being serious.

"All the folklore about gifts and exchanges, and eating the fruit. Those are all true enough. Dozens of things more. Walking by the greenwood or the dangers of May, as a month, also October, or warning people away from a particular person or a particular place at a particular time. Most of us are - like people, really. Most of us don't like hurting others. Some of us do. Some of us don't mean to, and, and we do anyway."

There was something there that caught his attention, the way his mind would snatch on a tiny participle in the text. It could be the thing that turned the phrase from a statement of certainty to one of uncertainty, or the way a beautifully deployed middle voice turned the entire sentence from a statement of action into one of protecting one's own interests.

"There's a story there." He let it hang there, to see what she did with it.

Vivian had not expected this to come up. Certainly not when they should be walking down to Robin's rooms like sensible people with a plan and a project and a task that needed doing. This was why she didn't like working on investigations with other people. They kept having complicated questions at the oddest times.

She looked Cadmus up and down. If you asked her, this topic wasn't important for their goal. But standing there, sturdy and solid, it sounded like it mattered to him. Then she nodded. "There is a story. More than one."

He just waited. She would grant him that, he was quite capable of forcing her to take things at his pace, not hers.

"My commitments, to my foremothers, my duties." Vivian shifted, moving to lean, not quite perching on the sturdy table she'd been using to lay everything out. "They are about being a go between, between our set and other people." This was an awkward part. It wasn't as if Vivian wasn't human too.

"Your set."

Vivian shrugged. "Think of it more like the difference between French and Belgian and English. There are differences, the law works differently, the government, and so on. You are in our country without knowing it, and you do not know the rules and the customs."

"It is not your country. Good solid land, been in my family back past the Pact, one way or another."

She snorted. "The physical land, yes. It is like a glass overlay, in places. Overlaying one another, but not necessarily touching. Except at the portals." She gestured. "There's one a few miles away, on private land. One of my cousins describes it as the warp and weft of fabric. And the other is embroidery, that goes in and out through the open spaces, so they are intricately, beautifully, interconnected, but they do not combine. They stay distinct, in some ways, while making one picture."

Cadmus tilted his head, thinking through that. "And you go back before the Pact? People like you?"

She nodded. "Well before. We trace the maternal line, as I said, but each generation, there is more mortal blood, and less of the Fatae. Which is fine, the - " She gestured, vaguely, down toward the kitchen. "I can't abide red meat. Some of my younger cousins, two generations younger, are fine with it. Some of my grandmother's generation can't touch iron, but these days there's so much metal around. We can't avoid it, unless we're in a place we have always controlled. That's not everyone, of course. Different lines, different challenges. Just an example."

He furrowed his brow, thinking, as if making a connection. "And the signing?"

That made her laugh. "Merfolk. And selkies. Well, not the signing, them. Up north, in Scotland. It's why my vocabulary is a bit odd."

Cadmus blinked at her, owlishly. "I knew they existed, I didn't know they talked to people."

There was a moment where she wanted to correct him, but then she realised that to him, talking with your hands was still talking. She didn't think at all before she offered, "I could take you up there sometime. When this is over. Introduce you."

Something in that tempted him, and she couldn't tell if it was the new knowledge or the fact he signed, or the fact she'd invited him. He was rather difficult to read, a lot of the time. She liked the challenge, and the fact he'd often tell her if she asked the right question. "I did tell Lena that it was merfolk. Well, she guessed and I confirmed it."

"Ha." Cadmus looked smug. "Mrs Cooper is exemplary." He considers. "Would you bring her too?" It had a wistful sound to it.

"I already offered the same to her, if she would like. Why do you ask?"

Cadmus lifted his hands. "She would love more people to talk to. Unless all your cousins know how to sign."

"Oh, no. Unfortunately. Or we could set Robin to some useful purpose, relaying messages when you aren't around, or interpreting radio plays for her pleasure, or something of that kind." The moment made them both laugh, and then they both realised what they were putting off. She coughed and took a breath. "When this is done, I will be glad to arrange it."

"I'll have to see to Farran, and that's a whole other problem."

She shook her head. "I have an idea or two for that, but that's not for tonight. Come on. We're both dreading this, and we're dragging our feet, and we'll feel better when we've done it."

Cadmus wanted to argue with her, he opened his mouth and closed it. Vivian just watched him, waiting for his very sharp mind to come to the same conclusions she had. Then he nodded. "You're right."

She turned, picking up the dowsing rods and the little wooden knob again. "Lead the way, then, it is your proper place."

Cadmus nodded, waiting until she had everything in her arms, then held the door for her. Once she was through, he said, "Let me go first. I do hope we don't run into anyone."

"Only one way to find out. If Robin's the room on the end on the right, who's opposite?"

"No one, at the moment, but some of Richard's books and trunks. A favour while he sorts through repacking them."

Vivian waited, out of sight around the corner into the family wing, and let Cadmus go across to the stairway up. He waved at her, signalling the coast was clear, and she followed. Then it was up another flight, and repeating the process while he attempted to wander down the hallway. He was exceedingly bad at looking innocent at this kind of thing, but he was doing his best. They both paused, when there was a creak of the house, but it didn't seem to be anyone coming or going.

There was a nook halfway down the hallway that was meant for some sort of table and floral arrangement or alabaster bust of some classical figure. It was currently empty, and they both ducked into it, in very close quarters. Vivian thought she was the one breathing quickly until she managed to get her breath under control, and realised he was as wound up about it as she was. Blinking at him, she asked. "You all right?"

He shrugged minutely. "Better when it's done."

She took her cue, and lifted the two rods. They swivelled, the sound of metal tubes spinning against metal suddenly quite loud to both of them, the way Cadmus started. But then they settled in, and Vivian felt the little precise jerks of the rods. She slowly angled them along the wall, getting a sense of what responded and what didn't.

Opening her magic to this felt queer, it always did, like a rush of cold water in her veins, something not quite natural to her. That cold, though, made the pulses of sudden warmth, of resonance, clear to her, down to her bones. It was enough to make her grunt with it, the effort almost physical. There were three places where it pulsed. That strongly suggested three separate objects. By the angles she thought they were stored fairly close together. His wardrobe, perhaps, or his trunk. Somewhere the cleaning staff wouldn't interfere with.

Cadmus, to his credit, didn't interrupt. He waited until she eased back, bracing against the curve of the niche. "Something?" His voice was quiet.

"Yes."

Then they both heard the footsteps. They were light, lighter than Madam Etna's, certainly. And a man's shoes, not a woman's, she thought. More to the point, they stopped outside Robin's door, and there was the faint tangible pulse of magic from the door lock, then the rattle of the handle turning. Neither of them dared to move.

It took forever for the door to close. Certainly it felt like forever, neither of them breathing. Once they heard the click, Vivian raised the rods again, expecting to feel the same thing. This time, no, there were four pulses, not three, like the first time.

She didn't think she'd missed one the first time. What it

meant made her bite her lip to keep from swearing. Not only might it give them away, she suspected it would discombobulate Cadmus no end.

"There's another." Vivian kept her voice low, trying not to hiss. That would carry, worse than the sound itself. And they could rely somewhat on the soundproofing charms, meant to keep noise in the hallways from bothering residents in their rooms.

Cadmus blinked at her, not understanding. She cursed herself for not explaining earlier.

"There were three items in there. Now there are four."

That made his eyes widen, and he looked from her to the door and back. "What do we do?"

She shook her head. "Retreat and figure out the next steps. Not here." She felt more and more out in the open the more they waited. A ridiculous thing to feel when she was in a tightly packed nook in the wall, but reality was fickle at the moment.

Cadmus nodded. "Let me look." He peeked around the edge of the wall, and then nodded, setting back off toward the stairs, back past the door to Robin's room. It wasn't until she followed him, walking about ten feet behind, that the hallway started to shift. Whatever Robin was up to, it was accelerating, and far too quickly for him to be taking proper care with it.

THIRTY-SIX

FRIDAY EVENING

At first, Cadmus thought it was just some trick of the light, but then the world shifted and he knew something was desperately horribly wrong. It was like being on a ship battling high seas, only the floor mostly stayed put and the rest of the world changed around them. There were flickers of light and a high pitched noise that made him clap his hands over his ears. Not that it helped, the noise kept going, and the lights kept shifting.

Finally, after what felt like minutes and was probably only a few seconds, he managed to look behind him. He saw Vivian moving, her hand flickering in and out, like light going on and off. He could see past her, down to the end of the hallway, and the effect didn't seem to be happening there, but it was hard to tell. Turning back to the way they were going, he had to shake his head and blink several times, as the walls around them dissolved into something else.

There was a flicker of the carpet on the floor disappearing. Then they seemed to be on the ground, all of a sudden, in knee-high grass, a meadow in full summer. He couldn't see clearly for a moment, it was all light and moving grass.

The land felt like his land. He couldn't begin to explain why he knew that, but the certainty filled him. It felt like springtime, though, not cresting into winter, the land had a give and softness to it.

He heard a sound that was absolutely a sheep, where there should not be a sheep. When he looked around him, he found himself at the head of a herd of twenty some sheep, grazing amiably and unperturbed by his presence. Only then did he wonder where Vivian was, and she wasn't there. Just the sheep.

He frowned, but at least he had not fallen into some queer myth where the sheep were about to turn lethal. He hoped. They seemed to be completely ordinary sheep, except for the fact they should not be there. He didn't want to move far in case it changed his ability to get back. But he took another step or two in the direction he'd been going, to see what happened.

Nothing changed for a minute or so. The sun shone. The wind blew. The sheep ate the grass. He couldn't hear anything off in the distance, or even find any way to figure out where he was, or when, other than the balmy weather.

Before he entirely found his bearings, the world shifted again, and this time the noises he heard before his vision cleared were much more frightening. That was a battle, and somewhere quite nearby. He found himself blinking, flashes of light or gunpowder making it hard to focus. It was gunpowder, or at least that was part of it, because a cloud of it had settled in the valley, down where he expected a valley to be.

He wondered for a moment if it were a hallucination, but he'd never been overly prone to them, especially not if Afghanistan had been some real if legendary being. And he'd never been particularly interested in battles with guns, beyond the most local history. Cromwell had staged a number of sieges along this part of the country. He could hear the clashes of arms, the roar of the guns.

None of it seemed too near him, fortunately, because he wanted no part of that battle. In the actual War, they'd shut the house up tight with magic, made it so no one could even stumble into the grounds, and hunkered down as best they could. One of his ancestors had built something very like the seven legendary gates of Thebes, twining magic around seven archways that permitted only certain people or materials in. The distraction, the reassuring touch of classical history, made him almost fail to notice the next shift until he was well into it.

This time, he landed somewhere in stillness, and he took a step or two forward again, in the direction he'd been going. This time the land was untended, there were thorny vines and brush near him, about where the doors of the hallway should be, he thought. It looked not like there was a battle, but like there had been one. A battle that had trampled things down, a year or two ago, all the plants that grew up in disturbed ground.

He turned and looked over his shoulder. There was a hall there, but a much earlier style, one he'd only read about in the family histories, much smaller than the current footprint of the house. It was made of rough stone, and some part of him desperately wanted a notebook, to sketch out all the details. It made him suddenly sure that whatever was happening, it involved time, more than space or hallucination.

He could see blackberries, and he knew from pulling out hordes of them as a boy, they grew over shallow stone. There was shepherd's purse, with the little buds growing off angular stalks. There was butter-and-eggs, as Mrs Cooper called it, with the sunny centres and the white flowers. Toadflax, some people called it, which was just as curious a name. Plantain, plenty of that, and the broad flat green leaves and ground cover.

He found naming the plants reassuring, a reminder that he was on land he knew, even if he didn't know it like that. All of these grew from time to time in the Thebes he knew, they weren't distant and foreign. But there was something faintly wrong about the landscape, and he suspected, if the others had been history, this was further in the past. He glanced down, and spotted a circular metal pin, a fibula, scuffed and half buried. He picked it up, turning it over in his hand, and then the world around him started to flicker again, and he made a decision, and kept it.

Somehow, he had the courage to take another step, and another, into the unknown. It was easier here than it had been in Afghanistan. Maybe it did make a difference, to be on your home ground, where you knew everything, even if it had changed and changed again. Another shiver of time around him, and he was in the same house, in a hallway, but looking quite different. The walls were wood panelled, but it was different from the wood he knew. He glanced up, at the intricate knotwork. He flashed back to a trip to one of the great Tudor palaces, with his father, who thought he should see how the other half lived. It had that carved intricacy, he could pick out paired initials, like in Hampton Court. That would make it 1500s, probably.

He almost forgot to look where he was going, but this time, when he looked around, there was Vivian, two feet behind him. He turned and offered her his hand. She took it, her grip strong about his wrist, like she refused to lose him, or become lost herself. Her mouth opened, she was making words, and his lip reading was only barely good enough to get the sense of it.

"Move. Keep moving." He agreed. He turned, so she was behind him, awkwardly gripping, and he managed to get a better grip on her wrist as well. Then they forged forward, as if pushing against a wall of water. It felt like a tremendous force, entirely impersonal, moving through honey, everything somewhat sticky. One step in front of the other, his chin tucked, like he was battling through a sand storm.

The snow, when it hit his face, was decidedly a surprise. He looked up, gasped, and the cold of the air around him chilled him and shocked him instantly. But Vivian had come through with him, hand still gripping his. They came to a stop, not because of any desire, but because they were both now better than knee deep in snow.

"Hold a minute." Her voice was cracking, edged with something he had no idea how to name. "Take a breath. Sort ourselves out." Her words were coming in short little gasps.

He nodded, letting go of her only long enough to offer an arm to link with hers. "Easier to manage this?"

She nodded, interlacing her arm with his, and then for good measure, threading her fingers with his. It was a sudden intimacy, one he hadn't expected, but it was practical. More strength in the arm.

"Do you know what's happening?" Then, hurriedly, he added "Besides the time slip. All here, I'm fairly sure. Just different times."

"Ice age, I expect." She gestured at a flat, featureless plain of ice and snow. "I don't know enough about it." She sounded frustrated. "Keep going, I guess. When we can." She looked down, and her skirt was getting drenched, well up her thighs. He looked away, it wasn't at all appropriate, but kept their arm linked.

"Is it the new object? How do we stop this?"

"I think we keep going. Down the hall, past the door. One thing at a time."

"That will get us free?"

"I hope so. If not, we'll - talk..." And then she swore, under her breath, he could only make out the intent, not the words. It might well not have been in English, surely her family had its own languages. He was so distracted he almost didn't brace for the next shift.

This one brought them out into a pleasant twilight, much warmer, a pleasant evening, but Cadmus could immediately see a glow of a fire in - that must be Oxford. "Fire." Something in it made everything in his body tense, like he was missing something essential. He took a breath,.

"Do you know when?"

"There's several major fires, through the centuries. That's Oxford properly, though." He blinked at the skyline. "Early, I think. Eleventh or twelfth century, maybe. I can't see the towers well enough."

That, for some reason, made Vivian laugh, and then she squeezed her hand. "That's reassuring. What else did you see?" This time, she took a step forward, bringing him along with her.

"Sheep. Cromwell, I think, certainly a skirmish with gunpowder. A deserted space. After some sort of war, where the land was disturbed, I think. There was a pin there. I grabbed it. Something Tudor - that was in the same hallway. And then..." He stopped, because she was looking at him quite oddly.

"A pin?"

"A fibula." He opened his other hand, wincing at where

he'd been holding onto it so hard it left an impression in his hand. "This."

"Hah." There was triumph in her voice. "May I use this? It won't harm it."

He blinked, but said "Yes?" It came out about as uncertain as he felt.

There was another flashing grin from her, and then she was saying words that were decidedly not in English at all, and the world jerked, this time. Not nearly such a smooth transition as the other times.

THIRTY-SEVEN

FRIDAY EVENING

"Wait, where am I?"

Vivian was glad that he had come back to himself. She had forcibly dragged him, near enough, down the hallway, around the corner, and back to the outside of his private rooms on the second floor. Or at least she thought they were his. They had the little heraldic markers that suggested it was the space for the keeper of the house, and the warding felt right to be his.

At any rate, it was away from that dreadful feeling, of time going every which way, over and over, giving her a pounding headache.

"Where am I?"

She hadn't answered his question. "Your rooms, I think?" Vivian said. "I hope?" Her knees nearly gave out then.

"Wait, you - yes, they are, oh bugger." The swear sounded entirely like him and entirely not, both at once, and it almost made her smile. A moment later, he was offering her his arm again, elbow crooked properly, and he'd got the door open while she wasn't looking. "Come sit."

He didn't quite dump her on a sofa, but it was a near thing, and she blinked up at him, trying to figure out where to start. The headache was not helping, one bit.

"Tea? Brandy?"

"Brandy? Something for a headache?" The last came out sounding very plaintive, and she grimaced. He blinked at her, didn't say anything, and went off to another corner of the room.

It took him some time to come back, by which point she had at least managed to do a few sensible things. She had loosened the buttons at the top of her dress, to have more space to breathe, and peered at her still damp skirts and moved them so they would at least not be damp and cold right on her skin. She could do a drying cantrip, of course, but not with this headache. Later, maybe. That sent her off down a chain of thoughts about how few forms of magic she felt she could manage right now, and how vulnerable that made her feel.

Finally, there were footsteps again, and she'd got so lost in her own thoughts that she started, jumping.

"Whiskey, the brandy's downstairs. And a potion, one of the milder ones, sorry, is that enough?" He was babbling, which made her frown, which made her head hurt more. But any port in a storm, and she nodded and put out her hand. He settled the potion vial into it, a deep and rather uneasy green. But that was one she knew, that would work well enough, at least to get her back on the right track. As she uncorked it, he settled on the sofa beside her, peering at her.

She drained the potion, and blinked at him. "Problem?"t

"I was rather hoping you'd be up to being the one with sensible good ideas." There was an edge to his voice that sounded like her voice in her head, all angles and chaos and uncertainty. It didn't bode well.

The comment did make her half-smile. "Afraid we might have to do it together."

"What was that? Do you know? Is it something your people do?"

"Time shifts, I thought that part was fairly obvious. I have a few ideas. And there's no single 'your people' going on here, what we have is my very idiot cousin, and I mean that in the most Athenian of classical senses. And magics of a kind no one's had much truck with since at least the Pact."

As she'd half hoped, the classics comment gave him some sort of anchor. "An idiot being a person who acts on their own behalf, not thinking of the polis, the city." He was thinking out loud, saying it to soothe himself, but then his eyes widened. "Oh! I see. A unitary act, out of sequence and continuity. Is that what's making the time shifts, do you think?"

That hadn't actually been a thing she'd meant, but it was an excellent theory. Really only one of them should be busy panicking right now, and it was probably more useful if she left him the option. She would have to go on pretending she had a clue what was going on. "Possibly." she agreed. "It certainly fits the evidence."

"The evidence is bugger all useless." Then he looked away and flushed.

"Swearing's rather called for in the circumstance," she replied. "We have our experiences - I had a slightly different sequence, but you'd know the building history much better than I do, of course. But all - this space, this property?"

"Yes." He considered. "But not always - the same location on the property. Among other things, sometimes I was on the ground, and sometimes on the second floor."

"Point. Though I suppose with the ice age, there's no telling how much ice was under us."

He snorted. "No, but I was properly outside for Cromwell. And the sheep."

She nodded, then glanced down at her hands. "And wherever you got this." She held up the pin.

"Is that what I thought it was? And what on earth did you do?"

Vivian lifted her other hand, the left, wriggling it. "Used the magic inherent in this being out of time to take us back to the place with the strongest pull, the time we came from. It ..." She glanced at the empty potion vial. "Glad it worked, don't want to do that again for at least a decade."

He shifted on the sofa, and then reached out a hand to touch hers, tentatively, looking like he wasn't sure what she'd do. "Thank you."

A dozen things collided in her head. She'd been getting herself free, not just him, that it was her idiot cousin who'd caused the problem, she had an obligation to fix it. That he wasn't skilled with this kind of magic. Not that she was, particularly, but she at least knew there was a kind of magic that muddled time and a few tricks to deal with it. And then she looked at him, and all of those thoughts disappeared. Instead, she found herself saying, "You'd do the same for me."

Cadmus blinked at her, and then he nodded once, like it changed something fundamental for him. "I would. This is Thebes. I won't let it be destroyed. Or anyone in it." Then his eyebrows went up. "Are the others all right, what do we do?"

His sense of noblesse oblige was a fine thing, but perhaps a tad exhausting. She tilted her head, thinking. "I don't know. You ready to brave the hallway again?"

"What about trying the one downstairs, first. Do we knock, or do we just go and listen?"

"Listen, I think. Or - do you have charms, that would indicate distress? Something wrong in the house?"

"Yes, but they haven't been working well. My brother put them in. Look, I can show you."

She didn't want to stand up, but he stood there, waiting, then offered her his hand. "I can't bring them to you, I'm sorry. They're built into the wall." She nodded, and levered herself up. He walked her over to a broad swath of wall, facing the desk, where it could be instantly seen by someone seated there. It was a mural of a green growing garden, laid out like the gardens outside, but with little dots of light glowing steadily in different places. She peered at it, trying to make sense of it.

"Each of the lights is a resident." he said. "All highly symbolic, but they blink if there's a particular threat. The house is mapped onto the layout, and spots will glow really quite obviously if there's a problem with the structure."

She whistled under her breath. "That's a tricky bit of magic. How do you anchor it to a new person?"

"The signature on the agreement. Nothing they haven't agreed to, of course. You roll up the slip of paper and slide it into one of the containers, here. It was intended, I suspect, to keep an eye on the staff, in that patriarchal way."

Something in his tone made her look sideways at him. "You don't approve of that?"

"No. Staff are still people, they don't need us checking up on them more than anyone else in the house. If we still had, oh, under housemaids barely in their teens, there'd be some call for making sure they were in at night, and so on. But Mrs Cooper doesn't need any of that. Nor the day staff."

Vivian nodded absently, and looked more carefully at the map. "Nothing here is flashing. Nor is it being particularly obvious. Does that mean everyone is all right? That the house is."

"That, or the enchantments broke. But here, this is you." He tapped a spot by the folly and pond. "I moved you out there last night." It made her smile. "And see, you're blinking quite slowly. Look, come sit down again, unless you need to look at the map." She shook her head, regretted the movement immensely, and he took her by the arm, and led her back to the sofa, perching on the other half of it. "What do we do now?"

"We wait for daylight and have a long chat with my cousin."

"Daylight?"

Vivian spread her hands. "Liminal times are more in his family line. I do a bit better in the daylight, on average."

"Except when dancing by magic's light."

"It is a touch easier to get privacy at night." The words came out more prim than she meant, but she smiled at the end, and was pleased to see him smile in turn.

"The headache. May I escort you downstairs, and fetch another potion from the healer's cupboard?"

"Please. Definitely a good idea." The throbbing ache was definitely back.

The next morning, her headache was much reduced. Cadmus had escorted her down to her room, promising that he or Farran would keep watch on that intriguing enchantment all night, and alert her immediately if anything changed. He had invited her to an early breakfast with him upstairs.

"How do we do this, then?"

"I put on a bit of formality, and I ask him what he's doing. You have to understand, we are, as a culture, given to indirectness. And what we can get away with, in that indirectness, is permitted. But when pressed in a particular way, we might be cornered into confessing."

"And you can do that?"

"I have three principal advantages. First, I am of Electra's line. This is one of the things we are for, to protect the human places, and the human people. Second, I am older, wiser, and not going to fall for his wiles."

"And third?"

That got her grinning. "I know quite a few tricks he's never bothered to learn. Lazy boy." She kept her tone light, and was rewarded by Cadmus smiling. She added, "I do believe in precautions. Farran." He looked up, from where he was perched on a chair across from the sofa.

"Ma'am?" So polite, she appreciated that.

"This is a letter. If we do not reappear within an hour after talking to my cousin, or if you see any signs of distress on the map up here that do not settle quickly, within a minute, you are to leave the house immediately, and take this letter to this place. The portal sigils are on the envelope, and the seal will give you safe passage. The letter explains everything I know, and the people there will provide the necessary assistance."

"Your family, ma'am?"

"My terrifying aunts, yes. I would rather not involve them if we don't have to."

There was a long silence, and Cadmus finally nodded. "This will not get easier. Are you ready, then?"

Vivian took a deep breath, and then pulled various items out of the leather-bound case she had brought up with her. They gleamed, not with polish, but with magic.

Cadmus shifted in his seat, and then asked "May I?" She nodded at them, gesturing. There was a blade, made of flint and bone, a copper wand, rounded and smoothed, a small bowl carved out of ancient ivory. All her own personal treasures. He didn't try to touch them, which she was grateful for. She wasn't sure what she'd say, if she'd have permitted that particular intimacy.

Vivian nodded, and stood. The walk to Robin's room felt unusually difficult. He had not left the space, they were fairly sure of that. But the air around felt oppressive, like the worst humid day in the tropics, where every movement was like swimming through water thick with plants and hiding unknown dangers. She knocked on the door, three precise raps.

The pause that followed felt like minutes, but it was really only three heartbeats. Then there was Robin's voice, sounding almost resigned. "Come."

She cast a quick charm on the door, to check that there was no trap, and found no magic on it whatsoever, even the usual locking magics of the house. It was as if something had wiped it clean entirely. That done, she glanced at Cadmus, and opened the door.

Robin was sitting on the bed, his feet tucked up and crossed at the ankles, looking about six years old, and forlorn. There were various items scattered on the floor around him, a ring of guttered candles in a circle around the room. Copper bowls at the compass points held offerings that had gone to ashes and foul-smelling dust without any hint of form.

She was careful not to step inside the circle, gesturing for Cadmus to stay beside her. "That's quite a ritual circle you attempted, Robin. Do tell." She kept her voice even, solid, unyielding.

"It didn't work." Robin sounded small and defeated now. "You know it didn't work."

"It didn't do what you wanted. That is not quite the same thing."

He looked up at her, wide-eyed. "It did something. But that stopped. Last night. And then everything..." He gestured at the ritual items, then at the four items in the centre of the circle. They were small, simple, almost blending into the rug, which was rather singed where they sat, now she looked more closely. It was hard to tell against the pattern at first.

The items were small. A piece of stone, likely meteorite,

if it did what she thought it did. There was a brooch, not unlike the fibula Cadmus had found last night, a common enough item through more than a millenia. The third was a geode, with a glow to the stones inside that was decidedly Fatae-touched somehow. The last was a vial, and she rather suspected that was the most recent addition, because it had a deep red liquid in it. She rather thought that would be made from elderberries from a portal tree.

All appeared undamaged, but she didn't want to vouch for the state of the glass vial more than strictly necessary.

Vivian turned, to make sure the door was fully closed. "What were you trying to do, Robin?"

Robin glanced at Cadmus. "Family business."

"It's his home, he's responsible for everyone living here, and you've made it dangerous. He has every right to know." Cadmus, beside her, nodded, crossing his arms, and looking as stern as he could manage. He was not particularly made to look stern, but she appreciated the effort.

Robin let out a long sigh, and then looked away, but he began to answer. "I wanted to give the things back. Things from that house, that manor, you know."

"The one not that many miles from here, yes." She tilted her head. "How did you get the items?"

"It took a lot. They didn't hire me on, as one of the early consultants, damn them. But I got a chance, later, and a chance to take a thing or two that were small enough, and I thought might be worth a trade. The vial I got from someone else."

"That's not from the house, then?"

"Portal nearest it." Robin sounded entirely grudging and grumpy. Vivian let out a sigh of relief. That was less difficult than it might be.

"And you just got the vial last night, then. That's what caused the problem."

He nodded, minutely. Cadmus, next to her, shifted. Vivian said, "I'll explain in a moment."

"So you got the vial, you came back, you did the ritual. Why in here?"

"I thought people would spot me, in the grounds. And after that thing with Danae, she told me she'd felt really awful. I thought I'd have more control here." Now he was sounding sulky.

"This is the sort of ritual that needs a properly prepared and consecrated space. No shortcuts. And you took, oh, a dozen."

"The bowls were right! The bowls were a bloody nuisance to get right. And the plants, some of them out of season, though the greenhouses here are quite well stocked."

Vivian let her mind flick through the places there had been trouble. "Roses, and an orchid, and several different herbs, right?"

Robin nodded. Cadmus asked, "Why those?"

"Those are the places you had trouble. If he was using a ritually consecrated tool, a knife, to cut them, that might have been enough to trigger the problems." Vivian kept watching Robin. "What happened when you tried the ritual?"

"Time went wrong." Robin's voice was flat and small now. "You felt it, didn't you? Why didn't you come stop me?"

"Because it took quite a bit to yank the world back in place." Vivian's voice had a snap to it now. "It hadn't occurred to you that using items from hundreds of years ago might alter things? Never mind the fact they were held in a magical stasis for almost all that time?"

"I wanted to give the Grandmothers gifts. Proper gifts." Now he was back to sulking. "You don't understand. None of Electra's daughters and sons do."

Vivian cocked her head. "I understand we can't go back before the Pact, no matter how tempting and appealing it is." She tapped a foot. "You know that. For magic's sake, the Grandmothers tell us that, at regular intervals."

"Haven't told me." Ah, that was it. He was sulky he hadn't been favoured.

"And you thought if you just gave them presents, they'd open the door, and let you in."

Robin shrugged. "Hard to make a life here. I just, I just wanted to go through. Not be here with all the death and the dying, and the bloody useless War. And all the men going on about serving and being noble and heroic. And I couldn't, not any of it."

Vivian considered. In fairness, much as she wasn't terribly inclined to fairness about Robin right now, that must have been hard. She knew he hadn't served, at least not in actual fighting. Most of the cousins hadn't. Either they found iron difficult to deal with, or couldn't be in mud and trenches long enough.

She had gathered there were particular signifiers in the files, for the men who'd been reassigned to positions that wouldn't kill them in difficult ways to explain. As opposed to the relentless bloody and mud-soaked War that was obvious.

Cadmus spoke then. "Lots of us didn't serve in the trenches, and still served. Vivian's explained there are some things she can't abide, and I can see how that would affect War service, but she seems quite competent. Surely you could rise to the occasion."

It was quite probably the wrong thing to say to get

Robin to cooperate. But Cadmus had every right, as a veteran himself, and as the owner of the house and the land. It certainly made Robin subside into sulkiness.

Vivian tsked. "Do you have notes on what you did?"

"Nothing you'd find useful." It came out sharper and hard.

Vivian shook her head. "Well, then. Stay there, if you know what's good for you. Cadmus, I'll need a few things." She paused, then rummaged in her pocket for a small note-book, peering at it. She'd written a list last night, along with her letter, but she crossed two items off, and added linden to the list. "I suspect Mrs Cooper has most of the spices, and the chest I left in your rooms has the rest. Can you fetch those?"

Cadmus nodded. "I'll knock, when I come back. As you did, earlier." He was holding together remarkably well, given his discomfort with things beyond his usual routine, but she wanted him out of the room for a few minutes. Also, she did in fact need the things he was fetching.

Once she was sure he was well down the hallway, by his footsteps, she lifted her chin, and peered at Robin. "You know I'll have to tell them. Formally."

He shrank a little, but nodded. "When you turned up here, I... Why did you have to find out?"

"Because Albion is a small community, and Farran has useful friends." Vivian felt this was entirely obvious. "Also, honestly, you'd have got someone's attention by now. That stunt last night. This isn't even sensible ritual theory, Robin, didn't Auntie train you better than that?"

He mumbled something, completely incoherent, and she shook her head. "You stay there. I have a lot of work to do."

She knelt, carefully, by one of the offering bowls. She

began casting the painstakingly precise charms to unweave the ashes into something safe to touch. When it cooled, it could be mixed with the plaster of paris in her case to be neutralised further, and transported to the aunties for proper disposal. Failed offerings were one of the most dangerous things she knew. The objects themselves, though complex, would be vastly simpler. Also not likely to cause danger if someone breathed wrong near them.

It was going to be a very long day, and hard on her knees.

C admus sat down heavily. The day had honestly been largely baffling to him. Not the part about collecting the spices and the lengths of silk she'd asked him to rummage up. He understood the theory of that, using the various properties of the herbs and spices magically was a thread that ran through every society he knew. Most of them, probably. That set him to wondering about how that played out in other places. It was at least a pleasant distraction to think about how Herodotus would describe the different approaches he knew about.

Until he came back to whatever Vivian was doing. She had taken the herbs from him at the door, and asked him to check on everyone else, and make sure no one disturbed them. Please. She had been very careful to ask him politely, and he appreciated that, rather than assuming everything. She did have that tendency, he noticed, to take charge. He found it both unsettling and reassuring at the same time, and that was no help at all.

Except that it gave him a lot more to think about, sitting on a chair in the hallway. He'd settled there to make sure no one bothered them, or tried to go into Robin's room. But then he couldn't leave, he had no books, for rather a long time. Everyone else seemed to be sticking to their rooms or were away. Mrs Cooper had brought up trays with flasks of hot water for tea and sandwiches. He'd been able to check no one was hurt, but no one wanted to talk to him.

That stung. Not that he had any idea what to say, he'd just stood there and blinked at them, and held out the tray.

Which had left him here alone in the hallway. He wasn't even sure where Farran was. Somewhere on the grounds, surely, doing something useful, but Cadmus hadn't wanted him here, just in case something did go wrong, awfully wrong.

Finally, well after lunch, Vivian opened the door, holding the sturdy wooden box she'd got from her own room. It was the size of a tea crate with leather handles bolted to the sides, but made of a smooth and polished wood with a queer shimmer of flashing blue-grey colour to it, like something living. She looked exhausted. Her hair was escaping from the bun at the back of her head in little wisps, there were hollows under her eyes. Her skin had also gone a slightly sallow colour, and he was almost distracted into trying to figure out the right word for it.

"Are you - what can I do?" She visibly wasn't all right.

"Tea, please. And food, eventually. Somewhere quiet?" Vivian blinked at him, and he found himself reacting instinctively.

"May I take that, or must you keep hold of it?"

There was a long pause, as if she were attempting to weigh the various factors, and failing to make the basic maths come out right. Finally, she said, her voice careful. "Can you take one handle?"

He nodded, and she shifted to let him take one side. It

felt unevenly heavy, certainly much more than the small objects had suggested, and he was suddenly grateful for the amount of exercise he got, seeing to the property. "My rooms." Someone had to be decisive, and apparently he was the only option. "And then I'll see about some food for us both."

Vivian was entirely quiet on the way to his rooms, as if she could only focus on one thing, and that was carrying the box. Cadmus got her settled in there, the sturdy box tucked next to her, closer to the window. "Let me go fetch the food."

She nodded, and looked as if she might well be asleep by the time he got back. That was if his memories of how Farran used to exhaust himself were anything to go by. He couldn't do much about that now, so he slipped out the door, and down the back stairs to the kitchen.

Mrs Cooper had been three steps ahead of him. There was a crock of soup, in one of the keep warm containers she brought out for such occasions. It had a hearty leek and potato soup, along with ham and cheddar sandwiches sliced up into manageable pieces. He nodded, signed his thanks, and then took the tray upstairs with him.

Vivian was asleep on the couch, one hand drifting down to rest possessively on the crate. Cadmus set the tray down as quietly as he could, everything would keep, and then looked at her. He wasn't sure if he should put a blanket over her, or if it would wake her up. And if she'd be cross if he woke her up. He wouldn't blame her, she'd been exhausting herself and he'd barely helped, and that was a thing people got cross about, he knew that.

It meant he stood in the centre of the room, looking at her, for a good ten minutes. Finally, he gave up waking her as a worthless idea, settling down in the chair opposite her with a book. He couldn't just go away and leave her. He didn't want to go away and leave her.

It was getting on for sunset when she finally stirred, three hours or so later. He immediately looked up from his book. "Are you cold? Would you like a blanket?"

Vivian sat up, rubbing her eyes, blinking at him owlishly. "I. Wait."

Cadmus said, patiently. "It's about sunset. Four or so. You fell asleep. There's food, would you like some? Or you could go wash up, the bathroom is that way." He gestured.

She blinked again, then managed to get herself fully upright. "Yes, um."

It was entirely startling to see her without her usual self-possession. She had, to this point, always seemed like a woman who knew exactly where everything was. And, for that matter, what she was doing, and what she would be doing ten minutes from now, an hour, eight hours, a day, all marching down into the future like rows of perfect soldiers. Seeing her with her hair in wisps, baffled by the world made him feel better and worse all at once. If seeing her grandmother was a mystery, this seemed like blasphemy.

He could hear the water running in the sink, then the odd clank in his little library here, the pipe behind the wall that never quite worked right. It didn't leak, not anymore, but it grumbled like much of the rest of the house. He took that as his cue to start a pot of tea. Then the water turned off. After several minutes, she came out again, with a freshly scrubbed face, and her hair retwisted into a knot low on the back of her head this time. It made her look quite different, no longer so prim, somehow younger, the way it framed her face.

"Here, here's soup. I thought about finding a blanket, but I wasn't sure if it would wake you, and you seemed like you needed the sleep, do you want something now?" He was babbling, he must sound ridiculous.

She looked up at him, once she'd got settled on the couch again. "Yes, if you don't mind. I did take a bit of a chill. Is that soup? Oh, grand."

"Soup, and she's making something nice for supper. Soothing. Chicken pie, I think she said. Nice and solid. And easy to put a few little ones aside for us if we don't make it down." He moved to bring the little table over, then the tray, so she could reach the soup and sandwiches, and the pot of tea he'd made while she was washing.

That got her blinking at him. "Us? But you'll want to go down and check on people."

He waved a hand. "Farran and Mrs Cooper are keeping an eye out. They'll come find us if there's need." It was us, that was clear to him now. "You shouldn't be alone, I am thinking."

Vivian grimaced. "Probably not. I'm not sure what I need, but I admit, I feel better having you here. Handy. In case." Her voice got a lot quieter at the end of that, and he wasn't sure how to read it at all. "I'm fairly sure I'm not up for supper downstairs, so if you're willing to let me hide here."

"Hide? More like recover, I thought."

She blinked at him again, as if he'd somehow been translated into an entirely different dialect than she'd been expecting.

"What happens now? Not right now, I mean, but in the next days."

The question seemed to settle her, even though she began by saying, "I'm not entirely sure." She took a couple of sips of the soup. "I need to bring the objects to the grandmothers, but that will take a little while to set up."

"What do we do about Robin?" He then snapped his teeth together, because that had been quite forward.

She looked up, and there was a bit of relief in her expression, he was sure of it now. It was so blatant, even he couldn't get that wrong, how her shoulders relaxed. "We." She stopped, tried again. "I'm glad that you're not sending me away. Or making me do it on my own."

"Why would I?" Cadmus was baffled. "It's my house to take care of, but you know a lot of things I don't. But I don't..." He stopped and swallowed. "I want this to be fixed. Properly. And you know how to do that, and you care about doing it right."

Somewhere in the middle of that, she tilted her head. "What will you do when Farran inherits?" she asked.

Cadmus had no idea where that came from, or what to do with it. He did the only thing he could think of to do for the moment, and poured himself a cup of tea.

V ivian waited. Rushing him did no good, she had been clear when she first met him that this was a man who did things in his own time. Oh, she'd rushed him at their first meeting, to keep him a little off balance, make sure he didn't ask questions that would have required lies.

She hadn't wanted to lie to him, either. Curious. That usually didn't bother her overmuch. Now, she cupped her hands around the tea, giving him the space to think about the question he didn't want to answer.

"It rather depends on Farran. He'll still be an apprentice." He swallowed. "I hope."

"I believe solving that will be a great deal easier than solving this. And I am glad to help. He's a level-headed young man." She turned her palm over, a gesture of offering. "And he deserves better than his current apprenticeship."

Cadmus blinked at her, owlishly. "Did I do something wrong?" Oh, that was fascinating, how it came out as a baffled question, not the defensive posturing most other people would do.

"No, it isn't that. Let me figure out how to explain it." She took a moment for more tea, to gather her thoughts. And to figure out how to put this so it would make sense to him, so it would stop looming at him from the shadows. "You looked for a place that would take Farran, that might suit. But it was just you, you didn't have the broad range of contacts and resources. Not what a large family would have, have favours owed, the people helped in the past, all that. The things that would give you the widest range of options. No matter how capable Farran might look to be."

She had been thinking about this for a while, now. It wasn't Cadmus's fault, it was a combination of circumstances, and the games of social hierarchy she suspected Cadmus had no intention of playing, and less desire to.

Cadmus sat with that, more than a bit lost in his own head, with occasional sips of tea. After a good two minutes, he looked up. "And what is different now?"

Vivian shrugged. "You have me. And one of the benefits of being a well-aged daughter of Electra is that rather a lot of people either owe me a favour. Or would be delighted to have me owe them one. Even if it's the sort of thing that is a fair trade, working out well for all involved."

"And you think Farran could do better somewhere?"

"I do." She was watching him closely now. Getting him onto this topic, now, had been a risk, but one she thought worthwhile. He trusted her, for better or for worse. And whatever he thought of the balance of what was owed, she knew that this whole mess with Robin could have been much worse.

It would have been worse if Cadmus had not had such a strong connection to the house and the land. It would have been worse if he had let his fears win, half a dozen times. It would have been worse if he had thrown her out, when he discovered her. He had done none of those things, and if she could do good for him, and for Farran, she would.

"What would you suggest, then?" He was weighing things, and she approved.

"I would need to ask him to do some additional things, as a test, but I have a theory. That the ways he is interfering with his current apprentice master's work have to do with him responding to the energies, the materia, in the talismans. You had a good thought, sending him somewhere he could direct it. But I suspect, well, I suspect it makes his skin itch. In a way he can't pin down."

Cadmus blinked. "Like I do, only for different reasons?"

Vivian was not entirely sure what he meant. She must have made some sort of expression that made sense to him, because he looked down for a moment, talking into his lap. "When there are too many people, or too much noise, or too much light, it itches in my head. Or in the centre of my back. Somewhere I can't reach. A full dinner table is about my limit, if everyone's talking quietly. More than that is far too much."

"I have never been entirely sure what to do with people who like large gatherings." Vivian said, amiably, because that much, she understood. "They seem a much more distant race than my foremothers."

He blinked at her, and then there was a slow, warm smile. "I thought you were the sort of person who'd be at all the parties. Fancy events. Looking, you look. You always look so put together. In control."

The idea made her grin, suddenly. "Oh, no. I put on the show because then people don't fuss at me. And it is useful in my line of business, to be taken very seriously. But I leave the going to parties to other people, who go and come back and tell me all the things I need to know." She considered.

"Also, looking like I have presence is about a quarter having a superb dressmaker. And the other three quarters looking like I know what I'm doing, and am confident about it."

"If you say so." He was entirely dubious. "What did you think of for Farran, then?"

Vivian considered. "I have a number of contacts with the auction houses. Someone with his apparent gift for feeling materia, responding to it, that is very useful to them. The other thing they look for is someone who is amiable, sociable, can engage as a peer with people who have things to sell, who wish to buy. Farran has the family background to do well there, without being too awed by the higher reaches of the Great Families."

Cadmus chewed on that. "We don't move in those circles."

"No, but you've taught him good manners, you and his parents and Lena. He's thoughtful, he listens, he's consider-ate. Those go a long way, and frankly they go rather further than the attitude of a stereotypical scion of a Great Family. You know the sort who expects everyone to do as he says, no matter what he wants. The auction house work, appraisal, it requires a sense of one's self that is interdependent, but clear."

There was another long pause. "And you're willing?" Then, so tentatively, fragile as a flower petal, he asked, "That means you'll -" He couldn't finish the sentence, but she could hear the offer, clearly enough. Or the desire for an offer to be made.

"Are you asking me if I'll disappear back to Trellech, and be like some fleeting memory?" Better to put it into words.

His head jerked, a tiny shaky nod. He met her eyes for a brief moment, then looked away, out the window.

"Ask me to come back, and I will." She spoke gently, and as firmly as she could. Asking, oh, she wasn't sure if he'd be able to, but she needed him to be the one to ask. It was his home, his and Farran's, and they had their routines. She had disrupted them, she couldn't insist she do so over and over again.

He took a long breath and let it out slowly. "I don't know how. And the, and the classics, they aren't much help. They treat women so abominably, sometimes. Often."

Vivian nodded. "In so many ways. But we live in different times, don't we." She considered how to go about this, without frightening him more. "I enjoy your company, Cadmus. The way you care. This is a lovely home, when it isn't beset by magical dangers. Most of your residents are grand."

He looked up, with an amused smile at the qualifier. "Your cousin. And who else?"

She waved a hand. "I would not choose to spend too much time with Madam Etna." She watched him, looking for the little signs something was too much. She read people like this routinely, but she found herself catching things with him even faster.

Cadmus stood, somewhat abruptly, going to the window, and looking out, down across the grounds, as if it gave him strength and certainty. Then he turned around and said, "I don't know what I'm doing, but I haven't known that in weeks. Will you come back here, and visit? See how we are?"

She smiled at that, and then it turned into a laugh of delight, almost despite herself. "I will. You hadn't ever thought you'd ask someone, did you?"

He shook his head, then came and held out his hand to her. She gestured at the couch beside her, and waited for him to sit, close enough his leg was against hers. Vivian curled her fingers around his, her other hand on top, before she continued. "I have my settled ways, and you have yours. But I will come and visit, a few days each time, and you can show me all the things in the grounds, and the house. And we will find Farran something that suits him, and see what else we might do together."

That last had a teasing note, and she watched him blink, then flush a delightful shade of pink. Oh, he'd definitely had thoughts about that, then. She wouldn't push him to talk about them yet, that would be unkind at the moment, when she'd already pressed him this far.

"All those things." He let out a long breath, leaving his hand between hers. "It is rather a lot. What do... what do we do now?"

"Eventually, we go down to supper, so Lena can see that you are well, and I am well. Then we figure out how to go and have a certain complex discussion with my foremothers."

"Are there things you need? Do you need me to be there?"

Vivian took a breath, spacing this. "I would like very much if you were. I know it scares you, but I promise there is a structure to it, I can tell you what to expect to happen. And I will do most of the talking."

He considered that, then nodded. "If you explain it first."

"Of course. And you can ask as many questions as you like."

"Can I do anything to help?"

"You said, you were a devotee of the Smith. Does that extend to actual smithcraft?"

He blinked, and she mentally scolded herself for going

several steps at one. Then he nodded. "Yes. Not in practice for anything terribly elaborate, but iron work, copper work. I fix Mrs Cooper's pots when needed, that sort of thing."

Vivian nodded. "I would like a copper box, if you could manage it. And I would much rather not ask Danae, even if she is less likely to wish me ill than she was."

Cadmus smiled at that. "Awkward, yes. A complicated favour, that one."

"Exactly. She owes me for the attack, but this is not the right sort of repayment."

He tilted his head. "A particular sort of maths, then. You'll have to teach me your methods, I think."

"That." She smiled at him. "And quite a few other things, I suspect."

FORTY-ONE

SUNDAY, NOVEMBER 26TH

O nce Vivian contacted her aunts, things happened in a rush. One minute, Vivian was sending messages in one of the journals that had become more readily available after the War. Expensive, finicky, he gathered, but exceedingly useful. An hour later, the first of the aunts arrived. Each carried a small bag, a staff, and was wearing clothing that seemed specifically chosen, but by no pattern Cadmus could begin to discern.

Vivian had placed Cadmus in the library, the public room where he felt most comfortable. The doorbell would ring, or there would be precise raps on the front door. Vivian would bring each one to the library, introduce her, though none of the names stayed in his head more than a few moments. Most - all but two or three - were women. All of them had a sort of familial resemblance that had nothing to do with hair colour, or shade of skin, size, or build, but was about how they held themselves. They all moved like Vivian, more on the balls of the feet, and like they were keeping pace with a song they all heard and no one else.

It struck him that Robin had some of the same mannerisms, only dimmer, as if he were less connected, more distant.

Then Vivian would bring her to the door, where Robin was waiting. The aunt would begin talking to him in the low-voiced tones of someone providing another layer of scolding.

The procession seemed to go on and on. At some point, more than two dozen people in, Mrs Cooper brought him lunch, and signed that the visitors were being well-behaved and considerate, the ones she'd talked to. Which implied that signing was not purely due to visits like the ones Vivian had made under the water.

His part was simple, at least. Vivian had explained they would acknowledge him, with a word Vivian had translated as 'landholder', then go to the gardens and arrange for the ritual. Between their appearances, Cadmus found himself distracted by what that term meant in their tongue, how the translation shaded things, which was at least a familiar sort of confusion.

Finally, when it was getting on for sunset, Vivian came to the library door without anyone. "They're all here. You are most cordially invited to join us, it is your land and your home, but you are not required to, if you would rather not."

"What will be happening?"

"They have decided on a particular form of ritual, we will do it, and we will see what the grandmothers say."

"So like your ritual, in the woods?"

"Possibly rather a lot more showy. Well, likely."

"Loud? Scary? Fast?"

She considered, permitting herself to lean against the wall, as she thought. "Things may happen quickly, but I think flashing lights are more likely than loud noises. And this is your land, and you are the one who was injured, well, a representative. You have rights, and whatever else happens, you will be safe."

He frowned. The way she phrased that tipped him off that he ought to worry. He was, perhaps, getting better at figuring out the things she did not say. "And you?"

There was entirely too long a delay before she answered. "Probably safe. But nothing is certain for me." She looked up, quickly. "Our grandmothers can be quick to take action, and I had my failings here."

He swallowed his arguments, because he did not know the language or how to translate it, it was like he had waded into Linear A without realising it. For all he knew, that was literally true. That was too large a thing to get his head around in the time he had.

Cadmus stood. "I would rather be with you." It was true for the immediate moment, and true for further down the road. Being this brave, now, was terrifying, but it was much worse than living in a future where he'd made some other choice.

Vivian beamed at him, and even he could read the relief there, the way her eyes crinkled and her shoulders relaxed visibly. "Thank you. I need to change quickly, then I'll be right back. Wait here, all right?"

"Do I need to change?" He was in a tweed suit, one of his better ones, but he thought that was not the sort of clothing they'd be wearing at all. If, he realised with a start, they wore clothing at all, since so many of the vase paintings didn't.

She shook her head. Then, without saying anything else, she disappeared out of the library door. She was back ten minutes later, wearing the same outfit, he thought, she had worn the night of her personal ritual. Linen dress, belted at the waist in some intricate pattern, with a cord belt of blue and blue-green and dark red, with little charms and beads glinting along the surface.

Her hair was pinned up with the sort of comb that Herodotus would go on for paragraphs about. He'd have theories about what it must mean and why it was important, and that he couldn't interpret properly at all. The large amber pendant at her throat almost glowed, and she had sandals on her feet that seemed very impractical for a grassy lawn in November. Not that Cadmus would risk mentioning it, Vivian was entirely clear on proper dress at other times, and knew the weather.

Vivian held out her hand. "Escort me, then, if you wish? I do promise nothing we do will harm the garden. I can't promise about the grandmothers, but they are not inclined to take their tempers out on innocent plants."

That made him smile, and he suddenly realised she was trying to put him at ease. He offered his arm to her, and once she'd looped her hand through, covered her hand with his for a moment. "I trust you. I don't trust them."

"You don't know them." Which was part of the issue, yes.

"How do I address them?"

"Aunt and Uncle will do perfectly well."

He blinked at her. "Names mean things. Does that imply things to them?"

"There are other things you could use, yes. Ma'am. Sir. But Aunt and Uncle is also appropriate, and not just because you might see some of them in future, at more festive events."

Cadmus let out a breath. "All right. I suppose it would be rude to keep them waiting."

Vivian laughed. "We can't start until sunset, anyway.

There will be torches, and a rather large brazier, to prepare you."

"The lights."

"Some of the lights." She was being cagey, but she'd been fair about telling him the kinds of things that would happen. "You'll have a place to stand or sit that's out of the way, you just need to stay there, all right? And if it goes well, I should be right next to you unless I need to do something specific."

There were times he wished she were not quite so precise in her explanations, because now he was worried again, about what things going badly would mean for her. On the other hand, she was trusting him with that, where most people never had. She didn't lie to him to make things easier, and it made him more certain this was love, and not something else, that he felt.

Vivian led him out through the back, down the path of the garden, into the circular area at the middle of the formal garden. Torches had been put up, on tall bronze tripods. He could see the flames burning, mostly gold and red, but with flickers of a startling turquoise blue, like flashes of movement in water. Two of the women, who looked about Vivian's age, stood at either side of the entrance, holding long spears. They were crossed at the tips, tall enough that two could pass underneath more or less comfortably.

"Cousins." Vivian nodded, first to the left, then the right. "May we enter?"

There was nothing physical stopping them. But Cadmus, who did not consider himself at all observant about these things, could feel a sort of pressure. There was a long silence, as if they were being judged, then the woman on the left nodded. "You may."

Vivian made a little nod, that was not a bow, but had the

same sort of formality to it, and then stepped forward. Cadmus did his best to match her pace, stride for stride. He tried to evenly follow the slight pull of her arm, as she angled them towards a spot that he thought might be north, walking counter clockwise. There was a broad stool there, and she turned, as they got to it, so that he was standing in front of it.

"Aunts, Uncles, Cousins. Here is the landholder, to observe, as is right and proper."

"Khaire." He was almost startled to hear the Greek from them. But he supposed that if anyone would use an ancient Greek greeting, it would be people descended from those Gods. He wondered, suddenly and distractingly, if that meant Vivian were actually fluent in the language, and if so, which dialect and if she'd teach him all of it.

He managed a proper "Khairete," in response, and there was a hum of sound. He thought they approved, or at least did not disapprove.

"Vivian, if you would?"

Vivian dropped his arm, with one final squeeze, and stepped forward, her movements suddenly more measured and precise. There were no bells this time, not as there had been in her private ritual. Instead she took a torch from beside the nearest tripod, lit it from the flame burning above, and stepped forward to light the large bronze brazier in the centre of the circle. It lit up, with the same uncanny turquoise tint to the flame as the torches had, flickering and casting formless shadows.

As if they were all responding to some unheard cue, a bell or a gong, everyone straightened, and began to step. First in place, small precise movements, until Vivian returned to her place in the circle. He couldn't see their faces clearly, even with the bonfire now going, nor much except for the two nearest them. One was a tiny woman, a least in her nineties, who made tiny measured movements with a degree of control that awed him. The tall woman on Vivian's right looked like an Amazon, her robes and her movements were flashier, with a little kick that made the skirts of her robe flare out. Like Vivian's feet had moved, by the rose garden, he realised with a start.

When they began to clap, a precise pattern, one that required a dozen pairs of hands to do, he could feel something begin to rise. He couldn't tell if it was power, or presence, or danger. All he knew was that he must stay where he was now, and he sat, to make it harder to flee.

FORTY-TWO

SUNDAY EVENING

Vivian had reservations about this. She knew that they needed to contact the Grandmothers, to explain, to put things right. More to the point, to ask for help putting things right. But she hadn't been able to reassure Cadmus, because she didn't know how this was going to go.

She should have realised sooner what was happening. That Robin was at the centre of it. She certainly should have stopped things before the rose garden became vicious, or Danae was coerced into attacking her. She'd had all the thoughts swirling in her head, in the voices of her least favourite aunts, the ones who were so often right, but not kind about it. More than a few of those were here tonight, and she wondered if that would twist the ritual, somehow.

There was nothing for it but the dancing and the clapping, and the rhythm. This was one she'd learned long ago, dancing in a large circle behind the adults, one autumn, with her mother and her father somewhere in the shadows moving, circling widdershins. She gave herself over to it, to the little rock on her toes, the step back, then the step to the side. There were no bells on her ankles tonight, but she danced as if there were, as if each twist of her foot would make the sound shimmer.

Vivian wondered for just a moment what Cadmus was thinking. She couldn't spare a look at him, as the dance took too much concentration, but she could feel the magic stir her skin. The hairs on her arms stood on end, like being too close to a lightning strike, for an agonising few seconds. The world felt like everything was too dense, like she was beneath the waves again, in the salt and pressure of the ocean. Then, suddenly, something cracked open. There was a flash of light, a shimmer, a shift as if it was about to downpour. Instead, there was a wash of colour, the aurora borealis focused and contained on one spot.

They kept dancing. They would always keep dancing, until told to stop. That was how things were done, how they had to be done, the only way to keep the magic winding, moving in a direction that was controlled. They had all heard the stories of what happened otherwise, how it was like a harp string or a bow snapping, flinging all that power anywhere at all.

She could see the shape now, forming, or shapes, the figures above the brazier. They were insubstantial still, as Vivian looked up through her eyelashes, not daring to look directly. Certainly not yet.

It was like smoke was lingering, only it had a shape beyond what wisps of smoke would form. Heads and hair and robes and what might be feet and hands. Then the dance moved her, steps to the left, and someone began a soft chant, wordless. Others picked up the harmonies, at the fifths and octaves, the parallels made of open spaces that the modern ear found a tad eerie.

The chant wove around them, and around the figures

hovering over the brazier. Vivian could make them all out now, and it was all seven of them. She'd only heard about that, before, never seen it, she'd only ever seen Grandmother Electra, in person, directly. She had, quite honestly, hoped to go her entire life without more.

Instead, there was a sudden clap, like thunder. It rattled bones and stones and all the branches of the garden, before everything was quiet and still and everyone had stopped moving. Vivian wasn't even sure she was breathing.

The voice sounded out above all of them, with a sharp edge to it, a faint note of discordance in the background, and the resonance of a drum. "Family." It was in the Greek, the vowels rolling like another burst of thunder. "Oikoi." They all bowed, the robes shifting against their ankles. Vivian could manage a spare thought to be grateful that Cadmus should be able to follow this, or enough of it.

The figures were looking around, taking in the assembled people. Then one of them descended, like taking a single step, down a staircase, only she came to land a few inches above the ground, in front of Vivian. They were splitting hairs, then. The grandmothers had promised not to set foot on Albion's ground, after all, even if they'd done the proper invitations.

Vivian couldn't look up for a moment, then there was a hand on her chin, guiding her to look up. "Granddaughter." A strong, sure hand took hers, and Vivian could feel a shift beside her, then Grandmother Electra launched herself back into the air, bringing Vivian with her.

It made her stomach feel queer, to be standing on air, a few feet above the head of her tallest uncle. But her grandmother had been clear on what she should do. Even if Vivian had wanted to argue, she didn't know how to.

"Explain." The word was kind and terrifying, all at once, and Vivian knew she had to do this properly.

"Grandmothers, welcome." She began that way, as politely as she could. "Your family needs your help."

She could have sworn there was something best described as a snicker, from one of the grandmothers, on the far end. She didn't know how to tell them apart, not the way they were standing, the way they were still apparently made of smoke and mist and sparkling light. Sometimes they had distinguishing features, the tales said, but not tonight. "Someone attempted to open the gates." That was one of them, being mildly helpful. Not the one who had snickered.

Vivian nodded, and now she needed to figure out how to be accurate, fair, but not blame Robin more than he had actually earned. She had thought about this, on and off all day, what she would say if she were given a chance. "Robin wanted to feel your love and your warm regard, but he made poor choices. People were hurt, and scared, and time was shaken out of tune."

There was a little buzzing, from all seven of the sisters, something Vivian couldn't begin to make out, it was some language that didn't even seem a cousin to Greek. Then Grandmother Electra said, more gently. "What did you do?"

Vivian took a deep breath. "This land, this house, is tended by a family who have been here many years." She felt the appeal to family would make the most sense to them, it was something she knew in her bones they under-stood. "This man, here, is the steward of the land. His nephew, who will inherit, asked for my help." Somewhere in the last few minutes, Cadmus had stood up, at attention.

She did not need to explain the help, she saw. They knew what had happened, there were the little flickers of gesture, nods of understanding. Vivian was sure now that this conversation was entirely about whether her explanation was acceptable, and probably whether Robin's apology was sufficient.

"Robin." It came out like a bell ringing, the vibrations back. "Which is Robin?"

As if they didn't know. He, to his credit, looked up, made a formal bow, and stepped forward, though he didn't manage to speak.

Another of the sisters descended, like Electra had. This must be Celaeno, or at least Vivian could only assume so. She landed lightly just enough above the ground to make her taller than Robin, walking in a circle around him, as if she must inspect him from every angle.

Then, she bent to whisper something in his ear. It was not a word, nor even a short question, but several sentences. From her vantage point, Vivian could see his eyes widen, his chin come up. He went completely still, as if he were so busy thinking he couldn't do anything else.

Celaeno just waited, entirely patient. After nearly a minute, Robin nodded, and lowered his head, as if in some silent supplication or hope or something else. It was not like anything Vivian had ever seen, certainly not anything captured in a sculpture or painting. It had that kind of interior tension to it, where all the muscles were engaged, and all his mind as well.

Celaeno circled him one more time, then paused to say something in his other ear, before she launched herself upward, taking her place in the line of the sisters again. She nodded once, and the woman in the middle stepped forward. She looked a little older than the others, if any of these women could be said to look any age at all. Vivian thought this must be Maia, eldest of the seven.

Whoever she was, she walked around the remaining sisters, descending from their space in the air as if walking down a curving staircase. She came down step by steady step, until she stood in front of Cadmus. He was afraid, Vivian was sure of that, but he was holding fast, watching Maia come toward him. "We owe you a favour." She spoke now in modern English, her voice clear.

She reached to touch his cheek, and Cadmus almost flinched, before she said something quiet, something Vivian couldn't hear. Whatever it was, Cadmus let out a breath. She touched his cheek, then his forehead. "We will take what was shattered, repair the magic, and leave a gift. It is yours to do with as you will. No hidden snares."

Cadmus was wide-eyed now, but he nodded, then made a bow, the kind someone might have made in formal Court. Maia laughed, something joyful and amused, something kind, before she turned, her robes flaring out to almost brush his foot, and she climbed back up to the pedestal.

Vivian was suddenly aware of Grandmother Electra taking her hand, and leaping again, before Vivian had a chance to gather herself. She landed harder than she meant to, jarring her back into her body, but nothing hurt, nothing felt broken.

Then there were hands on her cheeks, cupping her face, and a kiss on her forehead. "Be joyful, my daughter. You have done well, and I am proud of you." Nothing but those few words, but they made Vivian's heart sing. Not punished, then, but praised. And whatever had been said to Cadmus had been some help.

She ducked her head, and felt the hands slowly pull away from her. As she looked up, Electra stood among her sisters again for seven breaths, seven of Vivian's breaths. Then they flickered out, like a curtain of darkness covering them all, leaving the faintest scatter of sparkling stars in their wake. The great brazier had gone out entirely, but the torches around the circle flared up.

There was complete silence for another thirty seconds, and then the sound of two dozen people needing urgently to talk about what had just happened.

T here was chaos, everyone talking over everyone else, and Cadmus didn't know where to go, or what to do. People kept moving across his line of vision, ignoring him. At least they weren't bothering him, or demanding he tell them things. He didn't know whether to stand up, and flee to his study, where he understood things, or whether that would be dangerously rude.

While he was trying to decide, he felt a shadow next to him, something between him and the torches. He looked up to see Vivian, her hair coming loose in wisps. "Come on. We can go off, safely, enough. Auntie Constantina said she'd make sure everyone cleaned up and got off safely."

"But, don't you, shouldn't I?" It came out as a stammer.

"You should come back up to your study, and have something to drink, and something to eat. And I have been told I should make you do that. I do trust Aunt Constantina to get everyone else packed up."

"Are they angry? What about Robin? Everyone was so loud, after - after." He wasn't sure how to explain that.

Vivian took his hand, drawing him away, out through

the opening in the circle that led through the gardens, back toward the house. He could see people at the window, now, looking out. Mrs Cooper, Farran, and several of the others he couldn't quite make out.

She spoke quietly, once they were a good twenty feet from the ritual space. "Robin is being looked after, and talked to. The grandmothers didn't punish him, so we won't, but Auntie Theresa wants to make sure he has things to keep him busy. I'm fairly sure he'll be moving out in the next day or two."

"Oh." He tried to mentally rearrange the maths about fees and expenses, and he couldn't make his head sort it out, not right now. It was going to be tight, though.

"Come on. Upstairs, and quiet, and we'll sort things out."

Cadmus didn't have the strength to argue, and he hoped he was wise enough not to. "Are you all right?"

"They weren't angry with me, I'm grand." He realised, suddenly, that she was giddy, as if she were drunk on something.

"What did - she, your, who was that?"

"Grandmother Maia, the eldest. I think. They don't exactly introduce themselves. I know Grandmother Electra, of course, and there are paintings and tapestries and things, but those aren't the same." Some part of Cadmus was now caught up in the question of whether one could photograph them or not. Besides the fact it was dark and lit by torches, and photographs didn't do well with that at all.

"She said something about repairing things? And a, a gift?"

"The repairing is straightforward. They'll put the magic back, heal all the places Robin left scars in it." Vivian paused, physically as well as verbally. "Does that part make sense to you? You can think of the magic a bit like the backing on the tapestry of the landscape, a layer right below what we can see. Robin cut slashes in it, with what he was doing, and they're reweaving that. Terribly easy for them, near impossible for us."

"And that will mean it's safe again?"

"Safe, and more than safe. I suspect they'll be adding a bit in the way of protection or blessing or something. Actual blessing, they have watched us for long enough not to get that terribly wrong. It used to be gifts from the Fatae were, were curses, not meant to be, but curses."

"And this isn't?"

"I'm pretty sure they'll restrain themselves to sensible things. You might have very abundant prize-winning roses for a generation, though."

Cadmus felt he could probably live with that, so long as they were prize-winning roses who stayed put. "And the gift?"

"That, I don't know." They were back at the house, now, and Mrs Cooper was signing at him. He had to blink a couple of times to get his eyes to focus and adjust to the light. Only then could he sign to her that he was all right, but he needed rest.

She gestured at the tray she had ready, of sandwiches and bottles of beer. He smiled, remembering her comments in the past about beer having good nutritious things in it. Farran said, "I'll bring the tray up. The others went off to their rooms. Everyone's all right, Uncle. Mrs Cooper fed us all."

Cadmus could only nod at that, and then offer his arm to Vivian. They made a little procession upstairs. When Cadmus opened the door, he found that Mrs Cooper had tidied, without moving anything, but she had built up the fire, left a couple of folded blankets, a knit shawl, and a pitcher of water and clean glasses. Farran set the tray down by the sofa. "Should I lock up?"

"Leave a door unlatched for Robin. But other than that."

Farran nodded, and went out, looking back at Cadmus once. Cadmus shrugged. "You might want to wash up?" There was a bit of soot on her cheek, he had no idea how that had got there. For that matter, he had no idea what he looked like. She blinked, but nodded, and went off to do that. He watched her go, the way the robe moved as she walked.

By the time she came back, he'd changed into a smoking jacket and loosened his shirt. She settled on the sofa, then glanced at him. "Mrs Cooper thinks of everything. Go wash, Cadmus, and then we should eat."

He did as she said. After all, it made sense. He had soot on him, too, a line along his forehead. He washed his face, then his hands, then his face again, before drying off on a towel, and coming back out. Vivian had tucked the shawl around her shoulders, and poured tea - she had her hands cupped around a mug of it.

Cadmus almost chose the chair facing her, and then, at the last minute, found himself picking the couch next to her. She smiled at him, something warm and encouraging, and set her tea down, before she reached to take his hand. "I think I figured out the gift. There's a box on your desk."

He blinked, and stood, drawing her up with him, and keeping hold of her hand, like it was an anchor to keep him grounded. She came with him willingly. On his desk, carefully positioned to avoid damaging any of his books, was a box, of carved wood. It had a pattern like a lightning strike on it, in copper work, against wood that must be ebony. He reached out a hand, almost touching it, before he drew back. "Is it safe?"

"For you? Yes. For anyone else? Possibly not."

He glanced at her, but she just nodded at it and dropped his hand so he could open the chest. He reached for the latch, and there was a little buzz in his fingers, like a hint of the lingering magic he'd felt outside, then he had the latch open. One more breath, and he opened the lid. Inside were a few dozen coins. The ones he could see were all common currency.

Vivian let out a little whistle, between her teeth. "There should be a seal on a piece of parchment." He didn't know how she knew that, but he peered inside, and found it, folded against the front edge, folded in thirds. When he opened it, he could see a copper wax seal, and elegant handwriting.

"If you give that to the bank, they'll know how to handle it. So long as it's one of the old families."

"We've always banked with the Scali." He touched the coins. "Is this, it's not going to..."

"She said no tricks, no snares. This is yours, in compensation. Is it - is it enough?"

"Enough to sort the repairs we need, and not worry too much about the apprentice fees. Especially if you can. I mean, are you still willing?"

"Oh, yes. This squares you up with the grandmothers. I still owe you rather a lot. And I want to help, as I said."

He let out a breath, like he'd been holding it for years. "This is. This is space to breathe."

"They do that. They rearrange space and time around them, and when they smile, it's wonderful." Then she wobbled, and he blinked, before he said, "Look, come lie down."

She was tired enough, worn enough, that she didn't argue when he led her into his bedroom, pulling back the sheets enough she could curl up, in the warm. He tucked them back over her, and settled on the edge of the bed. He wasn't sure what to do now, but this felt right. Taking care of her felt right, since she was letting him. She blinked up at him. "Not intruding?"

He waved a hand. "Not any more."

Two days after the rite, Vivian had been called back to Trellech. Those two days had been a pleasure. She had woken in Cadmus's bed, with him settled beside her reading, watching over her. It was a novel experience, in more than one way. She'd certainly known the pleasures of the body with others, before. He had made no particular move in that direction, not until later that afternoon, when he had asked, as carefully and precisely as he could, if he might call on her, in future, or if she might be willing to come and visit.

It had come out all stilted, like something out of a child's idea of a romantic overture, but she found his care charming. She had turned to him, and murmured, "I would like nothing better." There was no need to rush him, and every reason not to. She had wanted to kiss him, a desire she hadn't expected to feel, not at her age, but she had waited, simply reaching to take his hand.

When she left, he had driven her to the portal, and leaned in to kiss her once on the cheek, before she stepped through. He was as precise and attentive to that as he had been to everything else, and she found she quite liked his care for craftsmanship.

Now, though, it was three weeks later and writing was not at all the same. Even if she suspected he found writing to be somewhat easier. They had swapped letters every day, trusting to the speed of the mail via the portal. She had made arrangements already to get him one of the journals, one for him and one for Farran, as a solstice gift.

In between their letters, which had rambled from folklore to food to books to translation to a few of her more amusing cases, she had turned her hand back to work. She had come back at the request of the Minster of Materia, who was most concerned about a possible case of adulteration in a particular line of unusual ingredients that the Temple of Healing relied on. Not the sort of thing one could put off. And once it was known she was in town, there had been the expected run of callers asking for her help. Some of those she'd handed off to Eleanor's competent research, some she had hired other specialists to see to, and she had tended to a minor but intriguing question of an enchantment on a ring herself.

Today, she had finished all of her formal business before lunch. She was waiting on a final confirmation before she could write up the formal report for the Minister of Materia, but she had given him her informal response yesterday, in plenty of time to avoid the risks he'd been afraid of. The ring was back with its owner, and also safe to wear again.

She was waiting on Cadmus, now. He had come into town this morning to make the final arrangements about transferring the coins into a more usable form, and she was very much looking forward to showing him her own bit of home. She could not settle to anything, even her recent book, and was decidedly grateful when she heard the bell.

Vivian had sent Eleanor off home, already, so she came out to get the door herself, hoping it was not someone who would need to be put off. She had put on one of her more flattering dresses, a deep sea-blue silk with a bit of shimmer to the colour that gave a sense of movement, and some delicate embroidery along the cuff and hem in a rather Hellenistic motif in darker blue, that caught the eye just the right amount.

Cadmus stood there, in what she thought was his best tweed suit, with a deep holly green waistcoat, and he looked nervous. "This, oh." His mouth went open, and then he said, "You're beautiful." It was as if he'd noticed it for the first time. Certainly it was the first time he'd said anything like that.

Vivian laughed, and held out her hand. "I missed you. Come in, come in. We're entirely alone."

Cadmus let out a long breath, then he held out a bunch of flowers, in his arm. "From the greenhouses." He'd taken special care to pack them, if he'd been carrying them all day. There were several roses in the mix, and ferns, and a single white orchid.

She smiled at him. "Let me put these in some water." She turned away, letting him gather himself, going into the kitchen to get a vase and settle them in place. She brushed her fingers along them, with the little spark of magic that would keep them fresh for weeks. When she came back out into the front room, he had set down his satchel, and he was shifting nervously from foot to foot.

"Ask, please." Vivian had learned enough of him to know that was the sign of his nerves getting the best of him.

"May I, I'd like to kiss you. If you're willing. You said, your letters."

Vivian nodded, promptly. "I would like that very much."

She came over, close enough to make it easy for him. "I'm not rushing you, mind."

He let out a little gasp, and then shifted to kiss her, awkward at first. He'd had a dalliance or two himself, but was rather more out of practice, from what he'd said, than Vivian was herself. They managed the kiss well enough, especially after she got a hand against his back, to steady them both.

When he pulled back, his eyes were shining, and he was a bit breathless. "I've wanted that for weeks." Then, straightening up. "You said you had some ideas of our afternoon? I don't need to be back until supper, we're still settling the new people in."

"I thought I'd show you my office, and then take you to where the cousins spend our time. Tea, there, and then I can see you off to the portal."

He hesitated, then said, "And you'll come visit for solstice?"

"I will. I said I would, didn't I?"

"Mrs Cooper has aired your room out properly, and laid the fire, and of course if you'd rather stay with me, you can do that." He was tripping over his tongue, all the nerves burbling out.

They were back to one of them needing to be calm and have a plan, so no matter how much she found herself wanting to match those nerves and desires, she kept her voice calm. "I would like a great deal of time with you, but if you want time on your own, I will toddle along to my own room, and amuse myself. I promise."

"Or talk to Mrs Cooper. She's quite interested in a trip north, when the weather's warmer."

"Good. I'll make arrangements." She then tugged at his hand. "Come see my offices."

"More than one?" Cadmus was pleasantly baffled.

"One for formal meetings, one for people I like." She led him through the former, all fussy upholstery and the little details that told a discerning eye that she had both style and money. She'd chosen each item in that room carefully, from the Art Deco design in green on the china to the pale green silk of the furniture, and the precise layout of her desk.

He looked around. "This is your public face. There's nothing, nothing personal here."

"No, and there's not supposed to be. You'll like the other one better." Vivian drew him through the door to the side, into her personal office. When she had taken over the house, she had chosen the best view for her personal office, saving the formal parlour for her formal space. She brought him in, turning him slightly with a hand at his waist, to get the best view out the broad bay window.

Cadmus sucked in his breath. "That's your land, isn't it?"

"Not in the way Thebes is, I certainly don't own it. But down to the river, as the magic flows, I feel responsible for it, yes." She was delighted that he'd seen it immediately, then she stepped back to let him look around. This room was decorated in a deeper green. Vivian had deliberately chosen different shades of it, ones that complemented each other, but that changed as the light and seasons shifted, with little touches of other colours. A deep red teapot, or a hyacinth purple one, depending on her mood, and a set of tea cups to match in deep jeweltones and their paler hues. They went with the books on the shelves, bound in every shade of book-cloth and leather she had been able to find.

Cadmus spun in place, taking it in. "This is you. All of you. Space to be you. Not your masks."

She nodded. "You understand." Leaning to kiss him again, she lingered in the feeling, of someone seeing what she'd done with this, without her needing to explain it. His arms came up around her, and they stood there, for some time in silence.

"This is not all you wanted to show me." His voice was nearly a whisper, more than a bit rough.

"The cousins. Upstairs is for when we have more time."

That made Cadmus laugh, and squeeze her for a moment. "We might get distracted, then?"

"Quite possibly. And we do have an appointment. Let me get my coat. Bring the papers, I've booked us a room there, and one of the cousins is coming to check the new apprentice agreement."

"Like you said."

Vivian nodded. "Like I promised."

Once she had her coat on, he offered her his arm, and she found walking with him that way most delightful. They paused here and there to look at the displays in the shop windows, once they were back among the shops, taking their time without rushing. Once they had made their way to the bookshop, he followed her lead, as she'd explained, upstairs. She murmured to him, "You'll feel the wards." He squeezed her hand, but didn't startle beyond that.

Alfred was still there, just until solstice. She brought Cadmus forward. "Alfred, this is Cadmus. Cadmus, this is Alfred. And this is Amandine." The graceful, still largely humanoid figure beside Alfred had arrived a fortnight ago, to learn about her duties.

Alfred rustled his leaves, a sort of full shiver that she hadn't seen out of him in some time, as if he were peering at Cadmus. Then there was a flick of the outer leaves, his approval. Amandine waited until he had gone silent, and added, her voice a whisper, "You are welcome, Cadmus." Then she inclined her upper body.

"You apparently suit." Vivian's voice was teasing. "We're in the Pen Room, thank you, when Irundel comes along." That got another little shiver of acknowledgement from Alfred and a rustle of agreement from Amandine.

"Do we have a few minutes?" Once she'd shown him into the room, Cadmus had settled on the couch, setting his satchel by his feet. She had joined him, giving him a little space, but close enough to touch if and when he wanted.

"A few."

He let out a breath. "Did you ever sort out the spirit? In the seance? I mean, is that anything we need to worry about?" Not a thing he'd wanted to ask about in a letter, then. She'd begun to get a sense for when he felt there was something foolish in putting words to paper.

"The best we can figure out it was a trickster spirit, taking a name. He didn't say anything too easy to discern, certainly nothing that's happened yet, but it didn't seem dangerous. I'm just as glad Madam Etna's moved out, though."

Cadmus nodded. "I kept thinking what you'd said about Mistress Cole. She's staying on, it turns out. Her niece prefers it, and one of the new residents seems to be taking to her."

"Good." He seemed to be waiting for something else, and Vivian gave him space for that as well.

Cadmus reached into his coat pocket and pulled out a small box. "Are there customs about gifts?"

"Not among people who have decided to be friends. Or rather, no customs you need worry about."

"I'll have something else for solstice." He was near stammering now. "But I made this for you. First time working at the forge on anything decorative in a long time."

That gave her a hint, and then she opened the box, to

find a beautiful shaped penannular brooch, a curve of metal with a tongue. It was simply made, except for a polished ammonite set at the end of one curve.

"From near the house." He looked as if he might shatter if she didn't like it.

"This is, this is..." She ran her fingers along the metal. "The smith's touch. And the stone is beautiful." Much better than a gemstone that he certainly couldn't afford, as well, but she liked the living history of the fossil very much indeed.

She might have said more, but then she was interrupted by Irundel coming in, all business and proper etiquette. Throughout their discussion, though, she couldn't keep from reaching to touch where she'd slipped the brooch into her pocket until she could find a shawl to wear it with.

EPILOGUE

By February, they had settled into a most pleasant routine.

As had become her custom, Vivian had taken the portal from Trellech at eleven on the Friday, and Cadmus had met her at the other end with the carriage. After lunch, she claimed her new spot in his study, both of them settling in to do more work. He was deep in his translation project. It was moving along at a good pace, now, with cheerful footnotes about the flora and fauna of North Africa and the Near East. She thought she might be able to talk him into a visit there, sometime before the book went to the publisher.

Her own paperwork this afternoon wasn't complex, just finishing up the month's accounts and invoices for Eleanor to send out on Monday. It had been relatively quiet over the solstice and New Year festivities, as it generally was, though she had some new inquiries coming now.

At quarter past six, she put her pen down, closed the inkwell, and cleared her throat. "Farran should be here shortly?"

"Oh? Oh, yes." He held up his hand, for a moment, the gesture she'd come to know well, him needing to get just one more thought down. He scribbled something down, and then closed his book with the bookmark in. "Shall we?"

Cadmus came around the desk, and held out his hand to her. She slipped her hand into the crook of his arm. He was looking particularly well tonight. Besides the journals, she had talked him into accepting the visit of a tailor who owed her a favour. He was wearing one of the suits now, cut to be flattering and comfortable, of a woollen blend he found much more pleasant than his previous. Better, under it, he had soft linen shirts that didn't make him slightly irritated all the time. The colours suited him, a cool dark grey, and he was wearing a deep blue cravat and pocket square.

"You look well. And busy, your paperwork?" He gestured. "That's a new frock?" He wasn't entirely certain, and she leaned in to kiss his cheek.

"A handful of small things." Then, laughing, she added. "And yes, a new frock." It was a deep purple that she thought suited her quite well. Not particularly fashionable, the colour, but no one expected a woman of her age - apparent or otherwise - to follow every fashion. More to the point, it went well with both shawl and brooch in style, nothing fussy to catch on the shawl.

"How is Alfred?"

"Quite fixed in place, now, I went to check on him on Monday. Amandine is settling in nicely." The related chatter took them down to the dining room, comfortably.

By the time they got to the dining room, everyone else was there, including Farran, who was near-glowing with happiness. It was his first visit since starting his new apprenticeship, and they were all pestering him with questions, those who were there.

Robin was gone, of course, he had made his excuses and disappeared off into rustication at the direction of one of his aunts. Madam Etna had moved on to a boarding house in London, with more opportunity for her seances. Madam Gregson had gone with her, to keep house.

Mistress Cole had remained, but she was much more often in the company of Herr Professor Balsano, and one of the older women they had added. Emma and Andie had, after some reflection, and some additional apology from Vivian, decided they could recommend the place to several academic colleagues. Vivian was quite sure two of them were a couple, as well. Danae White had, thankfully, not left. Vivian had a few awkward meals before she managed to pin the other woman down for a conversation, explanation, and a set of mutual apologies to clear the air.

Enough people, Cadmus had said, to keep things running smoothly for the next few years, and besides, he'd found he liked the company. Mrs Cooper had brought all the food up, keeping it warmed through charm or chafing dish. She was settled at the end of the table, signing amiably to Farran, asking about what he wanted for breakfast.

"Uncle!" Farran stood up, abruptly. "It's very good to see you. And you, Vivian."

"And you, Farran. Sit, sit."

She smiled at him, and moved to her usual place for these visits, at his right hand. It meant she could lean and explain something, if needed, and if he wasn't following the undercurrent of the conversation. Cadmus pulled out the chair, and then pushed it in as she sat down. "Tell us about it, do." She signed as she spoke, and when Farran began, bubbling over with his news, he did the same.

"Well, I'm apprenticing at Ormulu. They're one of the

most respected auction houses, but they're not very large, just five senior masters, ten journeymen and women, and ten apprentices. Some go into other fields - someone just finished his apprenticeship and is going to be an art appraiser, and someone else is a conservator, with the museum now? I'm learning so much, and it's going so very much better."

She'd known that as soon as she'd sorted out the introduction. Master Philemon Ettis had taken a look at Farran, walked around him, cast three charms, and then been exceedingly willing to sign the apprentice contract at most favourable terms. He'd later told her privately that Farran had a knack for recognising materia, and that was a priceless thing for an auction house that handled estate sales, as they did. It made them most pleased with her, and likely to send business her way in the future, and Farran was finally blossoming.

"And the other apprentices?" she asked, when he finished talking about the work, what he was learning so far. That got another delighted outpouring, he was making friends with them already. They'd been to the apprentice league matches, and out to the pub, and how Eleanor's brother liked them.

He'd been much more isolated at the talisman maker, and hadn't much cared for the other apprentices he'd met there. That made Vivian want to take another look at that little network of people again. It could keep for Monday, though.

The conversation went on during dinner, working around to the others chiming in about their apprenticeships. From there, it devolved into a delightful set of rather raucous stories, including from the doctor. Vivian was not sure she'd get the image of him parading around the Healing Temple garden in Trellech wearing a nightshirt and a pointed hat any time soon.

When they'd finally drunk the last of the after-dinner coffee, everyone parted ways. Farran went off to his room, and Cadmus escorted her off to his. They had not progressed to particular intimacies, not yet, but they had begun sharing a bed over the solstice holiday, and found it suited them both. He was wary of new things, a little jumpy. She could be patient, and not press him.

Especially since they had sorted out that they both liked it very much if she curled up with him, so they could talk quietly in the dark. It wasn't deep conversation, most of the time. Bits about his travels, and things he'd read, and some of her cases, the ones she could talk about without giving someone's privacy away.

Once they'd settled into bed, she shifted to lean on his shoulder, propped up by the pillows. "Better, now you've seen him?"

"Better." Cadmus was quiet for a long time, at least a minute, by the ticking of the clock. "I wasn't sure you were right. But of course you were."

"I can be wrong. Have been wrong, in the recent past. But about Farran's gift? I was rather sure I wasn't."

Cadmus kissed her hair. "So. Tell me what you want to solve next."

IF YOU ENJOYED *Seven Sisters* and would like to read more of this series, please sign up for my mailing list to get all the latest news and fun extras. Your reviews (on whatever review site you use) are much appreciated, too!

Read on for more historical details about this book and an excerpt from *Pastiche*.

AUTHOR'S NOTE

Hello, and welcome to my author's notes for *Seven Sisters*.

First, this is the final book in the Mysterious Charm series. Don't worry, there's more charm and enchantment of the 1920s to come.

If you'd like more about these particular characters, Vivian also appears in *Goblin Fruit,* and there is also a brief appearance by Farran at the beginning of that book (which takes place after this one.) Robin's story continues in *Fool's Gold,* where Vivian plays a small role.

My thanks as always to my most excellent editor, Kiya Nicoll, and to my early readers. Any remaining issues are of course, mine.

If you've been trying to place **Farran Michaels**, he appears briefly in both *Goblin Fruit* and *The Magician's Hoard* after he's sorted out his apprenticeship issues. I was intrigued by him and his knack for materia, and couldn't resist bringing him back.

Thebes is a fascinating city, historically. There are a lot of myths and legends about it, and unravelling some of them gets tricky because the Athenians (from whom we get a lot of our surviving written material) basically used Thebes as their target for "people who are not like us" when they weren't doing that to Sparta. If you'd like to learn more about the history, the Thebes episode of the *In Our Time* podcast from the BBC was what got me started thinking about naming the estate Thebes, and why.

One of the most complex things about this book was making decisions about the **Fatae**. As you've likely realised at this point, while I'm drawing on a wide range of folklore traditions (mostly but not entirely British), the world of the Fatae is broad and varied. Elder bushes being guardians of portals to Faerie (or some other land not meant for humans) is one of the longstanding traditions in folklore, but most of our lore doesn't mention them talking and walking around before they settle down...

Cadmus is, among other things, a chance to excuse my **classicist background**. My father was a professor with a Classics PhD turned theatre historian. I not only grew up on tales of the Greek myths and the various surviving plays, but I've taken Greek and Latin (more of the former than the latter).

In general, if there's a passing reference to a classical name that I don't explain in the following, a quick search at Wikipedia will find you a great summary. I've tried to give enough context that you don't need to, however.

Herodotus is often referred to as the earliest historian, looking systematically at events and how they came to be rather than simply telling stories he'd heard about them.

His *Histories* looked at the history of the Greco-Persian wars. It's actually a little weird to read, because some of it is Herodotus talking about Persian customs of food, dress, and lifestyle, and the rest is mostly battles.

(When I was taking Ancient Greek in high school, my study partner and I decided and then proved that if Herodotus is talking about a battle, any verb you don't know can be translated as "to attack" until you figure out the details. There's a verb in his description of the battle of Thermopylae that can be quite reasonably translated as "to make pincushions out of one's enemies with spears.")

At the introduction of Mrs Cooper, we discover she is deaf. While many people these days identify with Deaf culture, Mrs Cooper would not identify herself that way, as she's been largely cut off from other people who are deaf or hard of hearing since her school days.

She is, however, fluent at **British Sign Language**. I leaned heavily on various online BSL dictionaries to figure out the relevant signs, but found it was illuminating how people signed, and what that added to understanding their mood or character.

And of course, there are other situations in which sign is extremely helpful. Vivian is familiar with its uses in spaces where spoken language doesn't work, such as with mermaids underwater. And she points out it's useful in a noisy room or somewhere you don't want to make noise.

One more linguistic note: sign language uses a different grammatical structure than English. I didn't attempt to duplicate it here, other than a few bits of flavour, but what you're reading of the signed conversations might best be considered their translation into English.

The use of **name signs** varies in different communities. In many places, it's customary for them to be given to someone by other people, not decided by the person themselves, and people might have different name signs in different parts of their life. In this case, they're all somewhat informative about the people they describe.

The **Fauvists** were a group of early 20th century artists known for their extremely strong and bright colour choices. Not the sort of thing you'd expect in a fairly traditional English manor house.

We get our first serious glimpse at some of the differences between Vivian and her cousins when she and Robin trade oaths. Clearly, while they're related in particular ways, they also have some important differences.

The seven sisters of the title refer to the **Pleiades**, about whom there are a lot of myths and folklore. One of those pieces is that they became what humans would consider fae (or something between deities and mortals). As Vivian says later in the book, she prefers not to think about if they're actually goddesses - grandmothers is terrifying enough! They clearly have magical powers far beyond what the mortal magics of Albion allow, and just as clearly, their human descendants who remained after the Pact of 1483 are not entirely sure what their scope or interests are.

The **epithets** used in the oaths are some of the traditional epithets applied to Caelano and Electra. (And the word anthropoi at the end of Vivian's oath is the Greek word for humankind.)

Cadmus reflecting on the lack of focus on **women in classical translation** is one of my favourite parts. If you're at all inclined to read epic Greek poetry, I highly recommend Emily Wilson's translation of *The Odyssey* (the first full translation published by a woman, ever.) The journey of Odysseus's journey home after the Trojan War includes Circe (a sorceress who enchants his men) and Penelope, his exceedingly patient and clever wife. Medea is the focus of a number of myths, and specifically for escaping with Jason, who then betrays her.

The dinner conversation about **Sappho** was a chance to show the kinds of things that Cadmus, clever as he is, misses. Sappho is an ancient Greek woman poet who wrote compellingly about having a woman as a lover, among other things. Much of her work only survives in fragments, but the quotations here are all from public domain sources.

There were plenty of women in **lesbian** relationships at the time, but it was still more than a bit socially disapproved of, even if it was a fairly open secret in some social circles. The concerns Andie and Emma have, about needing to move, or that it might affect professional options, are fairly common (on the other hand, few people would have blinked much at older unmarried women setting up house together.)

The **dance in the rose garden** is an old idea of mine. The first time I saw *Riverdance*, the travelling production of Irish dancing, I had the thought of how those sharp and precise movements would work as a method of fighting (especially with a bit of magic in the mix.) Vivian is obviously quite skilled at using it here.

Spiritualism became quite common in the mid-1800s and remained popular through and after the Great War. While it could bring a great deal of comfort, it could also quickly lead to abuse of vulnerable people (often women who had lost husbands and children in quick succession).

Many of the tricks Vivian mentions that were used by spiritualists to fake sounds or events can actually be done perfectly well without magic. People would learn to crack their knuckles, use bent metal tins strapped to their knee, or insert strong wires hidden in their sleeves to make a table rock. (Miss Climpson, in the Dorothy L. Sayers novel *Strong Poison* has a lot to say about these and other tricks in the course of helping Lord Peter solve a mystery.)

There's a tiny Easter egg bit of fun in this seance. If you've read *Goblin Fruit*, the portion that starts "a gentleman, falling over his own two feet" refers to Carillon falling over Lizzie outside the party that begins their investigation (and lives) together.

Vivian's ritual takes place during the point when the Pleiades are the highest they get in the sky. One of the things I thought about a lot in this book was the sense of the numinous power, that is about being exposed to a mystery in the religious or spiritual sense. Cadmus has experiences of his own. He has the terrifying one of stumbling into something not meant for him in Afghanistan, but also his experiences of belonging to the Smith, a more approachable sort of mystery.

Cadmus never quite explains this directly, but he is part of a mystery cult focused on **The Smith**, who might be Hephestus, or might be Weyland the Smith, or might be a number of other divine powers. It explains why he has such an interest in specific parts of the legends around Thebes.

Much of the rest of the book follows from the above, though you get a better sense of how Cadmus stewards his land. (**Telling the bees** is a folklore custom that insists that the bees must be told of deaths or other major events in the household, for example.)

The Belin appear and are further described in *Goblin Fruit* if you're curious about them.

The **historical settings** that Cadmus and Vivian walk through are pretty much as described in the text - including a major fire in Oxford, and the near approach of Cromwell's troops in the English Civil War.

Linear A is the name for one of the forms of writing and languages found at Knossos, on the island of Crete (and a few other places). Linear B, an early precursor of Greek used by the Mycenaeans among others, was deciphered in the 1950s, but no one has sorted out Linear A yet.

And that brings us to the conclusion of the book, and of this series. If you haven't already signed up, my mailing list gets the latest news about new books and tidbits of research, among other things.

If you sign up for my newsletter, you'll receive *Ancient Trust*, a prequel novella following Lord Geoffrey Carillon as he inherits the land magic in 1922. His story continues in *Goblin Fruit*, where Vivian plays a pivotal role in a romance.

AUTHOR'S NOTE